Fiction SUNDELL Joanne
Sundell, Joanne.
Artic shadow

ARCTIC SHADOW

ARCTIC SHADOW

JOANNE SUNDELL

FIVE STAR

A part of Gale, Cengage Learning

GALE
CENGAGE Learning

Farmington Hills, Mich • San Francisco • New York • Waterville, Maine
Meriden, Conn • Mason, Ohio • Chicago

Copyright © 2015 by Joanne Sundell
A Glossary of foreign language terms are included at the back of the book.
Five Star™ Publishing, a part of Cengage Learning, Inc.

LIBRARY OF CONGRESS CATALOGING-IN-PUBLICATION DATA

Sundell, Joanne.
   Arctic shadow / Joanne Sundell. — First edition.
     pages ; cm. — (Watch eyes trilogy ; book 2)
     ISBN 978-1-4328-3008-3 (hardcover) — ISBN 1-4328-3008-2 (hardcover) — ISBN 978-1-4328-3005-2 (ebook) — ISBN 1-4328-3005-8 (ebook)
     [1. Supernatural—Fiction. 2. Shamans—Fiction. 3. Adventure and adventurers—Fiction. 4. Survival—Fiction. 5. Chukchi—Fiction. 6. Siberian husky—Fiction. 7. Dogs—Fiction. 8. Ghosts—Fiction. 9. Arctic regions—History—20th century—Fiction.] I. Title.
PZ7.S954645Ap 2015
[Fic]—dc23   2014047854

First Edition. First Printing: June 2015
Find us on Facebook– https://www.facebook.com/FiveStarCengage
Visit our website– http://www.gale.cengage.com/fivestar/
Contact Five Star™ Publishing at FiveStar@cengage.com

Printed in the United States of America
1 2 3 4 5 6 7 19 18 17 16 15

To the memory of my beloved Siberian huskies

~

To those who pioneered the importation of the Siberian husky
to Alaska

~

To the Frontier Spirit in us all

AUTHOR'S NOTE

The Chukchi people of northeast Siberia, over thousands of years, wisely bred and developed the Siberian husky we know today. This work of fiction is set in the context of real events that took place in northeast Siberia and on the Alaskan frontier in the early decades of the twentieth century.

PREFACE

The first significant importation of the Siberian husky to America occurred in 1908, bringing the gentle Chukchi sled dog to the unbridled, gold-rich wilds of the Alaska Territory. Passage by ship across the great Bering Sea brought the isolated worlds of Siberia and the Alaskan frontier together in trade and exploration. Life on both arctic frontiers proved rugged for native and pioneer alike, survival ever the challenge. Spirits rose. Spirits fell. While the Alaska pioneers depended on the sled dog for much in their daily life, the Chukchi of far northeast Siberia depended entirely on their dogs for survival, with travel over tundra and ice to hunt for food impossible without them.

"The Chukchi believed that their dogs guarded the gates of heaven, and that the way you treated a dog in this life determined your place in heaven.
If this is so then surely when time comes for us to pass we will be assured of a place of great honor.
It is said that your dogs wait for you, asleep until you come across, then they pull your sled through and into heaven."
(National Sanjankah Dog Association)

Eternally vigilant, the Gatekeepers focus keen *Watch Eyes* over all on Native Earth and in the worlds beyond. The spirit of the People, native and pioneer, depends on them. Worlds ever brush past, both human and spirit. Good and Evil are born into each: some become master; some do not. Some suffer greatly; some do not. None from the spirit world can breach the world of humans, affecting anything in the mortal world. No mortal can breach the world of spirits, affecting anything in the spirit world . . . *unless* . . . their life force, whether created for good or for evil, whether born out of prophecy or fanaticism, naturally grows in power and strength, finally gaining enough momentum to crash through and leave a mark.

The mark of a fanatic grows wider, deeper; his power strengthening. The ice storm is coming.

The Gatekeepers can guard the heavens but they are not masters on Native Earth. The gods can destroy but they cannot mend. The human spirit must prevail over the darkness coming.

CHAPTER ONE

"There appeared on the horizon a harmless-looking white stripe—the most terrifying sight in the whole of the Arctic Ocean . . . By evening, the white stripe became a clearly recognizable ice field . . . For three days they ran, and the ice field relentlessly followed, always gaining . . ."
—Yuri Rytkheu, *The Chukchi Bible*

Nome, District of Alaska ∼ mid-winter, 1909
The ice storm persisted. Dark spirits cast their shadow over the dogs, and brought the storm.

The spent huskies lay in uneasy circles on the scattered straw. Their watch-blue eyes stayed open. Except for an occasional twitch of a paw or rustle of fur, none made a move. Each pant sent a small breath of smoke into the frosty air. The huskies dared not sleep. They waited as they had for centuries. Drums of the ancestors coursed through their veins, the connection palpable in the rundown stable. Despite hunger, thirst, and torn paw pads, not one whined in complaint.

Eight of the imported Siberian husky team had survived the four-day All Alaska Sweepstakes. One had not, their leader, Zellie. An exceptional young dog, her death on Native Earth did not come from running the four-hundred-eight-mile grueling race under impossible conditions, but from ghostly shadows collected beneath icy crags and in bottomless crevasses, lying in wait for her. Zellie never had a chance. Powerful forces from mystic worlds long thought dead found her and killed her.

Lost in their own secrets, Anya and Rune faced each other in the cold afternoon dimness. Anya thought of her gods, and Rune, his. Neither said a word about the burden they felt, about their fears for the surviving eight dogs. Neither had been able to save Zellie. Doubts flooded them both.

At fourteen years of age, Anya didn't feel like much of a shaman, despite having just traveled to the spirit world and back.

Nearly seventeen, Rune didn't feel like much of a Viking warrior, despite having the ancient mark of the gods on him.

They each kept silent when they almost burst with wanting to reveal their secrets to each other—that they shared a special tie to the ancients—that they each communicated with ghosts of the past who were very much alive in the present. Anya had sensed spirits around her the whole of her life, but Rune, only recently, when he'd been called on by the gods to step out of his normal life and come to Anya's aid. *It is time. It begins.* Both heard the same call to battle, the same clarion cry of ancient drums and animal horns sounding out their destiny. The wolf and the dog must battle as one if any are to survive.

The Chukchi dogs stayed silent and still on the stable straw. Nothing in their centuries of breeding and training prepared them for this new challenge, for the ordeal of trying to last in a world where they were prey. All the dogs sensed this new world and this new danger. Gentle by nature, their best defense was to follow the team's lead dog, to watch her, to run, to hunt, and to fight as a pack; their howls joined with the cry of the wolf. Their instincts told them that to stray from the pack meant death. Their leader had strayed, and had never come back to them.

Zellie was with the Gatekeepers in soulful sleep, waiting for Anya, for Xander, and for all the other dogs in the race just run to "cross," when she would awaken and help pull their sleds into heaven. Anya believed this with all her heart. It was the only thing that kept her going. That and Xander.

He lived still, but for how long? Marked and weakened by fits, he'd already been attacked too many times by whatever evil was after them. Why, grandmother? Anya obeyed Nana-tasha's ghostly commands to race the dogs in Nome—*for the survival of all*—but Anya still didn't know what was after them or why. She'd stowed away on the same ship carrying the traded Chukchi dogs from the Markova Fair in Siberia all the way across the great Bering Sea, far from the only home they'd ever known to the unknown shores of the Alaskan frontier, for what? So Zellie could die! Her grandmother had been wrong. Doubting herself all over again, Anya didn't believe she possessed any mystical powers of the shamans.

She couldn't help the Gatekeepers. She didn't feel like praying to the Morning Dawn or the Directions or any of the Chukchi gods for guidance. None had helped save her smart, brave, loyal, black and white beauty. She'd raised Zellie from a pup, selecting her as one of the elite, and now Zellie's life on Native Earth had ended in the time it takes for a heart to beat, for life to begin or end.

Not for the first time, Anya wanted to die. She believed she deserved such punishment for her deeds. When she'd released all the dogs in her coastal village in Siberia, she'd expected her cold stepfather, Grisha, an important breeder of dogs, to run her through with a harpoon. She was willing to pay with her life.

The Chukchi depended on their dogs for everything. She'd released them because she couldn't stand to see the dogs broken up and traded away at the Markova Fair one more year! After thirteen years of watching this happen, and especially after bonding with the pups, Zellie and Xander, she couldn't sit still and watch the cherished dogs scattered all over Siberia, some to good men, some to bad men. Some used the whip. Not the

Chukchi, but others did. Her death at the hands of Grisha, she'd expected.

She hadn't expected him to trade her away to the ugly Yukaghir, who held a whip in one hand and Xander's lead in the other! She and Xander escaped Mooglo, but not before she'd been marked by his lash across her hand, the bloody mark made not by any human touch but by dark spirits after her. She understood the sign and ran from it as fast as she could. All the while she hoped the dark spirits wouldn't follow her and the dogs across the Bering Sea to unknown frontiers.

But they had. Zellie was dead. So was Boris Ivanov.

Ravens cawed outside; a common sound in the Arctic. Anya cringed. The Raven was no Creator god as she'd always thought, but a powerful force that worked against her. Back in her Chukchi village the Raven god chose bad spirits over good, she believed; unforgiving and angry at her when she released the dogs. The sign of the Raven had taunted, tricked, and terrorized her ever since then.

She understood the Raven's upset at her but not at the dogs, and not at Boris Ivanov. The big Russian traded for them in Markova, the same as many who came to the annual fair in Siberia. He brought the dogs to Nome to race them. She'd stowed away on the *Storm* because he had.

Now Boris the bear was dead. Why? And why did the Raven cast its clawing shadows over the Chukchi dogs? Anya swallowed hard. Her spirit had to match the Raven and become master. There was no other answer; no other way to keep Xander and the rest of the dogs safe. Her beloved grandmother had said as much to her, foretelling of her divinations.

"You are a child of the spirits, little Anya. You are a child of the great storms begun when worlds collide in our heavens. You came to us on the arctic winds. The Gatekeepers watch over you. They have given you a great burden to carry, my little

Anya. But they have also given you great powers. The shamans have always feared you because of this. You are the first of your kind, the first Native-born of the spirits. There are others created by the spirits: some for good, some for evil. You must become master, little Anya."

Still upset by the unnerving caws of the Raven overhead, outside the loosely boarded stable, Anya recited Nana-tasha's words again and again in her mind, and searched for a way to best the dark spirits after them.

"Anya—" Rune's voice broke with emotion; he was still upset himself over the day's events; over Zellie dying.

Anya didn't hear him.

"The dogs have to eat, Anya." Rune tried to get through to her. "We have no food. I'll find some. There's a half-thawed water barrel in the corner, enough for the dogs. Why don't you water them?"

If only he held the magic to take away her sadness. He understood her grief over losing Zellie, but as for the rest, no. Questions plagued him. How did Zellie finish the race when she was, by Anya's account, "dead"? Why did Anya tell him their race finish was "good enough" when he thought from the start his sled dog team had to win to make a difference?

They'd finished third, not first, with eleven teams dropping out the first day from the sudden, violent blizzard. Rune's time was just over eighty-three hours. The winning team finished in just over eighty-two. Rune finished an hour behind. To him that didn't sound "good enough." He was no musher, but a seaman. Upset with himself, he should have stayed at sea. He knew how to navigate at sea; not on land. It was his fault they lost the race and no fault of the brave-hearted dogs; Zellie least of all. If he'd been a true musher, Zellie might not be dead and he might have won the Sweepstakes . . . for Anya.

Rune fought his emotions. More unanswered questions

plagued him. What was after Anya and her dogs? What could so stir the oceans and awaken the old enemy of the Vikings from its long-sleeping, hidden depths and bring it to the shores of Nome?

To Rune it felt like the ancient Midgard serpent lay in wait in every watery pool, beneath every icy creek bed and glacial lake, in every snaking river and stream, and looked for a way to strike Anya, her dogs, and him. The serpent almost broke through the thick ice of the Norton Sound on the first day of the race, but Zellie and his team managed to reach land before it could kill.

Again, farther along the trail over frozen lakes, it thudded its head beneath the ice and tried to break through. He didn't see the serpent but felt its impact ricochet across the ice. Before he'd met Anya, Rune never believed in the ghostly beast of Viking legend. He did now. The race he'd just run, proof enough.

"Anya," he said again. "I'm going for food. You water the dogs."

What Rune really wanted to do was put his arms around the little Siberian girl and reassure her all would be well. He was wrong about her. Fourteen going on fifteen, she wasn't a little girl, and he couldn't guarantee all would be well.

She did look every bit the lost, slight female Rune had spied on his father's ship, a young girl who'd stowed away in his locker below deck. He'd thought her a ghost then, pretty like an ice seal, elusive and shimmery like a mermaid who could have found her way above the water through a breathing hole in the ice. Maybe she was all three, as much a part of the Arctic as the ice itself, and just as unpredictable.

Still unsure of many things about Anya, he didn't question her love for her dogs. She'd do anything for them, even if it meant her life. On each of the dogs' husky-masked faces, he could see the same determined devotion. They were ready to sacrifice for her, too. Suddenly envious, Rune had to get out of there. It had been a long time since he'd thought about his family and their lack of devotion to him. He needed some air.

"Rune." Anya barely spoke above a whisper. She'd gone over to sit by Xander and began to pet him. She didn't look at Rune. "I'll water the dogs. They're hungry. Would you find them some food?"

He realized she was still in shock over Zellie. He'd give her all the time and space she needed to get through this.

"I'll be back soon," he reassured.

The dogs stirred at his leaving, mindless of their injuries. He was a guardian. The Gatekeepers trusted his loyalty. Little Wolf, the gray and white husky runt of the pack, got up and started to follow Rune. So did Magic and Mushroom, the copper-red and white pair.

Xander settled under Anya's touch; neither acknowledged the movement of the others, too numb and distressed over Zellie. Despite being from different litters, Xander and Zellie had been together since furry, black and white pups; inseparable until now. She would guide and he would trail after her. This was a new world for him, a world without Zellie. Too weakened to howl in mourning, he whimpered under Anya's touch. Her hand, the trusted, comforting hand of his guardian, soothed him, and told him he was not alone. His canine senses reached out to Anya in the same way. He nestled under her touch, content to have her near.

Rune dropped down to give the three huskies following him a pat behind their ears. He didn't want the exhausted dogs to come with him. Their paw pads needed care. Besides, he didn't want any of the race-watchers still hanging about to approach him or the dogs. They'd likely prod and poke the animals to try and understand how the "Siberian rats," as they'd been called by Nome residents, even made it to the finish line.

All bets were against him and his team, "a hundred to one,"

with no one believing the smaller huskies could possibly run against the much larger, mixed Alaskan huskies. The Eskimos thought better of his team, but no one else did. He'd go to their trade store to see if they'd help him again with food. He had no money. Later, when he could, he'd pay them back. It was worth a try.

"Little Wolf, Magic, Mushroom . . . you guys stay," Rune commanded, then gave the hand signal for them to do so. They stood outside with him in the fresh snowfall.

Magic and Mushroom sat at once, but Little Wolf began to lick the hand giving him the command.

Rune's heart went out to the smallest husky in the pack. He remembered how hard the dog worked in his harness during the race to help bring the team home from the halfway point of Candle, across the finish in Nome. The little guy had been attacked at least three times, the last time poisoned. Rune knew who the culprit had to be. He'd find the bastard, all right, and take care of him! Not now, but soon.

Little Wolf nudged his hand again, looking for a pat. Rune obliged then led the stubborn pup back inside the stable and over to Anya, at the same time he gave Magic and Mushroom the command to follow.

"Anya," Rune said gently. He hated to disturb her. They'd finished the race over an hour ago and the dogs needed attention. "Anya," he repeated, and this time he put his hand under her soft, shapely chin. Her tears wet his fingers. Her pale complexion had lost its sparkle.

"Rune, I told you, didn't I?" she asked all of a sudden, her face flushed with upset. "I told you we didn't have to win the race but just finish. Your finish was good enough. I told you, didn't I?"

She abruptly let go of Xander and stood, then looked up into Rune's handsome features. She searched his glacial blue eyes, the same watch-blue as her dogs and the Gatekeepers. Confused about what she'd said to Rune after the race, she panicked when she thought she might have told him she'd traveled to the spirit world and come back to Native Earth, taking Zellie's place across the finish! If he knew everything about her, he might leave her and the dogs, thinking her "possessed by bad spirits," just like the shamans always accused her of being.

All her life she'd been shunned because of the shamans' poor opinion of her. Only two ever accepted her: her grandmother and Vitya. Nana-tasha was dead and Vitya wasn't here, but back in their home village. Rune was all she had in this strange place, Rune and the dogs. And now Zellie was gone. The ache inside her gnawed at any confidence she might have had before the race; before Zellie had been killed.

"Yes, Anya, you told me," Rune answered her, worried about the faraway look in her dark-lashed, seal-brown eyes. Her long hair had come loose from its tie, falling in soft, shimmering, dusky and brown folds over her shoulders and down her back. Now wasn't the time to have a discussion over the race finish or what the future might bring. He remembered what she'd said, all of it; especially the part about how they were still in danger.

She'd said, "It's just beginning." She really didn't have to tell him. He knew already from the pain at the back of his neck; from his birthmark of the ancient runes. The ghosts, good and bad, were not done with him, or Anya and the dogs. The ache, which only started after he'd met Anya would come and go. Until now, the mark had never once called his attention. The scar raised now where it had not before, pulling him out of his old life and into the unknown.

Odin himself, Rune believed, had traveled from his ancient golden realm to seek Rune out on Nome's deserted beaches. Odin, with his ravens and wolves and spear of war and wisdom, had stepped out of the shadows and into the light, for only

Rune to see. Rune remembered every detail of the otherworldly encounter.

Expressionless, the man had looked old . . . even ancient, in his musty travel robe, long gray hair and beard, with one good eye showing beneath the brim of a timeworn hat. Rune could just see where his other eye had been blinded. The oddly dressed traveler said nothing. Uneasy about the spear in the old traveler's hand, Rune waited for it to strike. What else could this mean but death coming for him, not ripped apart by wolves, but speared through the heart! Agitated by the fact that he had no spear of his own so he could die a Viking warrior, Rune raised his fists to Death and charged forward.

The razor sharp point of Death's spear stopped him, puncturing his chest to draw blood, but not kill.

Rune had stepped back, mindless of pain, helpless to do anything but stare at the deathly figure holding the spear, with its strange markings clearly visible to him now. The old man's ice-blue eye pierced through where the spear had not. Then the old man began to speak.

"I hung on a windy tree nine long nights, wounded with a spear, myself to myself. I took up the runes, screaming I took them!"

Rune hadn't cowered at the thunderous echo, but instead tried to pick apart what the old man said. He'd never heard anybody talk that way, like he was reading from some ancient book. And his name was mentioned? The old man said "runes." A memory had stirred, causing the birthmark at the back of his neck to burn hot, the same mark of the Viking gods for which he was named, his father had told him. Rune had never thought about this before—that his name held any real meaning.

"The Gatekeepers of the Chukchi have summoned," the ghostly figure then whispered secretively.

Rune had strained to listen.

"From nine seas you are born and nine serpents you must slay. Gungnir has found you and the wolf is awakened. In one hand you hold wisdom and in the other, war. But beware. Hel is coming. The wolf and the dog battle as one. The power of the runes is cast in human hands. It is time. It begins."

Never one to be afraid of unknown waters or ghosts and legends, Rune was uncertain about what the Viking gods wanted with him. He'd accepted the fact that he'd been singled out to help Anya and the Chukchi dogs but he still questioned why. He still questioned his skills to be of any help. Zellie was dead. So was Boris Ivanov.

Rune kept his hold on Anya's frail shoulders, not yet wanting to let go of her. His life was tied to hers by this time. He'd no choice but to follow the signs and help Anya and the dogs. To do otherwise would anger the ghostly gods of the Vikings. To do otherwise, he'd never forgive himself. He couldn't leave Anya alone anyway. She needed him.

His father, his mother, his own sister . . . none of them needed him.

Anya did.

"I'm just going," Rune said, yet kept hold of her.

Anya stared up into Rune's blue eyes, taking in the strength she felt from his touch. He looked every bit the Viking warrior of her imagination, with his straw-colored hair, his tall, powerful body, and his proven skills at sea and on land, too. He'd been able to drive her sled dog team in the All Alaska Sweepstakes when she'd doubted he could. She shouldn't have doubted him, she realized.

He did everything he needed to do to get the dogs across the finish. It wasn't his fault Zellie died. But was it Anya's? Sick to her stomach at the thought, she stepped out of Rune's reach. Was there anything she could have done to save Zellie?

Agitated, Anya knelt back down to Xander and ran her fingers through his thick fur, to feel him close. She naturally put one hand to Xander and held out the other to Zellie . . . but Zellie wasn't there. New tears fell.

Although it was hard to do, Rune left Anya alone and exited the stable, then headed into the snowfall. She needed time to get over all that had happened; so did he. He'd go and find food for the dogs but what after that? It was the middle of winter in the Arctic, in the wilds of the Alaskan frontier, and the thick sea ice would keep any ships from coming close. It would be months before his father's steamer, the *Storm,* or any others could reach the waters of Nome.

Isolated and penniless, Rune forged through the fresh, foot-deep snow toward the native trade store on the far edge of the booming city. He'd never needed money before, not caring about wealth like his mother and his sister. He'd kept the same five-hundred dollars in his duffle for years, working on board his father's ship, and didn't even think about it until he needed money for food and shelter in Nome.

He'd been careless last summer when he'd taken a room at the Nugget Inn, and had been easily robbed of his money. His own fault, he knew. It gave his father one more reason to doubt his abilities. Once Rune mentioned his name and was asked about his father, he might as well have left his door, room number nine at the inn, wide open. Based out of Seattle, Johansson and Son Shipping was widely known. Nome was the claim-jumping capital of the far north, known for lawlessness and gold fever. Rune shouldn't have been so naive and loose-lipped. Now he had no money. As for himself, he'd figure it out; but as for Anya and the dogs, he needed to find a way to take care of them.

Summer work in the mines was shut down until June. He'd look for winter work at the Pioneer Mining Company, one of the big operations. Its owner was one of the "lucky Swedes" who'd first discovered gold on Anvil Creek in the fall of 1898.

Rune needed to make a good wage. He didn't know much about gold mining other than the difference between open mining in warm weather and the potential for underground mining in cold, but he could learn.

He hadn't known much about dog driving either, but had managed to learn enough to finish the All Alaska Sweepstakes. At what cost? Did Zellie die because of any mistake he'd made? Did the rest of the dogs suffer injury because of him? Had the Viking gods given him too great a task?

The arctic winds picked up, and right away turned the snowfall into tiny shards of ice that cut across his face. Rune faced into the wind rather than away. He needed to sharpen his memory and go over every step of the race in his head and see if there was anything he could have done to save Zellie. He'd made mistakes, he knew. Had one of them killed?

This worry gnawed at him, weighted him down and slowed his step. The dogs didn't have time for his worries. He picked up his pace and ignored his own hunger and sapped strength. He headed for the Eskimo store, hoping they'd take his mark in trade for fish or meat for the dogs. When he could, he'd pay them back.

The Board of Trade Saloon was still jam-packed with miners, dog drivers, sled team owners, members of the Nome Kennel Club, tourists, other gamblers, and interested race-watchers.

Conversations went in all directions, from the bizarre, early onset of winter to the unusually violent storms; to the cut-short racing season; to the long months of isolation left; to questions about changing race rules; to Scotty Allen's big win of ten thousand dollars in the second annual All Alaska Sweepstakes; to bettors from the Outside; to losing telegraph communication from many of the race checkpoints; to dog driver Frank Lundgren's obvious mistreatment of his dogs and the consequences for such mistreatment; to allowing dog drivers to guide with whips; to how the smaller "Siberian rats" from across the Bering Sea could have fared so well against their larger, stronger, Alaskan mixed-malamute huskies; and to whether or not rookie dog driver Rune Johansson, with his nine Siberian dogs, had been bribed to slow down and lose the race. This rumor made the saloon circuit.

Some scratched their heads that the Siberian team did well in spite of being snowbound by the blizzard. Johansson was close behind Allen and Lundgren even after getting such a late start to Candle, the halfway point in the race. Then Johansson's team, after having covered over a hundred and fifty miles, turned around with little rest and still raced close behind the other teams. This is what made some wonder if there had been interference with Johansson's team to slow it down and come in third. If his team had crossed first, the Bank of Nome might go bust, the way bets had been placed. But with telegraph lines down and communication poor, chances were all of this was just rumor. Besides, no one had put much stock in the "Siberian rats" anyway. Yep, all just rumor.

"What's that?" Albert Fink, still seated at his corner table in the saloon, almost pulled out his Smith & Wesson .44 when the surly miner standing before him pulled what Albert first thought could be a gun on him. Pretty much everyone in Nome carried a weapon of some kind. Since Albert was the president of the newly organized Nome Kennel Club, which was responsible for the newly organized All Alaska Sweepstakes, he expected a disgruntled gambler or two might come at him and blame him for any losses they'd suffered. Albert, a racer himself, had kept his gun hand relaxed yet ready when he'd come back inside the Board of Trade Saloon after the last team crossed the finish line.

The atmosphere in Nome had been tense all winter even

without factoring in the important sled dog race and any upset bettors. Unexpected fierce, arctic weather on top of expected fierce, arctic weather coupled with long months of inaccessibility were not a good mix. Then add a small team of huskies from Siberia that should never have entered the race but that actually finished the race in decent time and that put some of the District of Alaska's finest dogs to shame. And yeah, could be some upset folks who lost good money or their good name.

A lawyer by trade, Albert was more than aware of the easy sleight of hand in the exchange of gold dust between even the best of friends. It was all about the gold in Nome; the gold and sled dog racing. The fever for both ran high.

"This here is my Bible, Mr. Fink. I've carried it with me ever since the weather turned on us last year."

Albert kept his focus on the man in front of him. He remembered more than one Nome resident took to their Bibles last year when violent winter storms hit early, turning summer to winter and day to night in the blink of an eye. He recalled all the talk of "doom and damnation." This man could be one of those or just another down-and-out miner.

Albert studied the nervous man's hand, and the Bible he held. His dirty fingers shook against the worn leather cover. The man's sunken eyes readily shifted focus, going from Albert to the crowd around them to the Bible in his hand. He looked to Albert like he hadn't slept in days. Gold fever could change a man. Gold fever could make a man crazy. Desperate, more like it. From the looks of this miner's poor clothes, he hadn't struck it rich on the red-and-black-streaked beaches of Nome or in the gold fields beyond. The unforgiving tundra hadn't given up any of its riches to this man, Albert could see.

Wary of the unpredictable miner, Albert eased his hand below the table to his holstered gun.

"Mr. Fink, I've come here to warn you of the end coming.

I've come here to warn you all," the man preached. "The wrath of God is upon us!" His voice started to rise.

"What's your name, friend?" Albert hoped he could calm the guy down and get him out of the saloon. He didn't want any fights going on; especially right after the race when everyone needed to settle their wins, their losses, and any tempers that flared over the unexpected show of the Siberian team.

The miner pulled back a little, seemingly surprised at the question, as if no one ever spoke to him in a normal tone. He smiled a little and lowered his Bible to the table, but didn't let go of his holy book.

"Name's Joshua of Jericho."

Albert realized then that the man had a new kind of fever, one he hadn't reckoned on: Bible fever. Albert didn't have anything against the Christian faithful but he recognized this man went beyond ordinary, spiritual belief to a place where someone or something had put the fear of God in him. It could have been the violent storms or his empty pockets; hard to know. Otherwise, he wouldn't call himself Joshua of Jericho and have that half-crazed glint in his eyes. He didn't look to Albert like a drunk. At least he didn't smell like one.

"Yes sir, Mr. Fink. I did help bring down the walls of Jericho. I obeyed God then and I must now." The man calling himself Joshua readily announced, "You are all in danger here. Someone is coming! Something is here!" He looked afraid, then picked his Bible back up and held it shaking in the air.

Albert glanced around the crowded saloon and then focused again on "Joshua." Damn, he wanted to get the guy out of there. He had no way of knowing if the upset miner packed a gun.

"Say, Albert," Bartholomew Granger said as he approached, and paid no attention to the man who stood at the table. "How long do you want me to keep the chalkboard up with the posted results? I can't tell if it's keeping bettors happy or making them mad."

"Someone is coming! Something is here!" Joshua of Jericho leveled at Bartholomew.

"Huh?" Bartholomew looked at the stranger and then quickly back at Albert. "What do you want me to do?"

"I want you to keep the board up," Albert calmly answered his friend, yet kept his eyes on the nervous man holding the now-lowered Bible. "I'll be over there in a minute."

A raucous cheer suddenly rose over by the posted results, only to be followed by angry shouts.

Bartholomew all but raced back to his post, and left Albert and the stranger alone.

"Mr. Fink, your days are numbered. So are the days for all in Nome. The beaches will be overrun by the waters of the Bering Sea and the city will perish!" Joshua of Jericho pointed his finger at Albert. "I've come to warn you all to leave before the end." His tone eerily calmed.

Albert decided to wait the guy out and let him finish. He didn't seem violent, just nuts.

"God has told me about the dogs, the Siberian dogs. They should not be here."

Oh, here we go, Albert thought. It's about the race after all, he supposed. The miner must have lost his money, all of it, betting on the wrong team.

"All right, Joshua of Jericho," Albert said and got up from the table. "I've heard enough. Why don't you get yourself a drink and settle down." With that, Albert brushed past the open-mouthed miner with his Bible still in hand, and charged over to the race chalkboard in the middle of the crowded saloon, to join his fellow kennel club members and to help deal with the race results and their consequences.

"You'll see, Albert Fink. All of you will see." Joshua of Jericho replaced his Bible in his jacket pocket and looked for the door of the Board of Trade Saloon.

Vitya looked out over the ice for any sign of a seal breathing hole. Seventy miles away from the shoreline, he and his trusted dog team of twenty had been out hunting seal on the frozen Bering Sea for three days. The days were actually nights since the Siberian arctic stayed in shadow this time of the year.

So far Vitya had two kills in the bed of his sled to show for his efforts. He wanted one more to ensure a good food store for his family in their coastal village. His parents and his sisters relied on him. He hunted alone now and liked it that way. Lately his father talked of herding reindeer instead of hunting the whale, the walrus, and the seal. Times like this Vitya missed Anya more than ever. He used to talk to her about everything. No more. Anya was gone.

It had been almost a year since he'd last seen her. She left during Days Grow Long at the end of the last winter season. Still in the Extending Days, Vitya knew winter would stay until New Summer Growing, before the ice would begin to thaw and let go its grip on them. The short summer season meant good hunting in the arctic waters off the coast for his village and good grazing tundra across the land for the villages of the reindeer herders.

Summer also signaled time for the Markova Fair on the Anadyr River. Vitya gulped down his continued upset whenever he thought of the Markova Fair. That's why Anya had to leave their home village. She released Grisha's dogs so they wouldn't be traded away at the fair. Grisha could have killed her for such an unforgivable act but he did not. He took her with him and the Chukchi dogs he selected for trade at the fair. Grisha returned to their village, without Anya. To this day Grisha wouldn't say a word about what happened to her.

Was Anya dead? Had Grisha left her out on unknown tundra to die? That's how he killed his own mother when she no longer could work. It was the Chukchi way, for children to kill their parents when they were of no more use. Vitya believed things must change. He didn't think he could kill his parents when the time came. He didn't think he could ever leave one of his children to die, either. That is, if he had any. Sixteen years old, unmarried, and with no babes of his own, Vitya gulped back more upset. He should be married now, to Anya!

If she made it to the fair, what happened to her? Surely Grisha wouldn't trade Anya away. No, he would not do such a thing to his own child. Anya had helped Grisha raise and train all of their valued sled dogs. It was wrong for her to let them go, Vitya knew. It was a terrible offense, punishable by death. Death for Anya would be better than trading her away.

Vitya didn't have special powers like Anya, the same powers as the shamans in their village. He couldn't sense things the way she always could; otherwise he would know for sure if she were dead or alive. It was "killing" him that he didn't know. There were days he wanted to kill Grisha for not telling him. Maybe he could force Grisha to talk and use the torture methods of the shamans.

It wasn't the first time he'd thought of it and it wouldn't be the last. When the shamans had to do something terrible like order the sacrificial killing of somebody in their village, that person could torture the shaman to make sure of the truth of the divination. If the shaman survived, he or she would be telling the truth. Would Grisha survive? Vitya wondered.

Before he used any force on Grisha, Vitya suddenly knew what he must do. He needed to go to the Markova Fair this year and see if he could find out what might have happened to the girl he loved, and had loved since they were children. He didn't know he felt more than friendship until he kissed her last year on the cliffs overlooking the great sea. His friendship turned to love in that moment—in the same moment he realized he didn't want her to leave their village and *him*.

Willing to help her get to a neighboring village where he could secure a dogsled team, he'd wanted to leave with her. She'd refused to let him leave his family and was determined to face Grisha with her deeds. Why didn't he follow his gut and take her away then, out of harm's way, out of Grisha's way! There wasn't a day gone by where he didn't regret that he hadn't run away with Anya then. Not a day. Did she have the necklace still, the one he made for her? Not a day passed when he didn't wonder about that, either.

Vitya stared out over his dog team. They raced across the ice at a steady pace, helping him search out seal holes in the ice. Good hunters, good runners, light eaters, energetic, gently bred, he'd miss his loyal Chukchi dog team when he traded them away at Markova. If Anya were here at this moment, she'd refuse to let him.

But she wasn't here.

The only way he could find her would be to take his dogs for trade. His father wanted to leave their village and make a new life for them all following the reindeer herds. Vitya would make sure to get the value of the traded dogs back to his family, but he would stay in the Anadyr region and look for Anya. It was only a start in his quest to find her, but it was all he had.

CHAPTER TWO

"He became quicker of movement than the other dogs,
swifter of foot, craftier, deadlier, more lithe, more lean
with ironlike muscle and sinew, more enduring, more
cruel, more ferocious, and more intelligent. He had to
become all these things, else he would not have held his
own nor survived the hostile environment in which he
found himself."

—Jack London, *White Fang*

Xander broke from Anya's hold and stood. Never before had he
done this, pulled away from his guardian's comforting touch,
first.

His canine instincts forced his weak body to stand and try to
shake off the wet, the misery, the emptiness that coated him.
On unsure legs he began to search the stable for Zellie.

The other dogs watched but didn't get up and follow, as if
they understood Xander's intent. One of their pack was missing. Drums of the ancients sounded out Zellie's death, sharpening their intuition, their awareness of what happened to their
leader on the last run. Still shaken themselves, the surviving
dogs needed to eat and to sleep and then run again; next time
faster and harder, to escape what hunted them.

Until coming to this new place, the dogs had always been
part of the hunt. They helped search out food for their masters
over tundra and ice. Used to circling their prey, they would wait

31

for their humans to kill, for the survival of them all. The dogs could kill if they had to. It was in their blood to survive, no matter their gentle breeding. To stay alive now, their instincts told them to stay together as a pack. It was their only chance. Their leader had been separated from them and she was gone.

More uneasy than afraid, the dogs sensed they must keep alert, watchful for anything coming at them. They were prey now, the hunted and not the hunter.

"No, Xander!" Anya called when he went outside the stable, in a panic she might lose sight of him. She knew he hurt for Zellie and had to be confused about what to do next, without her. He'd never been separated from Zellie until the Markova Fair when Grisha traded him to the ugly Yukaghir, to the dark spirits.

Xander's life forever changed in that moment; set on an even more dangerous path in a world without Zellie. She was his guide in all things, his forever and best friend as only dogs can understand. Xander never made a move without her, never ate a meal without her, and never ran before any sled without her. A young dog like Zellie, Xander was almost three now. He could have many years yet to live.

Anya was a Chukchi shaman with spiritual powers, but she couldn't foretell the future, at least not so far. Maybe that wasn't such a bad thing. Maybe she didn't want to know when the dark spirits would find Xander, as they had Zellie.

They would. Anya knew it was just a matter of time. She must become master over the Raven and the dark spirits, as her grandmother prophesied, to try and save Xander and the others. Too late for Zellie; she was gone. Anya had witnessed her passage into the hands of the eternal Gatekeepers who would keep watch over Zellie in death. Spirit, Anya's husky counterpart in the mystic world beyond Native Earth—the Chukchi spirit world—would also keep watch over Zellie. Anya and Spirit, one and the same, could exchange places, shape-shifting from human to husky and husky to human . . . all to fool the dark spirits.

That's exactly what happened right before Zellie died. Anya and Spirit, in mist and magic, switched places so Anya could be with Zellie a few precious moments as death came, then race across the All Alaska Sweepstakes finish, in Zellie's form. "All dogs that start must finish," the rules demanded. Zellie had to lead her team across the line for their sled to qualify; to make a difference. Zellie's team finished but at the cost of her life. Too late, neither Anya nor her Spirit had been able to master dark spirits and save her.

This fact struck new fear in Anya—fear that she could lose Xander, any day, any time, any place. She could lose Xander and the rest of the brave seven to an unknown evil; not giving up; not satisfied until they were all dead.

"Yes, English," the hard-edged Eskimo informed Rune. "I speak good. You race good," he said, and nodded to underscore his point.

Tufts of the storekeeper's black hair stood out as if ruffled by the wind, not yet returned in place. His heavy oilcloth parka had no fur trim. This wasn't the same Eskimo Rune had met before the race, the one who gave him extra provisions for his dogs. Anya and Rune didn't have enough money to buy all they needed then, but at this native trade store, they'd received charity donations. Embarrassed to ask for more, Rune had no choice.

His pockets were empty and he'd no way of knowing when or if he could fill them with gold dust or anything else. His pride wouldn't stop him. He couldn't afford to have any pride with hungry dogs. Anya needed food, too.

"I have no money." Rune looked the older man in the eye. "No gold, either."

"No *kanosak,* no gold?"

33

Rune shook his head in a flat no.

"You have good *issorartuyok*, good leader dog."

Rune's insides jarred. No, he did not. Zellie was gone. This Eskimo must want her in trade for goods.

"She's not for trade," Rune said flatly. No need to tell anybody about Zellie and what happened. Rune still couldn't answer that question, himself.

The storekeeper grunted something and then turned away from Rune.

"I will give you my mark in trade for food. I will give you anything I have, anything but the dogs. I will not trade any of the dogs," Rune said with finality.

"Your dogs, *makoktok amarok*, like the young wolf. Your dogs, *sivudlit*, like the ancestors of the wolf. They race fast, *pialaksaur-tut nakkertok*. They could finish the race first, *tikikrautauwok;* easy, I think. Why they not finish first?" the Eskimo asked, his brow furrowed deep in question.

Rune had no answer, at least none he'd give to this stranger. He kept silent, the plea in his eyes obvious. The dogs were hungry. He and Anya were hungry. He didn't want to stand at this sawbuck counter any longer than he had to, thinking of Zellie being dead and the rest of the dogs in danger of the same fate.

The wily Eskimo appeared to scrutinize Rune, his slant-eyed stare hard.

"*Piktaungitok tonrar* must have stopped you—evil spirits. Your dogs faster than the others and should have finished first. *Piktaungitok tonrar* must have stopped you."

Rune couldn't believe how close this Eskimo had come to the truth. Rune quickly dismissed the native tradesman's words as superstition and old beliefs; nothing more. This man didn't really see ghosts; at least not the ones after Anya, the dogs, and him.

"I am Chinook. I speak for our village dog races. Our dogs race faster if bred with yours. It's a good plan, yes?"

"No," Rune shot back. He didn't have to think about his answer. The dogs belonged to Anya. He would never go around her for any such decision. Besides, now was not the time; not with their very survival on the line.

The Eskimo gave Rune a curt nod as if he accepted his answer, yet kept up his stare.

"*Kringmiluardjuk?* If there is a pup, would you think about trading a *kringmiluardjuk* to me then?"

"Listen . . . Chinook." Rune tried to remember the man's name. He needed to get out of there with food, *now.* "My name is Rune Johansson. The dogs are not mine to decide such a thing. I will ask your question of her. That is all I can promise."

"Good," the Eskimo smiled, showing a few missing teeth. "I give you meat and fish. You will need more for the winter. If you want, you can come and hunt with my village. It is in the Bonanza Hills. Ask for the village of Chinook."

Rune offered his hand to shake.

"Thank you," he said, taken aback by Chinook's friendly offer, since Rune hadn't made any agreement with him over the dogs.

The Eskimo shook Rune's hand then turned away to fill a gunnysack with food for the white boy who could drive dogs. Chinook was impressed with him. He liked the boy's spirit, too. Chinook sensed that something upset the boy, still. It had to be *piktaungitok tonrar.* Evil spirits were in the air all around the boy. Chinook wanted to help if he could. He would speak to the shaman in their village. The same evil that changed the summer to winter in the blink of an eye, bringing the unusually fierce storms . . . was still here. It followed the boy and his dogs.

★ ★ ★ ★ ★

The crude entrance of the stable faced east, the most important direction to the Chukchi. Anya had finished watering her dogs. It was time to see to their injuries. Their paw pads needed care. They'd run over too many miles of jagged ice and unknown terrain, thrown off the race course more than once by evil and trickery. Normally the dogs would be fine. They were tough and had well-padded feet. But these were not "normal" times.

She immediately prostrated herself on the ground, at once believing she must appeal to the Morning Dawn and the Directions for guidance to save the dogs. The eyes of the Gatekeepers were on her. The dogs were her responsibility and she must protect them; but how? In this hostile place, in this unknown land where dark spirits followed, how could she find safe haven for the Chukchi dogs? Her face flat to the cold earth, her eyes pressed shut; she forced herself to think on what she *did have* to help save the dogs instead of what she did not have.

She'd learned to speak English well enough since she'd arrived in Alaska, whether by magic of the ancients or her natural intelligence. Growing up she'd picked up some Russian and some English words from passing whalers, but not enough to get by in this crowded, busy village of Nome. Back in her home village, men and women spoke differently, too, but that was because men usually roared while women whispered.

Here in Nome men and women spoke at the same volume, confusing her. The sounds of the words were the same, too. Chukchi women spoke with female accents on words. Here in Nome it was all the same. Here in Nome there was writing, signs on buildings Anya couldn't read. The Chukchi had no written language, only oral. Frustrated and anxious over her inability to communicate well with the English-speakers, she didn't know exactly when she'd mastered the white tongue. But she had. She could not read and write, but she could speak and understand.

Anya remembered her grandmother's words, telling her she must become master over dark spirits. Anya also thought of the times in her life when she dreaded spirits coming to her. They'd always made her anxious and sick to her stomach. Nana-tasha would tell her she was special and not to be upset by such visitations. Anya never believed she was special, not really; not until she realized the burden placed on her by the Gatekeepers; not until she truly needed her powers as a shaman to try to save the Chukchi dogs.

Now she could speak English in this "English" land. It was also the land of the Eskimo, the old enemy of the Chukchi. No more. From this point she must look to the Eskimo as a friend. Their native spirit would match hers, she told herself. Anya felt more native than white, despite the blood of a Russian whaler running through her veins. Her mother was full-blood Chukchi.

How Anya wished she could have known her mother. Tynga died giving birth to her. Grisha was not her real father. Grisha hated Anya because of Tynga's death, she believed. He'd never forgiven her. He believed all the accusations hurled at her by the village shamans, that she was possessed by bad spirits, because her birth ended Tynga's life.

In truth Anya did feel responsible. If not for her, her mother would live still. Her grandmother told her it was meant to be, but Anya never accepted this. Her birth would always be an unhappy mystery to her; unhappy because her mother died and a mystery because she sometimes felt more husky than human. She remembered the soft down of the huskies coming inside during the coldest of winter nights in the Extending season. They lay down next to her, and cuddled her as if she were their babe. Then, growing up, when she discovered she was a shaman, this only added to the mystery.

Was she human or spirit?

Was her father a faceless Russian whaler or a ghostly husky divined by spirits?

Anya pressed her face harder against the frozen earth. She didn't have time for such mystical thoughts. She must pray to the Morning Dawn and the Directions for help in saving the dogs. They mattered; she didn't.

Besides a miraculous ability to speak the local language, she had her crude knife with her still. It was "a gift from the gods," according to her grandmother. Anya ran her hand inside the pocket that hid the small blade to make sure of it. In her home village she'd used her blade only for cutting away ties and bindings, to free the dogs from their tethers. Never intending to use the crude weapon, she'd needed it and used it to release the dogs; ready to pay for her actions with her life.

The knife symbolized life and death.

The knife would only be used for the dogs.

If it truly was "a gift from the gods," then Anya would only use it to protect her beloved huskies. All of a sudden she opened her eyes and rose on her elbows to look at her hands. She watched them as if they were not attached to her but acting on their own, as if they still held her knife. Her fingers splayed over the part-frozen earth, and rubbed across caught-up pieces of straw and ice as if trying to wipe away all traces of blood from her knife and her hands. Anya sat up fully, upset when she remembered what happened soon after her arrival in Nome, when her knife had been covered in blood.

She'd kept hold of her knife . . . wiping it against her dress to help wipe away the smell of death. The dogs were bloodied but they were alive. Down on their sides now, stretched out and unmoving, only their eyes twitched open. They looked dazed, but they lived. Anya had sent a silent prayer to the Morning Dawn and all the gods for blowing enough breath in the dogs to sustain life. She'd found all nine huskies coiled in the tentacles of a grotesque snaking whip, just as her nightmare had foretold. The dogs were being dragged away to a sure, suffocating death, unable to cry out. Her crude knife overpowered the monster from her nightmare, cutting each lashing tentacle away and freeing each dog from death. It all happened in the time it takes for a heart to beat, giving life to all things and ending it just as fast.

Anya eased back down onto the stable floor. Instead of shutting away the memory of the attack, she'd keep it foremost in her mind and determined to keep up her prayers. She'd need them. Nightmares were something she'd never had until her arrival on these unknown shores. Dark spirits brought them. Dark spirits followed the dogs. Dark spirits followed her; Rune, too.

She pictured her knife inside her pocket, ready to strike down what tried to come at them all. Anya saw herself as the hunter and not the hunted. Sudden arctic winds brought the drums of the ancestors to her ears, at first low then growing in force. The music of the Chukchi coursed through her and renewed her spirit for the fight ahead. Wolves howled across the tundra, their cries stirring her dogs.

Xander came over and lay down next to her, then rested his head on his paws, eyes closed.

She put one hand to him and kept the other outstretched in prayer. Nothing was more precious to her than the warmth of his downy fur, his familiar smell, the heave of his breathing, the gentle blue of his watch eyes, and his kind spirit. Ever a mischievous pup, he was an innocent, not meant for life in any kind of hostile world. He was meant to run free across tundra and ice, one with the land and sea.

Under attack since he'd been traded at the Markova Fair, he'd suffered much. Changed now, forced into a fight he didn't start, he had to stay strong or die. Without Zellie, he would need time to find his way. Maybe one day he could be that innocent pup again. Anya prayed to all the Chukchi gods for that day to come.

The winds outside died down. Xander sat up, disturbed by something. Anya sat up, too. An eerie silence permeated the sharp atmosphere inside the stable. All the dogs had stirred, restless, whining. Loud caws from above the roof boards suddenly carried down through the wide spaces in-between.

The Raven is here.

The Arctic had many ravens, ordinary everyday ravens that never traveled in flocks to blacken the skies. Ravens were loners. Not these above the stable now. These ravens could gather and blacken the sky in a heartbeat, in the time it takes to give life to all things or take it away. These ravens were sent by the Raven god to trick, taunt, and terrorize. These ravens brought the ice storm.

Snow sifted through the cracks in the makeshift roof. The claws of the ravens overhead scratched where they could. Anya ran her fingers over her little blade, making sure of it, then placed herself in front of a growling Xander and the rest of the dogs. Her throat was dry; she tried to swallow. Her heart thudded. She steeled for the fight. Whatever was about to come at them would have to kill her first.

"Rune!"

"Who else did you expect?" He bent his head and entered the stable. "You don't have to yell," he lightly scolded. He cracked a smile. "All of Nome doesn't need to know where we are."

Anya let out the breath she'd been holding. She eased her hand off her knife but automatically wiped it across her fur parka to clean off the blood. There was no blood on her knife, yet the action helped calm her nerves.

Rune's smile faded. Something had frightened her; her and the dogs. He'd never heard Xander growl before.

"Who was here, Anya?" He kept his voice steady.

"They're gone," she answered before she wished she hadn't. How could she explain that a bunch of birds scared her?

"They?" Rune repeated. He had an idea what frightened her. The ghosts after them, the same ones who'd taken Zellie's life, must have shown themselves. He wondered in what form they'd appeared. Over land now and not water, they could not have been any serpent that lurked under the ice, and waited to kill. Still, he wanted to ask Anya. Before he could, he stopped himself.

How could he explain that the Midgard serpent of Viking legend stalked him during much of the race they'd just run? Anya knew of his gods. He knew of hers. At least they knew they came from different traditions and beliefs. But to tell her of the Midgard serpent and its legions would scare her more than she already was. Why do that? He would wait. She'd find out soon enough.

"It was the Raven," Anya said. "Whatever is after us sent the Raven." She dared a look at Rune, and waited for him to walk away the moment she said anything. All her life people walked away from her, accusing her of being possessed by bad spirits. Why did she have to open her mouth and tell him of the Raven? She knew why. He needed to know the enemy. He had to be warned.

"The raven is a good sign, Anya," Rune countered, staring down into her sad eyes. She carried nothing but worry on her pretty face. He wanted to bring back her smile. He wanted to take away her worry. The raven had helped guide the Vikings more than once through the darkest of storms. Odin himself had ravens as guide. Anya should know of this. Rune should reveal this to her even if she would be put off by such beliefs.

"The raven means you no harm, Anya. To my ancestors the raven has always been a welcome sign. You should not be frightened by the raven."

"You should not be so foolish, Rune," Anya shot back. She didn't care if she made him mad. He needed to know about the Raven to protect himself. "The Raven god of the Chukchi is angry with me. The Raven has joined the dark spirits after us. The Raven does not want the dogs to survive in this new land. You must be watchful for the Raven," she warned.

Now Rune understood.

"So go," Anya said and turned her back on Rune. She didn't want to see him leave. She didn't want to see the look of disapproval on his handsome face before he did.

"Go where?"

Anya instantly pivoted; her face lit up in a smile. She couldn't help it. She couldn't believe he stayed with her—with her and the dark spirits after them.

"That's my girl." He lightly chucked her chin. "Smiles are better than frowns."

Beaming inside and out, she forgot all else between them. She liked it when he called her, "my girl."

"All right, meal time, guys." Rune stepped around Anya and set down the loaded gunnysack he held. The dogs gathered but didn't rush him; their tails wagged and they already licked their chops. They smelled the fresh catch. Rune tossed a fish to each dog in turn then watched as each found his own spot to satisfy his appetite. He still marveled at their orderly behavior, not fighting each other for food as most dogs would but patiently waiting for their portion.

Yes, of course. Rune! Anya suddenly thought of the things she *had* to help save the dogs instead of what she didn't have.

One, she could speak English.

Two, she had her crude blade.

And three, she had Rune to help her. He just had again, she realized. Tilting her head upward she knew before she looked that the ravens scattered when Rune returned.

The Raven god was afraid of Rune. Since the time Rune pulled Xander from the jowls of the Bering Sea, and saved his life with a strength Anya didn't realize Rune had, she knew the Raven had to pull back. Just like now. Anya thought of Rune's Viking ancestors. He had their gift of striking fear in the enemy, their gift of war and wisdom.

War and wisdom?

How odd to come up with that. They were not her words. An eerie sensation shot through her. Were other spirits from worlds beyond the Chukchi trying to reach her, talking of *war and wisdom?* No, certainly not. The Vikings might have ravens but they didn't have shamans and spirits . . . or did they?

"Anya," Rune said, his tone serious.

She turned her face up to his. Her heart skipped a little at what he might say; at what she might want him to say. Each day she warmed to him more. It scared her a little. She had enough to be scared about without her worry over feelings for Rune. Besides, feelings only made you hurt.

"Our enemies stay close, Anya. Too close."

"I know," she whispered back, in a struggle to push away unwanted emotions. She needed to focus on the reality of their situation; not on girlish daydreams.

"We need to leave Nome," Rune cautioned. "We need to outrun and outlast the Raven god and the forces of *Hel.*"

"*Hel?*" Anya tried to imagine such a god and what it might look like. "Is *Hel* a powerful god?" Afraid to hear the answer, she asked the question anyway.

"You might say that." Rune's jaw tightened. His fists clenched. Zellie was dead. He didn't save her from *Hel.* There were eight dogs left. He couldn't fail again. He wouldn't.

"You are talking of the gods of your ancestors, of the Vikings, aren't you, Rune?"

"Yes." He tried to relax his fists, without much luck.

"When I speak of the Raven god I am talking of my native ancestors, of the Chukchi," Anya explained, feeling a little better than moments before.

"I know," Rune said, not missing the glint of pride in her eyes when she mentioned her people. Not missing the anger there for the Raven god, either. Rune admired her all over again for her bravery and loyalty to her dogs. He'd never met any girl like her.

"War and wisdom, Rune . . . what does it mean?"

Taken completely by surprise, he looked away from Anya to every corner of the cramped stable area. Was this some kind of trick of the dark elves? Were they whispering in Anya's ears, bringing their mischief and upset? No, he saw nothing. Only eight dogs watching him.

He charged outside the stable to have a look around but saw nothing in the gentle snowfall. Straightening to his full height, all six feet, two inches, he folded his hands at the back of his head and exhaled sharply. His birthmark singed. He tried to remember if he'd ever mentioned to Anya what Odin's ghost had told him on the beaches of Nome.

"Rune?" She realized the words, war and wisdom, must carry great meaning, he seemed so upset.

Brought back to the moment by Anya's quiet summons, he headed inside the stable.

"Why do you ask this? Why do you speak of war and wisdom to me?" he accused more than asked. He didn't mean to sound so rough with her. Maybe it wasn't such a good idea to have this conversation about their enemies, human and otherwise. Disappointed in himself, he didn't want to frighten her needlessly. Unsure what to say or do, he supposed he already had.

"I don't know how else the words could have come to me but from the spirits around you." She told him the truth.

"Spirits? Spirits around *me*?"

"Yes, *you*, Rune." The time for secrets was over. The dogs didn't have time for this. Their enemies were on the hunt. She and Rune must work together with no secrets between them. She would risk telling Rune she was a Chukchi shaman. Zellie had died. Boris the bear had died. How many more would die before this was all over? Time had run out. She and Rune couldn't afford to keep any secrets. Like it or not, their lives were set on the same dangerous path with no going back.

The dogs started to whine, all of them.

Someone . . . something was coming.

Xander went to Anya's side.

Eleven years since the big rush for gold in the Yukon, the steamship business between Seattle and Nome stayed brisk. The route from Seattle cut past the Gulf of Alaska in the Pacific Ocean through Dutch Harbor in the Aleutian Islands, then north into the Bering Sea. Mining districts had been established over much of the Alaska wild, coastal and interior. Individual mining had shifted more to big company mines, but by no means was the individual miner dead and gone.

The red and black sandy beaches of Nome had been mined out, three times over; each time setting the panning and sluicing zone farther inland from the Bering Sea and toward the tundra. There were yet fortunes to be made, but miners had to travel farther and dig deeper for their gold, using hydraulic methods and the new method of dredging as well. Individual miners still worked creek beds and streams on their claims and checked each and every pan for any sign of "color."

Claim jumping wasn't as common now since corrupt lawmakers and judges had been tossed out of the District of Alaska when caught trying to steal claims from rightful owners. That being said, law and order in the Alaska wild wasn't always easy to come by. Several miles away from Nome, Fort Davis helped keep the peace. Where they were needed, other U.S. army posts had been established in the District of Alaska. Local town boards and law enforcement would become part of the landscape soon enough.

Lars Johansson set down his pen. He took off his spectacles, feeling every bit of his forty-two years. Shoving his stack of ledgers across his desk, he rubbed his tired eyes. Light still poured in through his office windows. No need to turn on the electrics. Noise from the busy Port of Seattle filtered up to him through the red brick walls of Johansson and Son Shipping. Lars got up from his desk chair on the second floor and went over to one of the large windows, and trained his eyes on the newest addition to his fleet of steamers, the *Nordic;* this ship larger and heavier than any other in his fleet.

While the *Nordic* wasn't an ice-breaker, it was sturdy and well-built, and Lars thought it would easily weather the rough seas of the North. He wasn't any explorer needing to weather polar ice like Amundsen or Scott, but a businessman needing to navigate port to port, trading during the warmer months. His fleet of steamers served him and his business well. Plenty of trade in summer and plenty of business at home during winter.

The *Storm* sat moored next to the *Nordic.* It was being outfitted for Vladivostok; the southern Russian trading port was never blocked in with ice. Men busied all around the trusted steamer, loading freight, laying in fuel, and completing the checklist before their departure. The only crewman not aboard the *Storm* at the moment was its captain.

Lars abruptly turned away from the window and flopped down in his desk chair. The leather creaked, unnerving him even more. If Rune were here he'd let his son at last captain the *Storm* to Vladivostok. Lars stood up again only to flatten his hands on the wood of his desk. He studied his splayed fingers. Rune wasn't here now, thanks to him. If he hadn't made Rune take the little Siberian girl and her dogs to Nome, and tossed Rune's duffle in the lighter boat in the process, his son would be right here in this office with him, chomping at the bit to steer the *Storm* on its next venture.

Lars slowly folded to sit again. He shut his eyes and leaned his head back against the worn leather chair. The familiar action brought little comfort.

His son would have a birthday soon, and turn seventeen, alone. Lars grimaced inside. Neither Rune's mother nor his sister would care. Margret and Inga cared little about anything or anyone but themselves. He loved his wife and his daughter, but he didn't like them. When he'd first met and fallen in love with Margret, she was a different person. Money had changed her, his money. Had he known, maybe he would have stayed a crewman and not worked to captain his own *skepp*.

Maybe he wouldn't have followed the ambition to own a fleet of *skepps* if he knew Margret would change so. His *dotter*, Inga, was just like her mother; his fault, all of it. He'd done nothing but spoil his daughter. With Rune it had been different. Rune knew his own mind from the get-go it seemed, and wanted nothing more than to work hard and be at sea. Lars didn't have any opportunity to spoil Rune. No such word existed on board any ship. Being at sea was all about surviving, trading, and returning home . . . every crewman, every time.

Lars twisted in his chair, then pulled the whiskey tray close. He poured a snap and swallowed hard. Liquor wasn't the answer. It wouldn't help get Rune home safe. He all but dropped his glass onto the mirrored tray, then shoved it away. The headache he'd fought off all morning returned. He'd had the same nightmare about Rune; about Rune drowned at sea by the serpents of Viking legend.

Sailors always faced the demons of the ocean, every time they'd throw a duffle over their shoulder and head to sea. Rough waters, high seas, fierce winds, impending ice . . . these were common fears that could swallow a ship and its crew. Not serpents of old. Only Lars dreamed of such nonsense, of such fears. But were they just dreams, or did the old enemies of the Vikings still exist?

Lars shot out of his chair again. He charged over to the window and stared hard at the *Storm* outside. The *skepp* looked fine. All the moored ships did. The day was cloudy like most in Seattle. Nothing looked different or amiss but Lars didn't like what he saw, rather what he didn't see. No gulls flew overhead or perched on pier pilings. Not a sound; their unmistakable calls silenced. No dogs, either. None ran up and down the pier, stray or otherwise. Men still worked but not a sign of animal life?

It felt to Lars like something had scared them off. Squinting, he looked out over the dark waters past the Port of Seattle. He knew nothing really lurked there, waiting to strike. Then again, he couldn't shake the image of Rune's ship struggling to stay afloat, under attack by the Midgard serpent. His nightmares again, he knew. Ridiculous as they were, he couldn't shake them off easily, even in the light of day.

Lars thought back to the day he'd set Rune ashore in Nome the summer last. He'd seen through his scope that the lighter boat arrived safely despite the sudden turn in weather and combative, high seas. There was no way the larger, sturdier *Storm* could have reached Nome's beaches with the waters too shallow and treacherous. No large ships could get past the two-plus-mile boundary. When his scope was able to penetrate the thick cloud cover, Lars had watched, relieved to see Rune and the other crewmen help Boris Ivanov, the artless Siberian girl, and the nine huskies traded at Markova, disembark.

They'd made it safely when Lars feared they wouldn't.

They were safe then, but how about now? Lars knew he

wouldn't be able to come back for his son before the following summer, yet he'd left Rune. Were they still safe? That's what ate away at Lars, his fears and the nightmares bringing them on. All because of what he'd chosen to name his son, *Rune*.

Named after the rune sign of the Viking gods, Lars thought it fitting to have his son's name match his birthmark. At this point Lars believed he might have opened the gates of *Hel* because of it, sacrificing his son's life. He'd always worried about Rune being at sea, but now he thought he understood the reason, told to him in his nightmares. Lars couldn't afford to ignore his nightmares any longer. His son had a connection to the ancient past that must be broken or Rune would pay with his life.

Not if I get to him first.

As soon as the arctic ice broke, Lars would make way for Nome. If the ice didn't break enough for a clean path, he'd ram the *isen* using the *Nordic*, his biggest ship. Willing to risk losing his newest steamer, knowing how the ice can nip and cut and breach the ship's hull, he wasn't willing to lose Rune.

Lars refused to think about the truth of it—that he might already have.

CHAPTER THREE

The bars of the prison cell shook. The man shaking them was no self-proclaimed "man of steel" but a golem[1], a creation of mystical fanaticism, a clay figure infused at birth with a demon spark giving it life—a life intended to bring only death. Its shape was human but its heart was monstrous. It was only a man, a mere mortal, yet born with a demonic spark powerful and willful enough to bring disaster and cause an irreparable breach between worlds.

The timeless layering of worlds, spirit and human, cannot exist peacefully—not when another golem appears. Not with the birth of this golem on Native Earth, shaking in its cold cage, raging across the frozen tundra and rattling its bloody saber for all to hear.

The ice storm is coming! I am coming!

It is time. It begins.

Some hear the golem's roar. Many do not.

While all of Siberia shakes, the waters of the Bering Sea roll and crash, and the wilds of the arctic frontier quake in the thunder of the golem's chill warning, only the Gatekeepers of the Chukchi and the gods of the Vikings hear and are called to the unnatural breach. They must prepare. The wolf and the dog

1 *Gendercide Watch.* July 3, 2013 <http://www.gendercide.org> "According to the historian Robert Conquest, Joseph Stalin 'gives the impression of a large and crude claylike figure, a golem, into which a demonic spark has been instilled.' "

must battle as one; this union only because of the chance meeting between Anya and Rune.

The hand of the guardian has brushed the hand of the runes.

Rune stepped in front of Anya and Xander.

Time stood still inside their shelter. The snow picked up outside. The gray day turned dark. The rest of the dogs crowded close, alert to someone, something, coming. They all needed to be "more enduring, more cruel, more ferocious, and more intelligent" than whatever was coming for them. Zellie's death was fresh. This was not a friendly place.

"*Awrite* there!" A man called out before Anya and Rune could see him. Enemy or friend, they'd find out soon enough. Both kept up their guard. Anya pulled out her knife and Rune steadied for a fight.

Xander bristled. Flowers stood next to him; the piebald, spotted female husky seemed to seek his protection. He didn't acknowledge her but stared hard in the direction of the voice. It wasn't a guardian. It wasn't a protector. It could bring harm. It could have a whip in its hands. He would recognize the coiled weapon. He remembered the blows and how they felt. Two humans had taken whips to him. Two humans had cut him. He growled low and waited to see what this human had in its hands.

"*Awrite* there!" A cheerful voice greeted again. The moment the young Scot reached the stable entrance, his smile faded. "What's this? You look like you're busting for a fight when I've only come for a *wee blether* with you." He seemed to know better than to charge inside the stable, uninvited.

The tension drained from Rune. He wondered what this unwelcome stranger wanted. He studied the man head to foot and saw no weapons, nothing that threatened.

For Anya, it wasn't so easy. She tucked her knife back in the pocket of her kerker and rested her fingers against the crude blade. The man didn't look like any dark spirit. She let go of her knife and brought her hand out of her pocket. The man didn't look like Mooglo, the ugly Yukaghir, either. But then Mooglo was never far. His evil spirit was conjured by the Raven god. His spirit traveled the Bering Sea and could appear anytime, in anyone, she believed.

She thought of the dog driver who whipped his dogs mercilessly on the race just run; nearly killing them. He'd tried to kill hers, too. She wondered if he really was a man named "Frank Lundgren" or the ugly Yukaghir, Mooglo? Wary of this stranger who appeared out of nowhere, she rubbed her hand where she carried the scar of Mooglo's lash, then slid it back inside the pocket of her fur parka, to her knife.

Xander approached the unfamiliar human and nuzzled both of his hands, to make sure of them—that they didn't carry a whip.

"*Aye noo,* there's a *braw dug,*" the young Scot knelt down to Xander but didn't try to pet him.

"A what?" Anya stiffened; jealous Xander took so easily to the stranger. She forgot about her worries over Mooglo and the Raven god.

"I meant nothing by it, lassie. You *cannae* argue he's not a *braw dug.*"

"A good dog, you mean," Rune said.

The Scot stood up and offered his hand for Rune to shake. Xander stayed put.

"Name's Fox Maule Ramsey. I'm happy to meet you, Rune Johansson." His broad smile returned.

"How is it you know me?" Rune shot his question, and half-heartedly shook the stranger's hand.

"I'm a dog driver, too, lad. I *didnee* race this one, but I watched you and your team. You have gumption lad and so do your *dugs.*"

"The dogs belong to her." Rune stepped aside, leaving Anya in full view.

Xander kept his watch eyes on the stranger.

"*Aye,* the *bonnie* lassie you say?"

Anya straightened, all five feet two inches of her. She took her hand from her pocket. This stranger didn't look like any kind of threat. In fact he looked quite the opposite. He had a kind face, with honest eyes and an honest smile. She liked his easy tone and accent. Most of all, she liked that he was a dog driver.

"The dogs do not belong to me. They belong to the winds, to the tundra, and to the ice. They are Chukchi. They have no master," Anya said, her voice resolute yet hardly above a whisper. For a moment she imagined herself back in her home village where Chukchi females spoke in hushed tones. She wasn't homesick for herself, but for the dogs.

"*Aye noo,* I *kin* what you say." The young Scot put out his hand to her. "I'm that pleased to meet you. Call me Fox," he insisted, his smile friendly.

Anya couldn't help but smile back. She shook his hand. This was the first time she'd ever been asked to greet anyone so. It felt funny to touch a stranger's hand, but it must be the way men and women greet in *Alazzkah.* "Alaska," she mentally corrected.

"You have a funny name," she blurted.

"I suppose I do," Fox agreed. "I *didnee* have a say. I was but a *wean.*"

She pulled her hand away and put it to Xander's back.

The handsomely furred, black and white husky had resumed his companionable position at her side, sensing the danger had passed. His white mask was intent on the stranger, still.

Flowers faded into the mix of huskies. Some had lain down but were still watchful.

"The *dug* there you be giving a pat, what's his name?" Fox asked.

"Xander." Her fingers stroked behind Xander's ears. It was difficult to say Xander without Zellie. It was difficult to not put her other hand out and give Zellie a pat at the same time.

"Why so sad *noo*, lass?" Fox could see something was wrong.

"Listen . . . uh, Fox," Rune interrupted and stepped in-between the Scot and Anya. "That's enough questions. Anya is tired. The dogs are tired. I'm tired. Speak your peace and leave." Rune knew Anya hurt. He needed to protect her. He *wanted* to protect her.

"You're right, Rune Johansson. *Noo* is not a good time. Are you *biding* here long? I can come back for a bit of *blether* with you both tomorrow." Fox made his appeal, then took a step back.

Rune thought of what waited outside for the dogs and Anya. The unknown, that's what. Still, he was anxious to get her and the dogs out of Nome. He didn't have a plan for their safe escape. Out of time, money, and ideas, Rune couldn't afford to stay but he couldn't afford to leave either; not until he had a plan and the dogs were rested and their injuries seen to. Best to stay one more night in Nome, he decided. Besides, he was curious about what Fox Maule Ramsey wanted. The man meant them no harm, he could tell.

"Tomorrow it is," Rune told him, giving a nod. "We're leaving early."

"I *willnae* be late, lad and lassie. You have yourselves a good rest *noo* and we'll have our chat in the morning." He offered a bright smile to Rune and Anya and glanced at the husky masks of all the dogs. They were a bonnie lot, they were. He turned and exited the stable, and needed to bend his head under the low timbers of the doorway.

Anya let out her breath, unaware she'd been so tense. The

ivory carving at her neck burned against her skin. This forced her attention to it. She tensed again. Why did her necklace burn, and at this time?

Gasp!

She could swear she heard the word, *gitengev*, call across the winds outside. Calmly as she could, she took her hand from Xander's back and put her cool fingers against her skin, under the husky carving—Vitya's gift to her. She kept the necklace inside her kerker because she didn't want Rune or anybody else to see it and ask questions. Some things she wanted to keep private. Vitya's necklace was one of these things.

Vitya always called her *gitengev*, "pretty girl" in Chukchi. He had since they were children and it always annoyed her until last year . . . until he brushed a kiss across her lips. Now she didn't know how it made her feel. She missed him, yes. She missed a lot about her life back in her village in Siberia.

What did any of it matter?

Zellie is gone.

Her tension left her, replaced by sadness and bittersweet resolve. *It mattered* because of Xander; Xander and the rest of the Chukchi dogs who had braved so much along their journey from Siberia to come to this new place. The Gatekeepers kept watch over her and she must keep watch over the surviving dogs. The Gatekeepers sent them to this new place for a good reason.

Is it a good enough reason for Zellie to die?

"Anya." Rune held out some jerked caribou for her.

She didn't hear him or take the offered food.

"Anya," he said again. "You must eat."

This time she looked at Rune. Mutely, she took the meat and absentmindedly bit into it. Her body felt unreal, as if she'd passed back into the spirit world where food wasn't needed. She ate out of habit and not hunger. Flooded with doubt, she felt more powerless than ever to help the dogs. A mound of powdered snow had more glue to it than she did. She felt as if the next arctic wind could sweep her away from the dogs and forever separate her from them! Landed on different ice floes, she could hear the dogs call out, howling to the heavens. She could see the punishing ice close in and trap them . . . with death their best hope.

"Anya, eat," Rune ordered. He knew her mind was somewhere else, imagining the worst. He read the fear on her face, and felt the same uneasiness she did. All the more important for him to come up with a plan to escape Nome and escape whatever was after them. Although at this point he had a pretty good idea what: the Raven god of the Chukchi and shadows from *Hel*. He just didn't know why.

Why dark forces from times past showed themselves in the present to harm Chukchi dogs was beyond his thinking.

Why he and Anya had crossed paths in the first place still mystified him.

He was just a seaman who worked all his life to one day captain a steamer, wanting nothing more, nothing less. She was just a girl who grew up raising dogs in her native village. It seemed to him that the dogs were her life, wanting nothing more, nothing less.

Why then had they been set on this dangerous course together, to fight dark forces that hid in shadows and waited for them around every crag and crevasse?

All because of nine dogs?

Rune's insides flinched. *Nine dogs. Nine serpents you must slay,* were Odin's words to him. Nine signified the gods. Nine was and is an important number. Still, this had to be about more than dogs. Something more had to bring together the gods of the Chukchi and the gods of the Vikings, tapping Anya and him to save the Siberian huskies.

Right after the race just run, when Rune believed Zellie crossed the finish line, Anya told him Zellie did not. She told him, "Zellie was safe in a world beyond ours; with the gods." Rune remembered finding Zellie's empty harness, still tied to the leader tug line, and even now he couldn't believe it. Then who . . . then what . . . crossed the finish line in Zellie's place, in her body?

Rune turned his disbelief onto Anya. Looking at her now, so lost and sad, he couldn't think about the unthinkable—that it was she who finished the race and not Zellie!

But then, if anyone had told Rune that he'd be visited on the beaches of Nome by Odin's ghost, who sent him to help Anya and her dogs, he'd never have believed it. If anything, Rune had learned the unthinkable *was* thinkable. He exhaled sharply. Whatever Anya was . . . ghost, ice seal, mermaid, or simply a girl . . . she was his responsibility. To him, that was clear enough. He didn't need any more prodding from mystic Viking gods to remind him of his responsibility.

Anya bit into the dried caribou. She didn't like it. Fresh meat with fresh blood would taste better. A body got more energy from fresh blood. When she could, she'd always give her dogs fresh fish and meat. They could go miles farther on it. Closing her eyes, she imagined she tasted blubber from the whale and oil from the seal; both greasy; both delicious. She didn't need any cook fire to imagine such flavors. A cook fire only wasted nutrients by boiling them away.

In the Arctic every bite counted. Nothing could be wasted. She'd learned early to use the rounded Chukchi knife to slice meat and blubber from bone with ease. The dogs were usually close and she would toss them a bit of bone or fat when no one watched. The Chukchi never spoiled or pampered their dogs, but gave them only what was needed for work; nothing more. Anya never stuck to this and rebelliously gave the dogs scraps from the hunt.

The hunt!

Anya opened her eyes to the reality of where she was, of where the dogs were, and to the fact that *they* were being hunted now. She couldn't swallow another bite of the dried caribou and shoved it back at Rune.

"You didn't eat enough," Rune scolded, then replaced the unfinished caribou in his gunnysack. She hardly weighed anything. He didn't think she could go on much longer with so little food in her. Remembering back on the *Storm,* when he'd tried to give her a loaf of sourdough bread to eat, she spat it out. She ate the dried meat he'd brought then, the same food he gave to her dogs. She should be eating the caribou. Something took her appetite. He had a good guess what it was.

Xander wandered in-between Rune and Anya, limping slightly. He weaved a little, as if off balance.

Flowers got up and watched him.

The other dogs stirred. They sensed something was wrong with him.

Xander let out a shrill whine, then dropped to the floor in a fit.

Helpless to do anything but watch, Anya and Rune hovered over him. Anya knew Xander had been weakened by whatever evil was after him, but until this moment she hadn't realized how badly he'd been struck with fits. She watched him shake and tremble and struggle for breath, and cursed the day she set him and Zellie and the rest of Grisha's dogs free so they wouldn't be traded away at the Markova Fair.

Her actions angered the Raven god of the Chukchi. This was her fault. If she'd left well enough alone, maybe Xander would be all right and Zellie would be alive!

Xander stopped his spasms and his body went rigid. His breaths evened, though his eyes remained shut. Liquid pooled under his backside and mouth.

Anya grabbed up straw where she could and wiped away the telltale residue from his fit. Not satisfied, she reached under her kerker and ripped off the entire bottom of her only dress, then gently pressed the soft calico to his face and mouth to clear the colorless foam.

He didn't stir and appeared unaware of her ministrations.

Flowers pointed her muzzle upward and howled.

Magic and Mushroom did, too. Then Midday, Midnight, Frost, and Little Wolf.

"Is he dead?"

"No, Rune. His sickness makes him sleep. He will wake soon," Anya said hopefully and choked back new tears.

Rune blew out a breath, relieved. He thought he'd lost another Siberian husky, ashamed he wasn't a better "slayer of serpents." He wasn't a good Viking warrior. A good Viking warrior would better protect Xander. Who was he kidding? He wasn't any kind of Viking warrior but a boy, a still-wet-behind-the-ears one at that.

The dogs quieted. Only Flowers approached Xander and lay down next to him.

"Do not worry, girl. Xander will be all right." Anya gently tried to soothe the piebald husky when Anya had no idea if Xander would be all right. Anya thought of their ties as a pack and as a sled team. She pictured their sled formation to help get her mind off Xander's illness.

Flowers ran next to Frost in her team position on the sled towline, "gangline" it was sometimes called. Flowers ran next to Frost, Anya mentally repeated, both hitched behind Magic and Mushroom, who ran in the swing position behind the lead dog. *Zellie had been their leader.* Anya swallowed back tears over Zellie and mechanically kept going down her list of sled hitches. The team relied on the two wheel dogs that ran directly in front of the sled, Xander and Midnight, to "wheel" the sled around dangerous curves and drop-offs, their combined strength critical to a successful, safe run. Midday and Little Wolf, in their middle team position behind Flowers and Frost, ran directly in front of Xander and Midnight.

Then Anya's thoughts wandered back in time to her home village.

In Siberia all of the Chukchi dogs ran in a fan formation, up to twenty on a team spread out for the hunt. There was no need to run in any kind of paired formation with so much room to "fan out" over ice and tundra. The Alaska wild was different. The Yukon was different. The terrain didn't always allow such formation, but required dogs running alongside one another in pairs.

This hitch covered freight dogs and racing dogs, with a whip used for guide and punishment. All of Anya's Siberian huskies had to learn this new way of harnessing, but she refused to use a whip. Chukchi dogs never needed the whip. Stubborn sometimes, yes, but they never needed to be coerced to run faster, longer, or stronger. To get them to slow down and stop was another story. Chukchi dogs were born to run.

They didn't need the whip.

Boris Ivanov never used one on the dogs, Anya remembered. He'd brought nine Chukchi dogs to Nome, but she didn't know the whole story behind why he'd done so. She never would. Boris Ivanov took his reasons with him, to his grave.

If he were still alive, Boris might have told her.

The big Russian traded for eight dogs in Anadyr but when the little Siberian girl stowed away with her *Sibirskiy haski* on board Lars Johansson's steamer, eight became nine. Boris didn't think he needed any larger number to win the All Alaska Sweepstakes. He knew about the speed and endurance of the Chukchi dogs and thought he could easily win the big race with only nine dogs. Killed before he could see the proof of his efforts and how well the dogs took to the new terrain, his Siberian huskies came within an hour of winning the four-day, grueling run.

Boris did live long enough to appreciate Anya and Rune's ability to teach the dogs the new hitch and harnessing. He just didn't know a little magic was involved. Anya and Rune were still mystified themselves at how she seemed to know the new hitch formation and he seemed to know how to dog drive. Magic or not, they both believed they had help from somewhere. Anya looked to the Gatekeepers and Rune to his Viking god, Odin. How else could they master so much so fast?

"Here, take this, Rune." Anya's mind was back on the present, on Xander, and on what needed to be done. She reached inside the deepest pocket of her fur kerker and took out a seal-skin pouch of paste, her home remedy supply.

Rune mutely took the pouch. He didn't look at her.

"Rune," she said more pointedly.

"*Ja*," Rune answered in Norse tradition, absentmindedly shifting the pouch hand to hand.

Anya stood up. Xander still slept at her feet.

"Use the medicine inside this pouch on the dogs' paw pads, Rune. Examine the dogs and give me an account of each one. I need to know which need help," she said, not missing the faraway look in his eyes. There were a lot of things that could put that look there.

"Rune," she said again, and hoped he might tell her what troubled him.

He didn't.

He didn't say anything, still full of self-condemnation. Anya had given him a task. Good. He had something to do. Clasping the pouch securely in hand, he gave her a quick nod, then knelt down to the watchful huskies. Flowers was the closest.

She sat up and let him take up one of her front paws, outwardly sensing her guardian meant to help her. Her other guardian watched over Xander. Only one of Flowers's front paws was injured. A jut of ice had sliced into it. It bled still. Rune took a portion of paste and covered her wound. She licked his cheek, then let him examine her back paws. Satisfied she was all right but for her front paw, Rune moved on to the red and white husky pair.

Magic and Mushroom lay next to each other as if waiting their turn. They sat up for Rune and let him go over their injuries. They had a mix of cuts and bruises on their feet, but nothing deep. Rune covered any abrasions with a coat of the healing paste. Four dogs remained. Rune moved around the stable to each one. Little Wolf was next. The gray and white pup wagged its tail when Rune reached him.

In an hour's time all the dogs had been seen to. Xander had awakened and paced in a circle around the stable on wobbly legs. Yet dazed, he hadn't returned to his full senses. Anya left him alone. She prayed he'd recover his strength. There wasn't anything she could do for him. No home remedy could take away his sickness. She didn't have any potion to counteract the work of dark spirits. Shamans could cast spells, too. The shamans in her home village went into trances and cast spells. She'd seen it with her own eyes.

Grown men in her village had been sent to the ground in pain, screaming for a letup to their agony. Many of the adults gathered for religious ceremony in the community yaranga tasted the same mushrooms as the shamans, Anya suspected. Some villagers even drank their own liquids, disgusting Anya. She never did taste the red and white mushrooms or go into any dreamlike state. She would keep her eyes and ears on the ancestral drums, believing she must keep a clear head at such an important time.

Besides, she had enough trouble already with spirits that shadowed her and tried to get her attention. She didn't need to eat any magic mushrooms to see and hear them!

Her grandmother warned her to take things more seriously than she sometimes did during religious ceremonies. She must not poke fun at the behavior of others. Nana-tasha said she must not anger the gods by questioning the power of the shamans, either. She, Anya, had been gifted with the same powers. She didn't need any help in communicating with the spirit world, but Nana-tasha warned her repeatedly to keep still, keep quiet, and try to learn from the shamans. Only a child, Anya "had much to learn," her grandmother had cautioned.

At this moment Anya wished she had paid more attention. She wished she knew exactly how to cast spells. If so, she'd cast her own shadow over the dark Raven god, and stop the evil coming for them!

Something or someone didn't want the dogs to live; or her, or Rune.

Something or someone killed Zellie and Boris Ivanov.

Yes, at this moment Anya wished she'd paid closer attention to every action and reaction of the two shamans in her village. Then maybe . . . just maybe . . . Zellie would still be alive. A little bit of Anya would die every day at this thought.

"Are you cold?"

"No," Anya answered defensively.

"Then why are you shaking?" Rune stepped closer, and slipped off his fur parka as he did. "Here, use this as a pillow and lie down in the straw. The dogs will keep you warm. You need to sleep. We have a big day tomorrow."

"I'm not a child. I'm not cold. And I'm not tired," she spat rebelliously, and refused to take his kerker. The truth of it was she *did* feel like a child. She *was* cold. And she *was* tired. Embarrassed, as if Rune could read her thoughts and her misgivings, she reacted angrily.

"You don't need to take care of me. I will take care of myself and the dogs. You don't even like dogs. You can . . . you can leave any time," she told him, but regretted her words the moment she uttered them. None of it was true. She shouldn't take out her upset on Rune.

"I will leave in the morning if that's what you want," he said with no hint of emotion. He kept his bundled parka in mind. "It's a three-dog night, Anya. Choose three and lie down, *now.*"

She flinched at his tone. He didn't roar like Chukchi men, but still, she flinched. Of course she didn't want him to leave. She was just too stubborn to admit it. The words wouldn't come.

Xander stopped circling the stable, his confusion from his fit ended. Unable to gather the strength yet to jump up and push his front paws against Anya in play as he used to, he nudged his body against her side, then leaned on her for support.

Anya dropped to her knees and hugged him around the neck.

"I love you, Xander," she whispered. She let her tears come.

Xander didn't try to break from her hold, despite his weakened stance.

"We have to go on without Zellie. We have to," she cried against his fur. "When it is time for us to pass, and for Zellie to help pull our sled across to heaven, we will cross together, Xander. I promise," she vowed and meant it.

This time he did break from her hold, only to lick her face as if he understood her words.

His watch-blue eyes pierced through the dim light in the stable, warming Anya, strengthening her resolve, and helping dry her tears. Whatever was to come, they would face it together. All his life Xander had never liked being alone. Despite being a rough and tumble Chukchi pup with the promise of being the strongest and most enduring of sled dogs, he never liked being alone. He used to cry and whimper as a pup, unless she or Zellie were around. He would snuggle close and only ease into sleep when they were near.

Zellie could no longer circle nearby Xander, but Anya could. Nothing on Native Earth could take away the cursed fits he suffered. The fits frightened Anya as much as she thought they traumatized him. At least she could be there when he recovered. One day he might not wake up or be able to get up. On that day she would give herself over to the Gatekeepers. Her heart and all her souls would set adrift on an ice floe and disappear into the ice fog. It would be done.

"Lie down, Anya. Get warm and get some sleep," Rune quietly insisted. He didn't like seeing Anya so upset that she cried. God knew she had reason to cry. He couldn't think of anyone he'd ever met with more reason. Crying was something Rune stopped doing years ago. Men didn't cry. Boys cried. He'd wasted enough tears on a family that didn't love him. He was done with wasted tears and with love. It wasn't for him. He wasn't a boy anymore.

Anya curled up next to Xander, her arm across his body. She forgot about the words between Rune and her. She forced her attention from him. Flowers lay down close, snuggling against Anya. Midday and Magic, the other females in the pack, snuggled close, too. The dogs' panted breaths evened to sleep in a manner of seconds. Anya fell asleep along with them, soothed by the soft down of the Chukchi dogs, warmed instantly on this obvious "four-dog night."

Rune settled in an empty stable corner and kept watch over Anya and the dogs. He knew Anya was warm now. He brushed off the cold and didn't put his parka back on. No sleep for him. He didn't think he could sleep even if he wanted to. Besides, his time would be better spent going over every detail of the past four days. What did he miss? What didn't he do that might have saved Zellie? Too late for her now, he realized. She was dead.

But then who, what dog, crossed in her place?

Anya?

He pushed the possibility away, not in any mood to ponder ghosts and goblins. Yet Anya must know what happened. She knew Zellie didn't finish the race. He thought Zellie had, while Anya knew she had not. When he'd turned to the sled and harnessed dogs, to reassure Anya that Zellie was fine, he was shocked to find Zellie's empty harness.

Anya wasn't. He thought again of ghosts.

Ghost or not, Anya's words moments ago hit hard. It was a toss-up, which ones: that he could leave anytime; that he didn't even like dogs; or that he didn't need to take care of her. She sure didn't think much of him, did she? No matter at this point. Whether or not he wanted to leave, whether or not he liked dogs, whether or not she needed him here, he wasn't about to go anywhere. He couldn't. Committed to the fight, to protect her and the Chukchi huskies, he'd not say any more. It didn't make any difference what he wanted. What did he care?

I don't.

If this fight didn't kill him, he'd end up a sailor, a seaman. It's all he ever wanted, to navigate the arctic waters and find adventure. He didn't need anybody; not his father's approval or his money; not his family's love; and certainly not the good opinion of any stowaway girl! He shot up from his stable corner and charged outside, not forgetting his parka. He needed to get out of there and put distance between himself and . . . all of it!

The dogs not sleeping with Anya—Mushroom, Midnight, Frost, and Little Wolf—stirred at Rune's leaving. Their canine instincts told them to stay with the rest of the pack, but even stronger intuition sent them to follow Rune.

He'd disappeared. The dogs sniffed the air. None picked up Rune's scent. Wolves howled across mountain and tundra.

Midnight was the first to react, to know where the howls came from. The all-black husky took off into the heavy snowfall. The rest followed with Little Wolf in front. Soon all four dogs had disappeared, the same as Rune.

Xander's ears pricked. He opened his eyes but didn't stir or get up. Sensing danger, he would stay with his guardian and protect Anya. The pack was split now. His canine senses keen, he knew exactly which ones were missing. Torn over which instincts to obey, he wanted to stay with his guardian but he wanted to find the rest of his pack.

He winced inside, intuitively remembering Zellie and what happened when she split from the pack. Xander didn't remember in any human kind of way but in the same way dogs can sense danger; in the same way dogs know what a whip means when they see it. Xander whined.

Flowers stirred at Xander's low cry. She lifted her head for a look around and right away spotted the danger. The pack was split.

The cry of the wolf easily penetrated the loose timbers of the stable.

When Flowers moaned, matching Xander's earlier cry, he gave a quick bark to quiet her; as if signaling they needed to stay put. Flowers whimpered, then lay her head back down against the cold straw. She didn't snuggle against Anya any longer, too disquieted to sleep. She would stay alert with Xander. Instinctively she would help stand guard.

Now Magic sat up, her copper-red and white fur carrying the hint of a glimmer even with the poor light inside their shelter. All-white, Midday's fur also held a bit of shine the moment she stood.

Xander raised his head and sent another quick bark to the two in his pack. Like Flowers, both females caught his signal. They stubbornly obeyed.

Wolves howled in force now, the faraway sound clear to the Chukchi huskies but barely audible along the streets of Nome. The four dogs in the stable stayed quiet, yet stayed.

Anya slept on, unaware of the nightmare unfolding outside.

CHAPTER FOUR

"What is it, Zeke?"

"Damned if I know," the exhausted miner said and climbed out of his bunk, then reached for his gun.

"You going out there?" Homer Jessup eased back down in his own bunk. He wasn't going out and didn't think it smart for his friend to, either.

Zeke Raney made sure of his ammunition and his reliable Henry rifle. Whatever was outside, wolves or wolverines, he'd find out. Could be they had a bear, ripping it apart. If there were enough wolves in the pack, they could bring down a bear . . . or a man, he worried. Used to hunting in the wild, Zeke had run into just about everything, every kind of animal prey or predator, since coming to the Alaska frontier to mine gold. This didn't sound like any ordinary tussle to him or anything he'd ever heard before.

Just then a man shouted, or at least Zeke thought so. The sound came from the same far direction.

"Homer, get up and get your gun. Might need two for this," Zeke drawled evenly.

"I ain't going. I didn't come all the way to Alaska to be chewed apart by a bunch of wild animals. No sir, I ain't going," the scared miner said, making no bones about how he felt.

"Get out of bed. Get your clothes on and get your damned gun, Homer, or by God you'll regret it," Zeke threatened. "How'd you like to be out there alone?"

69

"It's snowing, Zeke. The storm is getting bad. There won't be anything left of the guy when we get out there anyway."

"Homer, by God, you get your hide and that yellow streak up and down it, out of bed, *now!*" Zeke stepped into his gumboots, already wearing his *siwash* socks. He pulled his fur parka over his long underwear and kept his eye on Homer, waiting for him to do the same.

"Get on it, Homer," he said one last time, then flung open the cabin door. The snow picked up and made it harder to see despite the light of winter. Spitting mad at his friend, he had to get going, with or without Homer. Whoever or whatever was out there was dying.

There were other miners' cabins, others who worked for the Pioneer Mining Company, the Arctic Mining Company, or the Anvil Gold Mine, but they put up their cabins farther down the mountain in the Bonanza Hills, closer to Nome. Zeke meant to hunt and trade pelts along with his earnings in the gold mines. To hunt more easily, he liked living away from most humans, who scared away game. His friend Homer helped him build the cabin, and had come all the way from Colorado with him during the early gold rush days.

Those days were gone, but there was still gold to be found. Neither of the men were family men so they didn't leave anybody behind; anybody they had to send money to. Getting older by the day, Zeke wished he had a family; a wife at least; or maybe a son. Hell, who was he kidding? He didn't even have a dog. Clicking his rifle to make sure it was loaded, he decided he would get a dog . . . tomorrow. A dog would be a more reliable companion than Homer turned out to be.

More cries, animal and human, echoed across the icy ridge. Zeke trudged through the deep snow fast as he could; regretting he hadn't put on his trail shoes. His way would be quicker if he walked over the snow instead of through it. No time to go back to the cabin. No time to worry if Homer followed to help.

The skies suddenly lit up. Northern lights flashed in the heavens, sending red, green, yellow, and blue rays shimmering down. Thunder cracked like a whip across the colors and split them into dimmer and dimmer shards of useless light. The gates of *Hel* had opened, stealing the light from the sky, pulling it down through ice and tundra to its fiery domain. Glacial lakes warmed and melted. *Hel* brought the ice storm. *Hel* brought the golem to the Gatekeepers' door.

Lost in nightmares, Anya couldn't breathe. Something had her by the neck. The more she fought, the tighter the hold on her. A hot, sickening odor came from behind her, as if whatever held her had been dead a long time. Something once human held her, its demonic hands now like whips where fingers used to be. The whips wound around her neck and cut off any air.

Was it Mooglo?

She still bore his bloody lash on her hand and now realized the ugly Yukaghir meant to take her life. She would not let him have the dogs! Frantically groping for her knife, she couldn't find it in her pocket! She tried to scream for Rune to help but she couldn't make a sound. Her chest pained too much. On her last breath, she realized Rune couldn't help. He'd already been killed.

"Spirit! Spirit!" Anya woke up screaming for her counterpart in the spirit world to help her save Rune and the dogs. Sweat coated her brow despite the cold in the stable. Drugged with sleep, she tried to clear her thoughts. When she did, dread seeped through them. She saw Xander, then Flowers, Magic, and Midday.

The rest were gone; Rune, too.

Her hands went to her cheeks to cool them. She felt on fire. This was no dream. Rune *was* in trouble. He should be there with her but he was not. He wouldn't have left without telling her; not for good at least. He would never take any of her dogs, either. They must have followed him. They must be in the same trouble.

Quickly as she could, Anya prostrated herself on the half-frozen stable floor and began praying to the Directions and all of the Chukchi gods to help Rune and the missing dogs. She prayed the Gatekeepers watched over them. Pressing her ear against the ground, she listened hard for any sign from the tundra or arctic winds that could tell her where Rune and the dogs might be, which direction they'd traveled.

None came.

Weighted down with worry, Anya tried to sit up and face the reality of this hard day. She and Xander, and the females with them, might be the only ones in their pack left alive. She had to do something, but what? If she left, and Rune and the missing males returned safely to find no one waiting in the stable, that would be bad. Maybe she was upset over nothing. Try as she might to believe that, she couldn't. Her mind raced. Her head pounded.

The past year flashed before her eyes, from the moment Grisha took her to Markova to trade her and the dogs away. Determined to think through all the moments she'd experienced with Rune and their journey with the dogs across the Bering Sea, and then running the race for their lives in Alaska—Anya called on every spiritual bone in her body to help her remember anything and everything that might help her, help Rune and the dogs. There had to be some sign, some hidden clue she'd overlooked.

With her hand on Xander for comfort, concentrating hard as she could, Anya closed her eyes and gave herself over to the ghostly forces of the Chukchi. She called on her powers as a shaman to come forth.

"*Awrite* there, lass. I'm here for our *wee blether noo* on this fine morning."

Fox Maule Ramsey smiled from the entryway of the stable.

Anya didn't smile back.

Rune finally came to. His head felt like someone had taken it off and thrown it into the Bering Sea for fish food. Sharp spikes prodded and poked at him, eating away at his shipwrecked body. Icy water poured over and through him, and dragged him down, down, down into its depths. He fought to stay conscious and clear his thinking. He couldn't open his eyes. Was he dead? Maybe. He'd experienced this before—thinking he'd died—only buried in snow and not freezing water. The dogs had saved him from his snowy coffin. *The dogs.*

He remembered.

The dogs had dug him out then. His eyes flew open. He met the watch-blue eyes of the Chukchi dog and the gray eyes of the wolf. *The wolf and the dog must battle as one.*

He remembered.

Odin's very words to him. Rune sat up, able to do so now. The dogs and the wolves backed off. Rune still couldn't believe it, that the wolves hadn't ripped him apart when they had the chance. Wasn't that what wolves always did, ripped men apart? Viking legend was full of such stories. But then two wolves guarded Odin, always at his side. Rune didn't feel any threat from this wolf pack. These wolves guarded him, protected him.

Rune's thoughts still muddled together. He closed his eyes again and shook his head hard, ignoring the pain. Memory flooded back. Rune shot to a stand. He'd left Anya and the dogs in the stable, intending to walk off his upset; that's all. It was snowing, like now. There was winter light, like now. He'd headed down the alleyway away from the stable, thinking to find Front Street and then the Board of Trade Saloon. He'd

73

wanted to go over the race results posted and think on things by himself. The saloon ought to be open and the saloonkeeper ought to let him in even if he couldn't buy a drink.

Right when Rune turned onto Front Street . . . *Frank Lundgren* stepped in his path—the same Frank Lundgren who finished second in the All Alaska Sweepstakes—the same Frank Lundgren whose lead dog had attacked Zellie—the same Frank Lundgren who'd tried to poison Rune's team— the same Frank Lundgren who'd near whipped his own sled dogs to death trying to win the race—and the same Frank Lundgren Rune had intended to hunt down and reckon with.

"Your turn now," Rune remembered Frank saying. Ready for a fight, in fact wanting a fight with the unscrupulous dog driver, Rune had locked his fingers in fists. The second he went for Frank, he was hit hard from behind. Dazed and fallen to his knees, Rune turned enough to manage a look at his attacker.

It was a man, at least he thought so. More ghost and shadow than a man, still it was a man with the spark of a demon. The larger-than-life shadowy figure held a bloody saber in its hand, wielding it victoriously overhead. It didn't speak, but Rune could hear its anger nonetheless, the sounds unearthly. The last thing Rune remembered was fury at himself for not having his own saber!

But he did.

Back in the present, Rune drew his right hand up and saw the cold steel in it, a Viking short sword. He recognized the type of blade. It was covered in blood, just like his attacker's. The wolves backed farther away. So did Midnight, Little Wolf, Mushroom, and Frost. Rune stared at the exposed figure on the ground at the water's edge. *Frank Lundgren* lay dead in front of him. Rune stared back at his sword.

Had he done this? His gut turned. He'd never killed a man before. At that moment Rune realized he bled from his own wounds. He looked at the dead mangle of flesh and bone that was Frank Lundgren. Rune didn't see any weapon, any bloody saber on him or near him. Then again there was a trail of blood to the water. *The water?* The glacial lake should be frozen, not melted.

None of this made any sense.

But then nothing had made much sense since he'd met Anya.

The snow had stopped. The night sky turned only a hair, to the twilight of a winter day. Rune watched the wolves track around the site. The dogs, too, sniffed over the dead body and at the water's edge. Rune could see better now. The wolves were blood-smeared. So were the dogs. It looked to him like they'd all been in the fight. *The wolf and the dog must battle as one.* And so they must have.

Anya!

Whatever had just happened to him—whatever had attacked him—might have attacked Anya and the rest of the dogs!

Men shouted in the distance. Rune had to get his bearings and get back to Anya. Instinctively he wiped the bloody sword in the snow, cleaning it, then slid the short blade inside his booted leg, out of sight. The dogs stayed put. The wolves, too.

Two men came over the rise. They had their rifles pointed.

"You there! Are you all right?" one shouted.

Rune didn't answer and let the men come closer. They were older than he. About his father's age, he guessed.

"Son," Zeke Raney said low and even. "Don't make a move. Don't make a sound."

Rune shot his hand out to bury the stranger's rifle muzzle to the ground. It was pointed at the wolves and the dogs.

"No, don't shoot," Rune warned.

Homer Jessup had his rifle on target, and pulled the trigger.

Zeke caught Homer's gun in time, the bullets firing aimlessly at the sky.

The dogs and the wolves stood motionless, all alert; their eyes on the two strangers. The gunfire didn't scare any of them off. They stood by Rune.

Zeke kept his eyes on the predators in front of him. He'd seen the dead body on the ground but didn't look at the mangle right now. Despite the boy's warning not to shoot, the wolves could attack any moment. He wasn't stupid. He'd been in Alaska and the Yukon long enough to know better than to think wolves could be friendly-like. They'd obviously just taken the man on the ground apart. Judging from the boy's wounds, they'd tried to take him apart, too. Zeke tightened his fingers around his rifle again and raised it to take aim at the wolves. The boy must be loco telling them not to shoot and *he* must be loco to listen!

"I said, *don't shoot,*" Rune said menacingly, and this time grabbed the rifle from Zeke.

Homer Jessup tried to take aim again with his rifle but his gun met the same fate as Zeke's. Rune snatched it away, too.

"Listen, kid. You might be hankering to die, but I'm not. If you don't give me back my gun, then use it on me before the wolves set on us all." Zeke meant every word of it.

"Hold on there, Zeke!" Homer yelled.

"We don't need to shoot the wolves or the dogs," Rune said, breathing a little easier since he had the strangers' weapons.

"What dogs?" Zeke blurted his question. Damned if this boy wasn't plum loco, thinking this mess of wolves had any dog in them. This was a killing pack of wolves if he'd ever seen one.

"Yeah, whattt . . . dddogs?" Homer echoed his friend, afraid and shaking so badly his teeth chattered.

Rune turned back to the wolf pack and the Chukchi dogs. They all stared at him, all on alert. He signaled for the dogs to "come" and for the wolves to "go"; instinctively waving the wolves away with his arm, his wave outwardly serving as the universal sign in any language, to go. And go they did, as if by magic.

Stupefied, Zeke stayed frozen to the spot.

Homer stopped shaking.

"You all right, son?" Zeke found his voice but didn't make a move, still unsure about the so-called dogs that remained. The kid looked all right but Zeke wanted to see to his cuts, feeling fatherly all of a sudden. This kid had no business being out in the wild with nothing more than a handful of wolf dogs; small at that, come to think of it.

Rune watched the wolves disappear into the mountains, halfway expecting to see Odin himself reappear with his two wolves and two ravens for companion. That was stupid, but the Viking god could have sent the wolf pack to help him. Maybe they were all ghosts, him included. He couldn't tell what was real and what wasn't.

All the blood looked and felt real enough. He thought someone else attacked him back in Nome. Rune had obviously been in a fight. So had Frank Lundgren. Who with? Why did Frank Lundgren lie in a dead heap? Did Rune kill the shady dog driver or . . . did someone or something else? That same someone or something could have Anya! Rune wheeled around to the two strangers.

"I have to go. Thanks for your help. Here, take your guns," he muttered, and handed them back their weapons. In the next instant he started down the snow-covered trail to Nome. He didn't need to signal for the dogs to come with him.

"I'll be darned," Zeke mumbled. "Never seen the likes of this, no sir."

Homer didn't know if his friend was referring to the wolves not attacking them or the dead body bloodying up the snow or the glacial lake icing back over. Homer stared at the water as it refroze. He wouldn't say anything to Zeke. Zeke would just think he'd been into the hooch again, and had drunk too much of his homemade liquor. Zeke tried more than once to shut down his still and get rid of the molasses, flour, and sugar Homer kept stowed for ingredients. But sure as shootin' . . . that there lake water was freezing up before his very eyes. Homer had never been more sober.

"Hey, kid!" Zeke found himself yelling after the boy. "You and your dogs are welcome at our cabin any time! If you need help, me and Homer will be here!" Why he said what he did, surprised him. The kid was a stranger. Yeah, but he was just a kid who looked poorly, if you ask me, Zeke thought. Life on the arctic frontier was tough at best. This kid looked like he could use a friendly hand up. Zeke hoped the kid would come back. The wolf dogs, too.

Homer shook his head at his old friend. He'd never heard such talk, and from Zeke of all people. Nope, he'd never heard the like.

The two miners exchanged looks over the dead body left from the wolf carnage. Why the wolves went after one man and not the other confounded both of them. There didn't seem to be enough of the man left to bury. His face wasn't recognizable. Expect they should bury the rest of him but instead, they left him as he lay. Survival of the fittest. The unknown body just became food for the wild.

Rune could hear one of the men shout after him but didn't stop. He hurried down the trail as fast as his legs would take him; deftly pulling the sword out of his boot to tuck it at his back, inside his parka. The trail had enough snowpack below the fresh accumulation to help him make decent time.

The dogs ran ahead. They knew where Rune was going. Their canine senses took them miles down the same trail, back to their pack.

Rune watched the dogs disappear from sight, glad they

weren't too injured to run. He should know by now that nothing much stops the Chukchi dog. They were born to run. He knew Mushroom, Midnight, Little Wolf, and Frost all headed home to the stable, to Anya and the rest of the dogs.

Let them all be there, alive, Rune pled silently. He'd never learned to pray. He didn't know how. Maybe someone listened to him now. Never had he wished so hard for answered prayers, or been so scared.

"Lass, *d'ye* mind if I come in a spell?" Fox Maule Ramsey repeated his question, despite seeing something must be wrong. The girl looked upset. The dogs, too. He'd been around sled dogs enough to know something was wrong. And where were the boy and the rest of the dogs? *Aye,* something was wrong.

Anya felt Xander tense. She slowly took her hand from his back and stood up. Filled with the same tension as Xander, she looked past the intrusive Scot, and ignored him completely. Her heart skipped a beat; one, then two. Xander ran outside. So did Flowers, Midday, and Magic. Anya sucked in a breath and held it. Someone was coming. She stayed put when she wanted to run and see for herself who it was. What if it wasn't Rune? She was scared she might be wrong. Instinctively, she closed her eyes, and looked for the trance of Chukchi shamans to give her the strength she needed. Standing still as she could, she shut out all sound, and listened only for the voice of the spirits. She prayed they would come.

"*Hallo,* Anya."

She let out the breath she'd been holding. It was Rune! Or was it? She kept her eyes shut, afraid the Raven played tricks. Was this a dream or a nightmare? Caught up in fear, she fought her emotions and tried to swallow back her tears. In that pained instant she realized how much Rune meant to her. It scared her, how much. She didn't like it that he mattered so much to her, but he did.

All the dogs barked at once.

Anya opened her eyes.

Rune smiled at her.

Helpless to do anything else, she returned his smile with all her heart. She looked at him as if seeing him for the first time, admiring the hint of dimples in his cheeks, the glacial blue of his eyes, the color of his hair, like sunlight itself; the perfect cut of his jaw, the tall, strong build of his body, and the way his smile warmed her, every part of her. No Viking warrior was ever so handsome. No Viking warrior ever returned from battle so . . . *blood-smeared*!

Brought back to her senses, seeing the blood on Rune and now on Midnight, Little Wolf, Mushroom, and Frost, Anya knew they'd been in a fight for their lives. She dropped to her knees and kissed the ground, sending a prayer of gratitude to all the gods, Rune's gods and hers. She didn't care who saw.

Whatever had happened to them, whatever the fight, Rune had saved the dogs again. She shouldn't have said what she did to him last night before she fell asleep. She shouldn't have said she didn't need him to help take care of her and the dogs. *She did.*

She shouldn't have told him he could leave anytime. *She didn't want him to.* She shouldn't have said he "didn't even like dogs." That was the worst thing she'd said. Safely returned with the dogs and up all night in a fight, maybe he'd forgotten her harsh words. She didn't want him to hate her.

Rune stepped past the nuisance Scot and tucked his hand in the crook of Anya's arm, helping her up off the ground; relieved she wasn't any ghost who might disappear beneath his fingers. Sometimes he felt like she was. He squeezed her arm, just enough to ensure he touched a flesh and blood girl. His prayers had been answered. Anya was alive and unhurt. He didn't know who to thank, which gods. Maybe he should thank the Almighty . . . but he didn't know how.

Anya didn't try to wriggle away from Rune's touch.

"Are you hurt bad, Rune?"

Rune kept hold of her.

"I'm all right. Just flesh wounds. I'm all right," he said.

"Well now, this is a fine how *d'ye* do!" Fox suddenly exclaimed.

Anya broke from Rune's hold, a little embarrassed the stranger was there.

Rune chucked her chin lightly, then put his attention to the Scot.

All the huskies had come back inside the stable. They touched muzzles and sniffed around each other, then licked any wounds found—the pack reunited.

Anya breathed a sigh of relief when she saw the dogs come inside. They were wounded, like Rune, but they were alive.

"What happened to you, Rune Johansson?" Fox asked in earnest.

Anya looked at Rune. She wasn't eager to hear.

He gave her a quick wink to let her know he was coming up with a story.

She momentarily relaxed. She'd get the truth later when they were alone.

"I got into a scrap with a couple of upset bettors and the dogs got into a scrap with a couple of upset malamutes," Rune began. "Seems some in Nome don't like me or these dogs much," he offered jokingly, trying to make light of any fight. "Seems some here think Anya and I should take these 'Siberian rats' back to Siberia."

"Rats you say. I *didnee* agree when I heard that. I don't *kin* how a body could say that. You might as well call 'em 'outside' *dugs* from the states south of here, which they're not. They are *dugs* of the North, *braw* as any 'inside' *dugs* they are." Fox shook his head back and forth, disapproving of such bad language used on such good dogs. "Looks like the varmints couldn't *haud* you or your *dugs doon*. Get a good piece of 'em, did you?"

"*Ja*," Rune said, looking at Anya when he did.

"*Aye*, good lad," Fox smiled broadly. "They won't be coming back for you *noo*, I bet."

Rune didn't smile.

"I wouldn't be so sure," he said.

Anya straightened her back, alert to Rune's meaning. The fight wasn't over.

"I'm that sorry folks here *cannae* take a little healthy competition," Fox said, shaking his head a second time. "If you run into trouble again, I'll help you take 'em *oot!*"

"Appreciate it," Rune said, and meant it. He liked the Scot. He could tell the Scot liked and respected their dogs. They weren't rats to be laughed at but true huskies of the Arctic to be counted on.

Anya looked closer at Fox Ramsey, liking the brown-eyed, brown-haired dog driver, too. Still, she wanted him to leave so Rune could tell her the whole story of what happened. She needed to know.

"When you're all mended, I'd like to have a *blether* with you about your *dugs*." Fox looked to Anya and Rune both. "I'm keen on knowing more about your *dugs* and where you got 'em."

"The Markova Fair in Anadyr, Siberia," Anya answered coolly. She hadn't intended to say anything, and surprised herself when she did. Something made her speak up. She thought she heard Nana-tasha's whisper, but how could that be? Her grandmother was dead. Yes, but her spirit spoke to Anya on the arctic wind. Her grandmother was not dead to her and she should never have thought it! Ashamed of herself for having spiritual doubts, Anya believed the voice inside her, telling her to speak of Markova now, was the whisper of her grandmother. Nana-tasha wanted her to befriend Fox Maule Ramsey. Anya was sure of it.

"The dogs are from the villages of the Chukchi people," Anya was quick to add.

"*Aye noo,* you say. They be Chukchi *dugs.*" Fox brightened to the subject. "Anythin' else you might tell me about them, lass? I'm keen on knowing where they got such gumption to run."

Anya beamed at Fox, happy to praise her dogs—happy to do Nana-tasha's bidding. She looked to Rune, to make sure this is what he wanted, too. And that Rune was truly all right, as he'd said.

Rune shot her a smile, then disappeared to the far corner of the stable and removed his fur parka, and the short sword hidden beneath, out of direct sight of Anya and the Scot.

Anya turned her attention back to Fox. She would tell him all about the Chukchi dog but little about herself. Nice as the man seemed to be, he didn't need to know about her growing up. He didn't need to know the real reason she'd come to Alaska; escaped was more like it. For the first time in days, she thought of Vitya and all the dogs left in her coastal village. She even thought of Grisha and his mean family. They should have escaped, too.

This sudden revelation hit hard. Whatever was coming for her and her dogs would sooner or later come for *Vitya* and *Grisha* and *their dogs* and try to hunt them down like the Cossacks did in the old days. Why this truth hit at this moment, she couldn't know. But she did know it was fact. The bloodthirsty Cossacks failed to wipe out the Chukchi, but the darkness brought to them, with the help of the Raven god . . . *would not.*

"Lass, what's wrong?" Fox didn't miss the look of horror on Anya's face. "Why you look like you've seen a ghost," he said, trying to lighten the moment. "There are no such things, lass. *D'nee* fret so."

Oh, but there are, Anya wanted to answer Fox Maule Ramsey, but she held her tongue. There is a war of ghosts after us, worse than the Cossacks, worse than the Czar's cruelest troops, worse than the sharpest harpoon or claw of the bear, worse than the roughest of seas, worse than the thickest ice pack . . . coming for us.

Was this some kind of divination, seeing this truth in her mind's eye?

Was she able to see into the future?

She was a shaman. It must be.

Xander nuzzled her hand, then brushed his head against her fingers, asking for a pat.

Usually soothed by his nearness, by sinking her fingers in his thick fur and feeling his warmth, she barely noticed Xander and gave him an absentminded tap. Her upset thoughts were elsewhere, in the spirit world.

Xander moved away and settled in the corner near Rune. His keen instincts brought him to Anya's side to help comfort her and those same instincts told him to leave. He whined low and closed his eyes. Then he felt a human touch—his guardian Rune stroked his head and behind his ears. Xander settled closer to Rune, content.

Drums of the ancestors beat loudly in Anya's ears; their fateful message still confused her. The Gatekeepers stood guard. Anya shook her head looking for clarity. Was this a rite of passage for a Chukchi shaman: to receive such a divination, such news?

At fourteen years old, was this the next passage into the world of spirits?

Was her childhood behind her?

Yes, she thought so.

In this moment she could feel her grandmother's soft kiss on her cheek, a kiss of goodbye. She would never hear her grandmother's whispers across arctic winds, ever again. Tears trickled down Anya's suddenly flushed cheeks but she ignored them. Her fingers tingled as if they held the drum of the ancients, vibrating through her, touching all of her souls. The drums spoke of the times to come.

The days ahead will be dark. Expect the unexpected. Some will live. Many will die. Native Earth is ripped open. The hole widens. The ice thickens and fills the place where our People and our dogs live, trapping them, lost forever. The ice will never melt. The passage of time will not save us. The passage across the Great Sea will. The spirit of the Chukchi rests within you. You are shaman. You are spirit. You are warrior. You must become master. Your human spirit must prevail.

Trust only the runes.

Anya felt a light touch on her hand, enough to break her trance.

Fox had taken up her hand, concerned for her. She looked lost and upset to him.

Anya jerked her hand away as if burned. She was upset, but not at the Scot. Oddly, she was surprised she didn't feel sick to her stomach. All her life when spirits tried to come round in shadows and whispers, she would feel nauseated; later realizing it was because the spirits tried to pull her into their world. That tugging always made her feel sick. Sometimes she dropped to her knees, she felt so sick.

Why *not* now? Of all times, why not when ghosts of the ancestors came so close she could hear them clearly and even see their faint outline misted all around. She'd never been closer to spirits! Why wasn't she sick? The answer made Anya's knees buckle, but she caught herself and didn't fall to the ground. She wasn't hit with nausea but with the truth of it.

The spirits didn't make her sick because she was one of them now.

Chapter Five

"*Ja,* I'll get you there," Rune promised Fox Maule Ramsey.

Rune and Fox went too fast for Anya. Everything moved too fast, spirits moving in and out especially. The lines between worlds clouded. She fought for clarity. It didn't help that Rune and Fox made their plans without even asking her what she thought. Mad at both of them, she stomped out of the stable.

It had stopped snowing, and she needed to put distance between herself and the pair inside. Did they think she was just a girl, a simple girl at that! The Chukchi didn't put females above males, ever; unless a female was a shaman or the mother or wife of a dog breeder. Dog breeders were important and so it followed that those in their family were also to be treated with importance. Usually that meant soft, fawn-skin dresses with beautiful decorations of embroidery and beads. Still, most Chukchi men didn't think much of Chukchi women. That's exactly how Anya felt when she heard Rune and Fox go on with their plans, like an unimportant Chukchi woman, ignored as if she didn't have a thought in her head!

"Where do you think you're going?" Rune caught Anya's arm, enough to stop her from getting away.

"What do you or your new best friend care?" Anya huffed, angry and a little hurt. She tried to wrest her arm from Rune, but it didn't work. "Let go of me," she spat.

Rune held her fast.

"Anya, it's a bad idea for you to leave. I won't let you go." He tried to keep his voice low.

Xander trotted outside the stable, the other seven behind him. They circled around Anya like a trained group of soldiers, her watchful guard.

"What?" The dogs, too! Exasperated and defeated, she threw up her hands and went back inside the stable, still seething mad. For the first time in her entire life she didn't want anything to do with Chukchi dogs or Chukchi men—or men, period! For the first time in her life she was behaving like a woman—another rite of passage she had yet to realize she'd crossed.

Rune followed her and the dogs behind him, all still on guard.

Fox Ramsey made ready to leave. He'd witnessed the exchange outside and figured Rune and Anya had had a little spat, that's all. Even though he knew the dogs belonged to the lassie, it was the lad he was interested in. Rune Johansson promised to get him to Siberia, to the next Markova Fair, so he could bring back Siberian huskies. Fox figured on trading for sixty to seventy Siberian huskies, at least. Rune knew about steamships and arctic waters. Rune could captain a steamer to Siberia and help Fox bring back the dogs.

"I've done it before," Rune had said.

Skeptical the lad might be stretching the truth, Fox asked for details. Though sketchy, he got some; enough at least to believe Rune told the truth. He decided to trust Rune and entrust him with the money needed to prepare for the demanding voyage. Fox needed to travel to Siberia when the ice broke and he needed Rune to get him there. The lad knew about ships and he knew about dogs. Fox could hunt around for another to take him; able to pay any captain, but Rune Johansson had won his confidence.

Traveling from Scotland last year with his two uncles, Fox arrived in Nome to help oversee their already-wealthy family's gold interests. He loved dog racing from the start. When he wasn't helping with the family mines, he was out on the trail racing Eskimo sled dogs. He preferred the Inuit dogs to the freight mixes seen everywhere. The Eskimo dogs were faster. When he saw Rune's Siberian team cross the finish, against all odds, he was convinced of the smaller huskies' speed and endurance.

Ignoring the talk all around him about the "Siberian rats being outside dogs" and "not worth betting on," he knew right away the merits of the Siberian team. It should have been obvious to everyone watching, but it wasn't. Some applauded the smaller team, but most chalked their good finish up as blind luck. Fox knew better. He knew dogs pretty well by this time and he knew better. No one predicted such a decent finish for the Siberian team, including him. But once the dogs made such a good showing, Fox was surprised more locals didn't take notice and give them the full respect they deserved—all the better for Fox to race his own Siberian dogs in next year's All Alaska Sweepstakes!

"I'll be going *noo* and let you be on your way," Fox quipped, searching for his cap. He'd dropped his Ramsey Clan tartan cap somewhere in the half-frozen straw.

"On our way?" Anya parroted, shooting Rune an accusing glance. "Just wh—"

"Shush," Rune said, putting his fingers to her lips.

Anya swatted his hand away.

"*Noo,* you two be needin' to get along a *wee* bit better," Fox said, his face all smiles. "I'm going *noo* to fetch the money I'll be giving you for the journey. See if you can patch it up before I return," he joked, but meant it. He was putting a lot of trust and a lot of money in the lad and lassie's hands and he *didnee* want it all to be for naught.

Anya and Rune stayed silent and stayed put while Fox Ramsey exited the stable. The moment the Scot was out of earshot, the two began talking at the same time. Neither heard the other, each was so busy getting their own words out. The dogs appeared just as stirred up. Their whines broke into soft howls. Anya and Rune, practically at the same time, turned to the dogs and told them to "shush."

Then they both started to laugh, and the tension between them disappeared. The dogs immediately quieted and settled into sleepy circles, content to wait for their guardians' next command.

"I'm sorry, Rune. I didn't mean . . . I didn't mean—"

"No, I'm the one who's sorry," Rune interrupted. "I should have—"

"Yes, you should have," she teased, and interrupted him this time.

A smile crossed his face.

Hers, too.

"We don't have much time, Anya." Rune wasn't smiling. "Whatever is after us and the dogs got to me last night as soon as I left here. I don't know if it was a man or some kind of evil conjuring cloaked in shadows. Frank Lundgren was there, too; standing right in front of me before I was knocked out from behind. When I came to, well up the trail in the mountains, Frank Lundgren lay dead in front of me. I don't know if I killed him or something else did. The dogs had followed me. And wolves, a pack of them, all covered in blood just like me. Maybe the wolves ripped the dog driver apart. I don't know. If they did, I can't believe the wolves didn't rip me apart, too."

Anya put her fingers to Rune's lips as if she'd done it before. She hadn't.

"What killed Frank Lundgren killed Boris Ivanov and Zellie," she said, convinced of it, then let her fingers trail away from Rune's mouth; unmindful she'd touched him in the first place.

Rune wasn't.

"It's out there waiting for us, isn't it, Rune?"

He read all the worry in the world on her innocent face, worry over Zellie dying and worry the others would meet the same fate.

"What can we do, Rune? We can't escape," she said, ashamed of herself for saying so.

Rune took Anya by her slight shoulders and looked down into her soft brown eyes, willing the enduring ice seal and mystic mermaid in her to surface. She was made of stronger stuff. She was born in the Arctic, a girl of the tundra and ice. No matter she was part-Chukchi, part-white, she was all arctic, tough through and through. She had good reason to be scared though. He was scared, too. He wanted to let her talk about her fears and shed tears, but they didn't have time.

"What we *can* do now, Anya, is get our gear ready to trek out of here and head up into the mountains. There's an out-of-the-way cabin where we can all go. Two men there will help us." The wolves will help us too, it occurred to Rune. "The men are good men who tried to help me last night. We'll be safe there. The dogs will be safe there." Rune hoped he wasn't making empty promises. He decided to take "Zeke" up on his offer. He'd heard the name "Homer" shouted out, too. A secluded cabin sounded pretty good. At least they'd be well away from Nome where too many eyes and ears were on them. If their enemies came after them, they'd run. Chukchi dogs were fast. They'd outrun the enemy before on the Norton Sound and so they might have to again.

"Trust only the runes," Anya whispered; her voice far away.

"What did you say?" Rune couldn't have heard right.

Anya suddenly looked at Rune as if for the first time. Prophecy told her to *trust only the runes*. She made the connection to Rune.

"What are runes?"

"Viking legend, that's all." Rune kept his answer short. He didn't want this conversation. He gave her his back and grabbed up his parka from its corner. The steel blade of the sword clanked against the ground. He tried to shove the steel under his parka.

"Is that blade part of Viking legend, too?" Anya asked pointedly.

"Look," Rune pivoted back around, sword and all. "We don't have time—"

"*Guid* mornin' again." Fox Ramsey appeared out of nowhere. The dogs scattered, yet kept their ears pricked and their eyes wide for any danger.

Rune shoved the cut-off sword behind him and let it drop into the straw with his fur parka. He took steps over to the Scot to head him off. He didn't want Fox coming too far inside the stable.

Anya retreated to her own corner, gaining time to think. Rune could take the lead with Fox for the moment. She needed to find her courage, fast.

"All right, lad, here you go. Twenty-five-thousand dollars should cover the trip and all the expenses. I'll not be giving you a penny more. Spend wisely," Fox underscored.

He couldn't believe his own actions in this, giving so much money to strangers, young ones at that. It defied every ounce of business sense in him, yet Fox trusted Rune and Anya with his money. A voice inside him told him they wouldn't break his trust. That same voice had brought him to Alaska in the first place. So far it had all gone right. He didn't have any reason to doubt his instincts now. Withdrawing so much money from the Bank of Nome at one time, he'd have some explaining to do to his uncles. When the time was right, he'd tell them of his plans for travel to Siberia. His purpose was important, too important to worry about anything except acquiring the huskies from across the Bering Sea.

Rune took the bundle of paper money, dumbfounded to see it appear in his hand, as if a magician had just pulled a rabbit out of a hat. He was speechless.

"Lad, you and the lassie have your *dugs* to mind. You have my money to mind *noo*, to boot," Fox gave a wink. "I trust you to get a ship and crew ready to leave Nome when the ice breaks in summer. We've a voyage to Siberia to make. I trust you to get me there and back again with my own *dugs*. I can see you do *nee* have a place to bide, you and the lass and your *dugs*. Take some of the money and find a safe place to bide until we can leave Nome."

"I was thinking to work in the mines till summer," Rune mumbled, his concentration still on the bundle of money in his hand. "There's good pay, I hear."

It was all Rune could think to say. The money wasn't charity, but Rune couldn't shake the feeling. Rune had always worked as crew on his father's ships. He didn't know exactly how much money took the ships from one trade stop to the next, securing fuel, making repairs, and paying crew. Who was he kidding? He didn't know if he could even get a ship. His father wouldn't be waiting with the *Storm* for him to just hop on board and captain to Siberia!

Well, it's done now.

He had the money in hand to prove it. Rune had to find a ship and find a way to get the Scot to Markova. What had Fox just said? Find a safe place to bide until we can leave Nome. A safe place to *hide* is more like it, Rune thought bitterly.

"All right then, Rune Johansson," Fox conceded. He studied Rune's face hard. "Consider this money your pay from the mines, the Ramsey family mines. You've got good Alaska gold profit in your hands *noo*, and you're going to earn it. This is *nee* charity, lad. This is business. This is trade business, serious trade business."

"I agree. This is serious trade." Rune looked Fox in the eye. "I will get you to Siberia and back again with your dogs." Rune would give his life to keep their lives safe. He might have to—so long over water—so vulnerable to the Midgard serpent from *Hel.*

"*Aye,* then, we're in business." Fox put his hand out to shake Rune's.

Rune put the roll of bills in his left hand and extended his right to seal their agreement.

Anya placed her hand atop theirs. She'd been listening to their conversation. She didn't know much, or care much, about money. The Chukchi placed little value on money and no value on greed. A greedy person was a worthless person and should be punished. What made her get up from her corner was talk of the journey back across the Bering Sea. The waters had proved dangerous for Rune, for all of them. There was no safe place to hide or bide for them now.

Anya had found the courage she needed to at least face the reality of the moment.

Though she'd never again hear her beloved grandmother's voice in the music of the arctic wind, she'd never forget Nanatasha's parting message to her. Anya understood why Nanatasha wanted her to befriend Fox Maule Ramsey: the Scot wanted to *rescue* Chukchi dogs from Siberia. He just didn't know it. He thinks he's going to the Markova Fair to bring back dogs to race, but Anya knew better. Her Spirit knew better.

The Gatekeepers watched and listened. The ice storm had been slowed, allowing time so that *some will live.*

"*Aye,* lassie, we're all in business," Fox assured, then pumped his arm a second time to include Anya.

She pulled her hand away, the deal sealed. First Boris Ivanov, then Rune, and now Fox Ramsey were "in business" with her to rescue Chukchi dogs. Why hadn't she seen it before? Why hadn't she believed, truly believed, what her grandmother prophesied. The signs were right in front of her all the time. Part human, part *Spirit,* she was born to Native Earth for one purpose: to save the dogs of their People.

The Gatekeepers stood guard. Anya felt their presence. As shaman she could hear and understand what ancestral spirits told her. *Native Earth is ripped open. The hole widens. The ice thickens and fills the place where our People and our dogs live, trapping them, lost forever. The ice will never melt. The passage of time will not save us. The passage across the Great Sea will.*

Anya had no way of knowing how much time the People had left. Neither did she know who or what came after them. What she did realize was that the dogs of the Chukchi, the enduring sled dogs carefully bred over thousands of years—the lifeline of the People—would not survive unless they crossed the Great Sea.

Zellie had crossed the Great Sea and paid for it with her life.

Anya would rather it had been her.

Some will live. Many will die.

Anya would rather her life had been the one sacrificed.

"What do you say, Anya?" Rune broke into her dark concentration.

"About what?" she asked innocently, trying to keep her voice light and her thoughts secret.

"About us meeting back up with Fox regular until summer at the Board of Trade Saloon. Plans need to be made. We can't make them if we don't meet up. We're going to keep any plans we make to ourselves. Fox has agreed to that," Rune emphasized.

For his part Fox gave a clear nod. The last thing he wanted was any competition in the next All Alaska Sweepstakes. He didn't want other dog drivers in the District of Alaska to know he intended to race Siberian huskies. In fact he wanted to race three teams, driving one himself. That meant he needed at least forty-eight dogs to train, and would put sixteen to a team; the usual number in sled dog racing. Nine Siberian huskies had almost won the race just run. Imagine the thrill of what sixteen might do!

"Wait." Fox took off his tartan cap and scratched his head, puzzled over seeing only eight dogs gathered in the stable; not nine. Why hadn't he noticed before? Where was the lad and lassie's leader dog, the other black and white husky—the ninth dog? Fox had witnessed the team leave and then cross the finish line, all the *same* dogs. The leader finished the race.

"Where's your leader *dug*?" Fox looked from Rune to Anya, his question for both of them.

"She's gone."

"Gone, you say, lassie?" Fox parroted. He waited for more of an explanation. No one ever took their eyes off their leader dog.

"Yes." Anya wiped away new tears.

Rune tensed; worried over Anya being upset and worried about revealing too much to the Scot. The less said about things, the better. The less Fox Maule Ramsey knew, the better his chances to stay safe. No, Rune didn't want to involve the Scot in their troubles any more than he had to.

"What happened, lassie?" Fox asked, gently this time.

Anya swallowed hard.

"I don't know," she answered with a lie. She'd no choice. Uncomfortable under Fox's puzzled stare, she had to think of something to say, and quick. She looked at Rune. From the blank expression on his face, he didn't know what to say, either. She swallowed hard again, her mouth bone dry.

"You don't know?" Fox was unconvinced.

"I told you, I don't know," Anya said again. "Something must have spirited her away during the night and now she's gone. I know she won't come back. She would have at this point if she could. Something bad must have happened to her." Anya told the truth this time. She refused to cry. She refused to give the Raven god any satisfaction.

"I'm that sorry, lassie." Fox softened his tone. "Is there anythin' I can do?"

Anya shook her head no.

Not for the first time, Rune admired Anya's sharp-wittedness. She wasn't like any girl he'd ever met in Seattle or any other place. If he stopped to think about their meeting up and then working together, it still baffled him. Lives can change in a heartbeat. That's for certain.

Fox turned to leave, then abruptly turned back around to Anya and Rune.

"Do you *nee* tether your *dugs* like most? I do *nee kin* why your *dugs* are *nee* tied to posts to keep 'em from running off? I do *nee* mean to upset you both, but I do *nee kin*," Fox said, his observation genuine.

"You're right," Anya spoke up, her voice wistful. "Maybe if Zellie had been tied, she wouldn't have run and she'd still be with us." The words rang true. Anya fought new tears. If she'd just left Zellie tied to her post back in their home village, maybe none of this would be happening. She exhaled sharply. Yes, it would. The ice storm was coming, no matter what. There was no going back and Anya knew it.

"You're right that most sled dogs need to be tied, in winter especially. I will find a place for these dogs and make a proper dog yard for them when I can," she assured.

"Enough said, lassie," Fox put a brotherly hand to her shoulder. "If you need me for anythin', you can get word to me at the Board of Trade Saloon or the Ramsey mines. You have gumption like your *dugs*, lassie. I'm that glad to meet up with you and the lad here and that glad I'll soon have *dugs* of my own from your homeland. Maybe some of their gumption will rub off on me," he joked, his hand off her shoulder now. The lassie seemed thin, bonnie but a *wee* bit thin. "You and the lad find a place to bide and *doon* three squares a day," Fox ordered gingerly.

"A square is a meal, by the by," Fox joked again, in case the lassie wasn't familiar with frontier slang.

Anya smiled at the hint for her to eat more. She'd heard it all her life from Vitya, then Rune, and now from their new friend. The Scot managed to make her think of something besides losing Zellie. Fox Maule Ramsey was kind. She liked him, like a brother.

Xander came up to Anya, nudging his head under her hand, and asked for a pat.

She scratched behind his ears, then buried her fingers in his thick fur. She absentmindedly trailed her fingers along the back of his head.

Xander leaned against her side, almost shoving her over, wanting to play.

Alarmed, Anya shot Xander a quick look, worried a fit might be coming on. No, she could see right away from his friskiness he was all right. His watch eyes were clear, the bluest of blues. She ran her hand along his back and felt the strength in him had returned, mentally thanking the Morning Dawn and all the Directions for bringing him fully back to her. Anya dropped to her knees to hug Xander but he beat her to it, easily toppling her with his front paws. Giggling at his antics, she didn't even try to get up.

This black and white husky is special to the lassie, Fox thought while watching them play. He wondered about the black and white leader dog gone missing, if the lassie felt the same for Zellie. *Aye*, she did. The lassie's unshed tears told the story. Fox could read all the hurt she held inside. He wondered again what terrible fate Zellie must have encountered.

A bear?

Wolves?

A drop off an icy crag?

Or . . . did she encounter the end of an angry gun? He wouldn't put anything past the likes of some mean locals he'd met, like the whip-lashing dog driver, Frank Lundgren. Fox didn't like the braggart excuse for a dog driver. If Zellie had a bullet in her, it could well be from Lundgren's gun. Fox meant to find him, and find out.

"I'm on my way *noo*," Fox announced, setting his red and black tartan cap center on his head. "Meet me at the Ramsey Mining Company in four weeks' time. Come sooner if need be. Let's keep our business to ourselves. I *willnae* speak of it for *noo*, even to my uncles."

Rune nodded his agreement.

Anya, too.

"Mind my money," Fox said with a wink, then breezed past all the watchful huskies and quickly disappeared.

"We have to talk," Anya said the moment Fox had gone.

Rune turned his back on her and began shoving his few belongings in his duffle. He'd already hidden the roll of bills in a pouch inside. The sword wouldn't fit. Just then he grabbed up the nearby caribou blanket and wrapped the fur cover around the sword. He'd load it on their sled with the rest of the supplies they had left, with no one the wiser. Collecting everything in his arms, he headed outside, past Anya.

She followed him out.

The dogs stirred when they saw Rune go toward the sled. They were ready to run.

Anya headed the dogs off, ushering them back inside the stable. She gave the signal for them to stay, then made sure they obeyed before going over to Rune. They weren't alone. People walked by. One stranger after another eyed her, then walked on.

Some gave her a nod; most did not.

With the weather broken and the skies cleared, the streets and alleyways in Nome filled with men and women who needed to work and children who needed to go to school, white and Eskimo alike. The four-day holiday celebrating the second running of the All Alaska Sweepstakes was over and life went on, quickly returning to normal.

Anya watched Rune pack the sled, surprised that no one else did, surprised no one appeared to recognize him from the race. Otherwise, wouldn't they want to see the new dogs again? It puzzled her. Here she'd thought they all needed to stay hidden in the stable away from prying eyes and too many questions when no one really took much notice after all. Only one man in all of Nome searched them out, Fox Maule Ramsey. But then only one man had started their rescue in the first place, Boris Ivanov. Anya was beginning to understand.

"So let's talk," Rune said, turning around and facing her.

"Out here?" Anya wanted their talk to be private.

"Yes, out here. No one's hanging around to overhear us, and I don't want to leave the sled unguarded."

"The sword, you mean," she said.

"Something like that," he admitted.

Anya glanced around them. She scoured the area for anyone or anything suspicious. Satisfied no one lurked, no human, that is, she closed her eyes and listened for spirit signs warning her of danger. None came.

"Rune, you said it before. We don't have much time. You are not what you seem and neither am I. I'll go first. I'm a Chukchi shaman and I see and hear dead spirits of my ancestors. Your turn," she leveled.

Whoa. That explains it. That explains why he sometimes thought of her as a ghost, the way she seemed to shimmer in the light, then almost faded in thin air at the slightest touch.

She might not be a ghost but she'd just told him she talked to them. A numbing chill shot through Rune . . . so did he.

"Me too," he heard himself say.

"You're a shaman, too?" Irritated that he joked with her, this wasn't going well. He would leave her and the dogs the first chance he got now that he knew the truth about her. Well fine. Let him leave.

"Anya, where do you think you're going?" Rune caught her arm and held her to the spot.

She tried to wriggle free, huffing mad at him. She'd save the hurt for later.

"Just let go. You can go, too. I told you the other night to go and you're still here!"

Rune grabbed her other arm to make sure she couldn't escape him.

"I took my turn and answered your question. What's got you so riled?" Rune could see she fought her emotions and struggled to hold them in. He knew more than the evils of the Raven god upset her. He just didn't know what.

"No, you didn't answer me. You mocked me. You are *no* shaman," she accused. The fight in her suddenly gone, her arms went limp. She just wanted to get this all over with and get out of there. She didn't care where. Maybe even back to Siberia. Maybe she could better help save the dogs in her homeland. Her world spun. Her head pounded with the motion of it. She couldn't tell which world spun, human or spirit. She didn't care.

"Anya, I said, me too. I see and hear ghosts, too," Rune tried to explain.

A bolt of energy brought the life back in her. She shook her head to clear it, able to stand straight and steady at his words. His simple answer was the best thing she'd ever heard in all her complicated life. She had to know more.

"Ru—"

He cut her off. Time was short.

"The god of my Viking ancestors appeared to me and sent me to help you and your dogs. The sword was in my hand when I came to this morning. It must have been put there by Odin, himself. Nine serpents I must slay, he told me. One is dead. Eight are left. I will use the sword on them. I swear with my life," he vowed.

"We have to get the dogs in harness and hitched and leave this place. *Now,* Anya." With that, he abruptly let go of her and went to fetch the dogs.

Anya couldn't move and couldn't believe what Rune just said, yet she knew he told her the truth. He wasn't a shaman, but he came close. He could see and hear spirits like she did, only he heard the spirits of his ancestors, the Vikings. Odin must be a powerful Viking god. The queerest sensation struck Anya. Were there others like her and like Rune? The possibility stirred her. Suddenly she didn't feel quite so peculiar or so alone.

"Anya, hurry," Rune ordered, jolting her back to the present. He shoved a bundle of harnessing at her, then took some of the hide strappings himself to help get all the dogs hitched and ready to run.

One by one, Anya slipped harnessing onto Xander, Midnight, Little Wolf, and then Midday. Anxious to go and needing no prompting, all four dogs took up their assigned places in front of the sled; Xander and Midnight to their "wheel" positions and Little Wolf and Midday to their "team" positions. Anya watched them and watched Rune harness the other four. She'd never been more proud. Much had been asked of the dogs. Robbed of any kind of normal life for a Chukchi dog to run, to hunt, to protect and give their all to the People, they must endure on this new frontier. They must sacrifice all they've ever known for the unknown, where danger waited for them at day's end instead of the loving arms of Chukchi children.

It began to snow. In a heartbeat, the snowfall increased. The light of the winter day faded to gray. Arctic shadows crept in, giving an eerie darkness to the alleyway. The wind picked up and sent swirls of snow whistling past.

Anya took notice.

So did Rune.

A new storm brewed.

The busy streets of Nome quieted with most residents getting out of the coming weather. Snowstorms weren't unusual but this one came in too fast for comfort and right on the heels of the fierce storm that moved in on the race just run. The sudden, violent storm cut out eleven teams the first day with only three teams able to combat the storm and cross the finish.

Nervous teachers put chalkboards, readers, and sewing machines away. Boys and girls filed out of their schoolrooms to go home early. Some must return to their villages while others lived in town. Miners headed out of saloons, needing to get back to their company housing and their winter work of drift mining. Stores began to close and locals hurried to finish laying in supplies. Freight dog teams barked in the streets, waiting for their sleds to be loaded and their drivers' call to "Mush!" Hotels, brimful with businessmen, gold investors, and tourists, made sure of their registers to check for any open rooms. Bad weather meant customers through the door.

Storekeeper Chinook didn't close up his trade. Instead he found his pipe and lit the well-packed tobacco. He took his usual seat on the empty barrel behind the counter before he took a puff. Blowing slowly, watching the smoke swirl into disappearing trails, he didn't worry over his family or his village, and believed them safe from the storm. He did worry over the boy, the girl, and their Chukchi dogs . . . and knew they were not.

CHAPTER SIX

The copper-red and white pair of swing dogs pushed forward through the snowy gale. Magic and Mushroom ran at the head of the team under Anya's guide. The huskies didn't obey any called-out commands but the bidding of the ancestors, who told them instinctively to run until they could run no more. When the trail allowed, Anya or Rune would ride in the sled, then take turns dog driving. The dogs quickly picked up speed on the flats, making it hard for anyone running alongside to keep up. The extra weight didn't slow the dogs. Altitude did. When the team had to climb rough terrain around rocky bends, neither Anya nor Rune rode in the sled's basket but helped push it ever on, ever upward.

The dogs' hearts pumped as one, their pack mentality set. They ran with the wolves now, enemies no more. Four of the Chukchi dogs had just fought alongside the wolf to save their guardian. Midnight, Frost, Mushroom, and Little Wolf still nursed their wounds from the fight. They ignored any pain, any blood. They only knew to run. The thing after them wasn't any shape they could recognize or smell they could track and go after. The thing came at them quick, silent, killing.

Xander ran at the back of the pack, skillfully pulling and turning the sled away from steep embankments and uncertain ground. Partnered with Midnight the two wheel dogs worked together, both keenly intent on one purpose—to run and outrun what hunted them. Forced out of their gentle nature and generations of hard work and play, they sensed the danger. They knew to obey their masters, their guardians, only them. They listened now to the call of the wild, their canine instincts telling them they must kill or be killed. Collectively, all eight dogs underwent this change from gentle husky to prey mentality, but not to the same degree. Not all showed the same strength for what would come; some were more vulnerable than others.

Alert like her dogs to everything around her, Anya pressed their dogsled up the trail to follow Rune. She kept her eyes and ears peeled for any new signs of danger besides the obvious storm. Signs could come from this world or another. She traveled both worlds now, moving in and out of them like the tides; one moment a part of the ocean and the next a part of the sand. She couldn't predict when she might become *Spirit* again, and leave her physical body on Native Earth to inhabit her husky body in the spirit world. At least she didn't fear the world of the shamans enveloping her and changing her life form. Despite her Spirit's help, she hadn't forgotten what the ancestors prophesied when they told her that her human spirit must prevail over the darkness to come.

Rune, too, she realized.

He might have the help of spirits returned from the Viking dead, calling on him to join her fight, but he, and he alone, had to prevail. Our human spirits must prevail, she mentally repeated. If either of us is killed, then all is lost. Rune had been close to dying twice before. The dogs found him buried in snow and dug him out. Their aid and an air pocket saved him. Last night Rune almost died. Anya was sure of it. The dogs helped him, along with the Viking sword in his hand, but his human strength and will prevailed. He was alive, and that was proof enough for her.

She and Rune walked the edges of a dangerous crag together. Something monstrous waited in the shadows beneath; waited for her and Rune to slip and fall; waited for the dogs to slip and fall into the clutches of crushing arctic waves, buried in hiding beneath the ice. Anya's resolve stiffened. She wouldn't leave Native Earth without a fight.

She would ignore any pain, any blood. She only knew to run.

The golem would soon be let out of its cage. The whole of Russia trembled, and for good reason. The fanatic demon would spark the beginning of the End for so many, born and yet to be born. A human shape, yes, but there was nothing humane about the golem—nothing caring, nothing gentle, not a flicker of kindness in him. Though still imprisoned in Siberia, the revolution would soon come, the revolution that would free him. Once started, the waves of communism would build into an ocean of death and drown all in its Red path.

The Chukchi would try to stand in their way, as they had for centuries.

The Chukchi had been able to survive because of their dogs.

They fought the Czar and the brutal Cossacks, outrunning and outsmarting the enemy until a truce had been negotiated. Fierce fighters themselves, besting rival tribes, the People knew the Arctic and lived as one with the harsh climate; able to find food, shelter, to survive and maintain their way of life. They didn't have equal weapons, but they withstood the Czar and the Cossacks because of their dogs. The Czar had tried to kill the People before, wanting all the riches of the fur trade in the region. More than once, a plot of genocide was formulated and failed.

Once released from exile, the golem would not fail.

Because of the sheer power of his fanaticism, of the evil born in him, the golem caused a rupture in Native Earth. The ice storm was born in the belly of the rupture, the fate of millions instantly sealed. Enemies of the golem quickly began to fall.

Already the Raven god of the Chukchi and the fires of Viking *Hel* bent to the golem's will. There were more in his way. Evil sparks evil if gone unchecked. The golem had begun a war of ghosts, moving in the shadows, striking where he could. Still imprisoned in his cell, it was the only kind of war he could wage—war in the darkest part of the spirit world.

Once free, he could start a different war unlike any before on Native Earth. Where the Czar failed, he would not. Where the Cossacks failed, he would not. The idea of death breathed life into the monster within him.

Angry surf pushed up through the ice, crashing against arctic shores with whiplike force, nearly freeing the golem. Soon, he knew. He could already taste the blood of crushed spirits and destroyed lives congealing in the breaking waves. He thirsted for more, feeding on every shard of the growing ice storm.

"Ahoy there!" Rune called across the clearing.

The weather hadn't let up. He could make out a cabin ahead. This could be the right cabin. He didn't remember the name of the man who tried to help him last night, but he thought this could be where he lived. Wait, Zeke was one and Homer the other. That's all Rune had to go on, the two names and the stranger's promise Rune could come back with the dogs anytime if they needed help.

"Ahoy there!" Rune yelled again, hoping the man meant what he said.

Anya slowed the dogs, or tried to. Hard to hold, they wanted to run on by this place. She did, too. The storm had her on edge.

No one came outside the cabin. Rune couldn't see any windows; only a shut door. The place looked deserted, but Rune didn't think the men would be off hunting or headed to the drift mines, not in this storm. They could be in trouble . . . or dead. He pictured them laid out on the ground next to Frank Lundgren's mangled body. Rune conjured the image of the thing that attacked him last night. It wasn't wolves. It wasn't anything of this world. If it found the two men who had helped him, he hoped their deaths had come swiftly.

. Worried for the men and needing to learn their fate, Rune pivoted in the snow and motioned to Anya to mush the team in the direction of the glacial lake where he'd fought last night. He had to find out if the men were dead or alive. He'd use the sword again if he had to.

Wolves howled in the distance ahead, as if in warning. Rune imagined the scene, the carnage. He'd put Anya and the dogs in new danger and he knew it.

"Anya!" He stopped short. He'd changed his mind about them following.

"Whoa! Whoa!" She shouted to the team, and threw the snow hook to the ground to try and hold them. More on edge than she'd been moments before, she believed Rune had good reason for this.

The dogs must not have agreed, fighting Anya's command for them to stop.

"Whoa!" she had to call again.

This time they obeyed, but barked in sharp protest.

Despite the bad weather that hampered them, Rune strode over to the sled and grabbed up the sword from inside the caribou blanket. The weight of the short blade surprised him, momentarily pulling his arm down. He lifted it back up. The longer he held the steel, the lighter it became. Magic, he thought, this blade of war and wisdom.

Anya froze, not from the below zero temperatures but out of fear for Rune.

"Anya, stay here with the dogs and wait for me!" he shouted over the rising gale.

The wind whipped now without let up.

Anya took hold of the sled's handlebar to help brace against the strong gusts. Her fur mitts protected her hands well enough. She doubted Rune could make his way in this storm, sword or not. The blinding snow might do just that, blind him.

The dogs quieted, tied to their lines, ever watchful of Anya and Rune. Used to the worst of storms, they didn't fall away from their guard. Centuries of breeding taught them to hold fast. They meant to protect their guardians. Voices carried over the winds, through the storm, telling them to hold fast.

Anya watched Rune disappear over the rise. She shuddered at what he might find beyond. Through the handlebar of the sled, she felt the same tension in all the tethered dogs, their leather bindings held taut. The dogs pushed against their hold, enough to signal their upset but not take off in the storm. She felt the drums of the ancients beat in her heart, just as upset as she. Times were dangerous. Every step, every turn, every day could end it all. She worried for Rune and what he might have to face. Wolves called again over the distance. She struggled to understand their cries, her fears increased.

Xander unexpectedly let out his own piercing howl across the open, and matched the call of the wolf.

Anya panicked, her fears immediately transferred to Xander. Was a fit coming on? Please, Morning Dawn. Protect him. Please protect him, she pled silently. Positioned right in front of the sled, close to her, he stood tall against the storm and didn't appear to falter. Suddenly he jerked hard against the leather straps that tethered him to the sled. Then Anya understood his upset. He wanted to go with Rune.

"No, I can't let you," she whispered.

Xander turned his proud head, his watch eyes on Anya.

She instinctively knew he thought of her in that moment, that he might not come back.

Snow pelted Xander's husky mask while the winds tore at his thick fur. He gave a soft bark, then whimpered before he switched his attention to the leather that held him. Biting at the tug line, he shook his head back and forth hard, his teeth clenched on the line.

Anya reluctantly pulled off her mitt and reached inside the pocket of her kerker, and fumbled for her knife. She had to let him go. How could she not? He followed the call of the wild now; not her; not Zellie. If something happened to him . . . she wouldn't have any reason to stay in this cruel world, too unhappy without him and Zellie. Desperate to keep Xander close, she wished it were as easy as keeping him tied. But she couldn't and she knew it. Then she thought of the other dogs. She knew she couldn't just leave them alone and unprotected.

Xander barked hard at Anya, as if trying to hurry her up.

Her tears trickled into icy lines down her cheeks. She wiped them away but not before their salty taste brushed inside her mouth. Reminded instantly of sea water, of the ocean, she saw herself drift away from Xander, helpless on an ice floe, abandoning him. She'd no choice and she knew it; not the way he demanded she let him go.

Anya had Xander's ties cut in moments, acting quickly before she could change her mind. Then her mind went blank. Her body emptied of all emotion. It was the only way she could force herself to let Xander go—if she already felt dead.

And gone he was, in a heartbeat. He took off in the same direction as Rune.

Anya swallowed past her dry, raw throat and stared after him. Involuntarily she ran her tongue over her chapped lips, trying to find some kind of moisture to ease the pain she felt inside. Bad idea. Ice coated everywhere, sticking and stinging wherever she touched.

It would never let up—the ice—until it was done with them.

But not without a fight! Anya brushed the ice away from her face as best she could and stood tall against the storm, as Xander just had, and focused on the seven dogs that remained. She put her knife back in her pocket for safety, yet kept her hand firmly around the crude blade. If anything came for her or the dogs, she was determined to be ready.

Vitya was determined, too—determined to find Anya and bring her back to their village. He would stand up to Grisha and the shamans. If he had to, he would take Anya to live with his family and the reindeer hunters. If he had to, he would kill to keep her safe. Why didn't he stand up to Grisha the day Grisha took her away from their coastal village? He should have done more to protect her. The husky necklace he'd carved for Anya and handed her before she left was little protection against anything. But maybe it would help her remember him.

Maybe she would remember she had a good friend in him.

Maybe she would hear him call her *gitengev*, pretty girl.

Maybe she knew he wanted to be more than a friend.

His kiss should have told her he wanted to be her husband. If he found her, he would never let her go; never again. He would help her breed and raise Chukchi dogs. She loved the dogs more than her own life. He prayed one day she might come to love him just as much. She already had his heart. He longed to have hers. The husky carving was a start, he thought; a reminder of him. He imagined her fingers on the smooth ivory shaped by his fingers, touching him, pulling him to her.

The next Markova Fair couldn't come soon enough.

"Ridiculous, Lars! I'm not about to take our precious daughter to the wilds of Alaska! You can just forget that idea," Margret Johansson fumed. "You cannot expect us to be uprooted from our lives here in Seattle to traipse across some frozen wilderness where we're likely to be eaten by wolves or bears or whatever lives on the frontier up north." That said, Margret plopped down on the elegant settee, right next to a crying Inga. Fifteen now, Inga had dissolved into tears the moment her father talked of leaving Seattle.

"Not even to find our son?" Lars gritted his question.

"Humph," Margret huffed. "Rune is always running off somewhere, and never stays home. I don't understand him. He's never liked our beautiful home or going out in good society. Anyway, he's almost seventeen, able to take care of himself. I'm sure he'll come home when he's of the mind. I don't doubt you left money in his pocket. He'll be just fine," Margret pronounced.

"Money isn't the answer to everything," Lars said evenly. "You just think it is."

Lars was having a hard time remembering what he ever saw in Margret that made him fall in love with her and marry her. Oh, she was still beautiful, he granted; but only on the outside. Inside she'd turned uglier than the worst of arctic storms. He came around center, looking hard at his wife and daughter.

"When the ice breaks in the North, you will both be on the ship for Nome, District of Alaska. You will live in the frontier city for as long as I see fit. We will be a family . . . for Rune." Lars had trouble getting his words out past his frustration and anger at his wife and daughter.

"What will we possibly do in such a wild place? There is no society of any value in Nome!" Margret stood and faced her husband. "You must think of our daughter. Don't you care about her? Don't you want to keep her home and safe?"

His hand formed a fist at his side, and he had trouble keeping it there. He'd never hit a woman before but dammit, he wanted to hit his wife. No man should *ever* hit a woman. Forcing his fingers to relax, he wasn't about to harm his wife, but for the life of him, he didn't understand how she could be so uncaring about her own son. His wife looked so changed to him. Her blond beauty, her once-soft expression, her loving gaze were all gone. He shook his head in disappointment and took a step back from her.

"How dare you?" Margret whispered hard. "How dare you shake your head at me? I am your wife and Inga is your daughter. I repeat my question. How could you let our daughter be exposed to . . . to whatever waits in a nowhere place like *Nome*?"

Lars had no answer for his wife, no answer that she'd accept or understand. The truth stung. Her words stung. She didn't even think of their son, only Inga; and herself, he mentally added.

"Don't you want Inga and me to be happy? Don't you want the best for us?" Margret demanded, her voice every bit as hard as her expression.

"Don't you want to see your son again? Don't you want to help me find Rune and make sure *he's* safe and *he's* happy?"

Lars didn't want to hit Margret anymore. He didn't even want to look at her. Dragged down with disappointment in her, he needed to finish this conversation and get out of the house and back to Seattle's harbor. It always calmed him to be at sea. When the ice broke up north, he'd outfit the *Nordic* and get Margret and Inga on board, willing or unwilling.

"Where are you going?" Margret challenged. "We haven't finished this discussion!"

"Yes we have," Lars said curtly over his shoulder and quickly exited their velvet-cushioned, crystal chandeliered, high-polished mahogany parlor.

Wolves had Xander surrounded—a dozen yellow-eyed, snarling, circling in. He instinctively knew this would be a fight to the death. Slowly, he began to pivot around in the snow that pelted, looking each predator in the eye before the kill. His doglike memory and instincts went to Zellie, his companion in life. She waited for him in the sleeping wild, waited to help him across to the time of the ancestors. Soon he would wait with Zellie for their guardians, and help to pull each into the same wild. First he would suffer the bite of the wolf and taste the blood of death. Intuition told him the pain would be momentary; then he'd be gone from Native Earth.

He longed to be with Zellie, and whimpered for her, feeling every bit a pup again that wanted nothing more than to follow her and nestle close. His Chukchi canine instincts strong and fine-tuned over centuries of intelligent breeding, Xander naturally understood the circle of life in this hostile place as well as the animals born to it. The "call of the wild" deafened. Still, he pricked his ears and turned to each after him, then lunged at the biggest first.

The lights of heaven lit without warning. Red, green, blue, and yellow streaked across the darkened sky, enough to penetrate the thick snowfall and illuminate the circle of predators and prey. Xander didn't pull back from the largest of the wolf pack, and sank his teeth into its black-furred neck, beginning the destined fight. The wolf didn't fight back? Startled, Xander stopped his assault. Confused, he tasted the blood in his mouth, the blood of his enemy. Kill or be killed. It was all he knew, all he sensed and all he could understand now.

His heart pumped with energy for the fight. About to go after the wolf again, the animal surprised him with a howl instead of bared teeth. The wolf threw his head toward the heavens and cried to the lights above. So did the rest of the pack. Xander backed away from the wolf, still stunned and confused, the song in his blood still one of death and not life. The drums of the ancestors had yet to reach him.

Then he heard her—Zellie. The effect was immediate. Her call consoled him and broke through his confusion. *The wolf and the dog must battle as one.* He understood Zellie's ghostlike howls and whispers on the wind, his instincts keen. It wasn't the Gatekeepers, but Zellie. Her spirit spoke to his. He must not fear or fight with the wolves. They meant him no harm.

Xander stood alone in the circle of wolves.

The one he'd hurt, the leader of their pack, broke from the circle and reapproached him.

The eyes of the wolf changed color, now watch-blue.

Xander barked in soft apology, then lowered to the ground, his body flush with the snow in a sign of subservience. The great black wolf shook its head and whined in acknowledgment, as if he released Xander from any punishment for his attack. Xander immediately stood, still wary of the pack that surrounded him but keenly aware of his connection to them. This was new, to trust the wolf so readily. The wolves slowly backed away from him as if with the same wariness.

Other calls suddenly alerted the wolf pack; Xander, too. It wasn't the wolf or the dog. Something else bade them all come, inviting them to battle. The wolves took off, the black wolf in the lead. Xander went with them.

Anya heard Zellie's unmistakable howls. But it *couldn't* be her. Zellie was dead. Anya's imagination had taken over. She missed Zellie and thought she heard her in every cry. Snow swirled around Anya, so fast the Directions were confused. That's all. She hadn't heard Zellie, she told herself. It hurt too much to think otherwise. Even so, it wasn't Xander. So worried over him, Anya knew her thinking was blurred, her senses dulled. She clutched her knife hard in her pocket, and did her best to concentrate and sharpen her wits.

Flowers gave out a loud yelp, as if hurt.

So did Midday.

Then Magic.

The females, Anya realized right away—*only the females.* Her gut turned. She let go of her knife. Her female center felt cut. The overwhelming pain sent her to her knees in the snow. She got back up in a heartbeat and ran to her dogs the moment she suspicioned something had just happened to them. Praying to the Morning Dawn and the Creator god she was wrong, afraid to check the three females but knowing she must, Anya began with Flowers. The snow and high winds made her task difficult.

The piebald whimpered at Anya's touch, and flinched when Anya examined her. Anya found no injuries . . . that she could see. She tried to relax. It must have been her imagination taking over again, thinking something bad happened to the three females, all yelping at the same time. Just my imagination, she reassured herself again.

Anya examined Magic next because she was closer to Flowers. The copper-red and white husky looked all right. No observable injuries, yet the skittish female didn't want to be touched.

Uneasy all over again, Anya rushed back down the line of dogs to the other side of the gangline, to Midday. The all-white husky stood restless and obviously upset. She wouldn't let Anya near, growling low in warning. Anya's gut turned hard. Spirits were here—*bad ones.*

The males started to bark. They smelled danger.

Drops of blood drizzled in front of Anya's line of vision. She didn't need to look up to see the ravens circling; their loud caws audible over the dogs and the gale. She didn't need to question which bad spirits had come. The claws of the Raven god left their bloody mark. Dread coursed through Anya, sickening her, sapping her energy, her concentration. More caws. More blood dripped from the twilight skies and streaked through the storm as if pretending to be a part of the northern lights, trying to fool any watchers.

The Gatekeepers were not fooled.

Anya was not fooled.

The Raven god had turned on them. Something or someone had turned the Raven against the Chukchi and their dogs.

The Gatekeepers knew what guided the Raven now.

Anya did not.

The Gatekeepers had no way to communicate this to Anya. She was born to Native Earth to rely on her human spirit and understanding to discover the truth. Along with her Spirit, she must do battle with the darkness that shadowed them all. A holy woman, a shaman of the Chukchi now, the Gatekeepers must rely on her human skills and instincts to slow the ice storm long enough so some of their own might survive. They must keep watch at the Gates of Heaven. The ancestors had spoken.

Her head so heavy she felt dizzy, Anya did her best to look up and face the Raven. Dozens of black-winged birds pecked at the heavens, their claws sending droplets of blood toward *Hel*. Anya reached inside her pocket and pulled out her *gift of the gods*, her knife. She was determined to take the ravens down, one by one. If they alighted anywhere, she would kill, striking them through the heart of the Raven. Soon one did land; then another, then another . . . prancing victoriously across the snow-covered ground. They came closer, unfettered by the still-high winds, baiting Anya. She struck them down, each one and all together—in a heartbeat—in the time it takes to give life or end it.

All seven huskies, females and males alike, barked and fought their ties, jumping to get into the fray. Anya refused to let them. She meant to protect them and stop the ravens. She had; at least those that came close enough to kill. The rest flew off into the storm, which eerily quieted. Snowflakes drifted down through calm breezes, the storm over for the moment.

Dead ravens littered the scene. Anya meant to gather them in a pile and burn them all to Rune's Viking *Hel*. She must be master and so must Rune, over their enemies past and present; no matter if they were conceived in this world or another.

Anya wiped her knife clean in the snow before replacing it in the pocket of her kerker. She knew she'd killed many ravens, but was it enough to stop them from attacking again and keep the Raven god away for good? No, probably not. Had the Raven god injured Flowers, Midday, and Magic? She thought so. The Raven god was powerful. Someone, something, controlled the Raven now, sending it against the Chukchi dogs to bring such misfortune to them all.

On this day the Raven flew against the females.

Anya cringed inside. There could only be one answer. She didn't want to think it. She couldn't imagine any enemy so cruel, so evil it would harm females *there,* in the part of their body where they could conceive life! Afraid for the dogs, she prostrated herself on the ground, her face flush to the snow, and prayed with everything in her to the Morning Dawn, the Directions, and the Creator gods of the Chukchi to undo any evil visited on them by the Raven god. Turning her head, her ear hard against the frozen tundra, she listened for any drumbeat from the ancestors telling her the dogs had not been cut *there,* as she suspected. She felt the same cut, the same hurt, the same emptiness inside her.

Nothing came to her from the ancients. The Gatekeepers kept silent. No understanding drummed through the air to reach her. Slowly, with great effort, Anya pulled herself to a stand. This was an awful day.

She'd failed her dogs again, possibly allowing them to be harmed for life, unable to have pups and continue their bloodlines. The screams inside her head were her own. She called to her grandmother across worlds to answer her. Someone had to answer her and tell her what had just happened. But no message came, no answer across arctic winds.

"Nana-tasha, please," Anya whispered softly. "There must be a way for you to reach me. There must! You said you would always be with me, when I lie down and when I rise up. You promised me you would always be close. In failing the dogs again have I failed you? I am sorry, grandmother. I am—"

Unable to finish, refusing to finish, Anya dried her tears and straightened her spine. She was alone in this, dejected but not defeated. Spiraling around to the dogs, she checked each for any new wounds and made sure of their ties, that they were adjusted properly so as not to cause any chafing or sore spots. She would ignore the females' cold response to any attention, only for now. They would need time to heal from this day. She understood.

So intent on her task was she, Anya didn't turn back to see Nana-tasha's presence misting close by. If she had, she might have gotten the answer she desperately wanted. A shiver down her spine forced Anya to look up. When she did she saw nothing; nothing but light snow billowing in breezy curtains, blown away in a heartbeat. Her chest hurt. She ached for her grandmother. She longed to disappear into the spirit world and try to find her.

The moment Anya thought it, it began to happen.

Drawn suddenly into the world of spirits, Anya felt her body tingle, everywhere, all at once. She watched her arms slowly dissolve into sparkle and mist, knowing they would soon take on the shape of her husky counterpart, Spirit. *She* would soon become Spirit's husky being. This had happened once before, when Zellie was close to death and she'd become Spirit—the ache inside her to be with a loved one equally strong now, equally demanding. The sights and sounds of Native Earth began to fade. Flowers, Magic, even Midday barked loudly. So did the rest, with Little Wolf the loudest of all.

Anya felt powerless to heed their calls.

She really didn't want to leave them, but she ached for her grandmother, feeling like a child again, longing for the loving arms of Nana-tasha. She could go and come back in a heartbeat, couldn't she? Unsure of the answer—unsure if she could come and go at will—Anya realized she couldn't risk being away from her dogs for any length of time and leave them exposed to mortal danger. With every ounce of strength she could call on as a shaman, no matter the discomfort, she forced herself away from Spirit and back to Native Earth; her feet set firm on the uncertain ice and snow. Sight and sound rushed back in with a vengeance.

Smoke mushroomed out of the nearby cabin's chimney, choking black smoke. A fire had started inside. Anya needed to get the dogs away from there! Then two men rushed past her, shouting, and with guns blazing.

"Shoot the damn thing, Homer!" Zeke Raney yelled, limping hard behind, in a struggle to keep up.

"What thing, Zeke? I can't make nothing out!"

Anya held fast to the sled and her dogs. At least the men weren't after them, but something inside. *Hel* was all Anya could think—*Viking Hel*—Rune's ancient enemy.

"Dammit, Homer, the thing went inside our place. The cabin's afire!" Zeke tried to kick the door of the cabin open but his bad leg wouldn't let him. "Help me, Homer!" he yelled and tried to shove the door in with the butt of his rifle.

"I don't want to get in there with that thing," Homer cried.

"For God's sake, Homer, our place . . . *cough* . . . is burning down! If what's inside . . . *cough* . . . doesn't kill you, then I just . . . *cough* . . . might," Zeke choked out through the smoke.

Stiff breezes picked up, enough to carry the thick smoke high in the air and cloud the twilight skies overhead.

Homer and Zeke at last managed to kick open the door, able to see and breathe better with the smoke scattered. The two aging miners looked at each other, the same shock on both their faces. The cabin appeared untouched except for the door they'd just crashed open! No more fire. No sign of anything coming in there.

"What do you think, Zeke?" Homer pulled off his beaver cap and scratched his head.

"Beats the hell out of me," Zeke said under his raw breath.

CHAPTER SEVEN

"The boy done saved us, Zeke. Sure as shootin', he did," Homer Jessup said straight out.

"Yeah, and it wasn't with any gun," Zeke said, his tone laced with grudging respect.

Despite the men being inside their cabin, a ways from her, Anya could hear them. She knew "the boy" they spoke of had to be Rune. That meant he was *alive,* at least when the men last saw him! Anya had lost any clear sense of time. The days and nights in the Arctic still looked the same soft twilight of the Extending Days of winter. She thought it was late in the same day she and Rune left Nome; the big race just over and Zellie killed only two days ago.

Xander wasn't back yet. What if he'd been killed same as Zellie!

Anya tried to stay calm and think. Xander took off after Rune. If Rune is all right, Xander will be all right, she told herself. She'd know if he were dead, wouldn't she? Anya hung her head in worry. There was no end in sight to this awful day.

She raised her head back up only to find two rifles targeted on her. They could be harpoons for all she cared. She didn't care about her own safety, only Xander's and Rune's. Let the shamans kill her. Let Grisha kill her. Let the Raven god kill her. Let these men kill her. *Let them try,* she angrily finished her anxious thought, at once ripping her knife out of her pocket and going for the guns aimed at her.

"Hold on, young lady," Zeke said, then lowered his rifle to keep it out of her reach. He didn't try to restrain the upset girl. "We mean you no harm. No need to use that knife of yours on us. No need, young lady."

Anya kept her knife raised, eyeing both of the men. She didn't trust anybody anymore. These men could be Mooglo for all she knew. Grisha had traded her to the ugly Yukaghir in Anadyr. Mooglo could have taken the white men's shape now to fool her. His evil shadow followed across the Great Sea to the Alaskan frontier, bringing the monstrous whip to all their backs. He'd joined the Raven god to harm them; she was sure of it.

Homer let his rifle drop to the ground. He said nothing, and kept still and quiet as a church mouse.

The dogs began to bark again. Anya's attention shifted from the men to them. *Something, someone was coming!* The dogs leapt against their harnesses in the direction of the sound. Anya faced the same direction as the dogs, her knife clasped firm. She'd no idea what might come. No wind whooshed by to give away its secrets.

A small band of Inuit Eskimo hunters and their dogs appeared over the rise in fanned formation. They soon came into focus. Two of the sleds held dead caribou in their baskets, the third: *Rune!* His lifeless body was covered in a fur sleeping robe.

Anya held her dogs and held her breath. Overcome with new fears, she was all out of prayers. All she had left was hope—hope that Rune only slept and had not been killed—hope that Xander didn't lie dead next to him. Xander had run off after Rune. This fact gnawed at her.

The third sled that carried Rune approached. The drumbeat of death pounded Anya to a standstill. Her own will and rational thought deserted her. She let the dogs lurch the sled forward to reach Rune, mindless of how easily the sled's ties might entangle with the Inuit's. She'd been standing on the sled's runners and managed to keep her footing and at the same time hold onto the handlebar with both hands; her knife somehow back in her pocket.

Magic and Mushroom reached the Inuit team first, sniffing at Rune's blankets, then alternately barked. Flowers and Frost shoved into them. Their excited movements jerked the ties of the rest of the sled's team, with Little Wolf, Midday, and Midnight all bumping this way and that. The ties became a jumble, something that never happened with Chukchi dogs. Forced to come to her senses and fix the problem, Anya stepped off the runners and caught her dogs, then tried to prevent any more trouble with the Inuit team.

The larger-pawed, heavier Inuit dogs—mostly white with dense, even fur, triangular ears, and short, bushy tails curled over their backs—barked against the smaller Siberian dogs. Bred for work and in keeping with centuries of life in the Arctic, their Inuit prey drive stayed with them every step of the way. Now was no exception. A few tried to nip at the Siberians, their teeth bared. Their dog driver shouted and cracked a long whip overhead, immediately stopping his dogs' assault.

Anya jumped at the sight and the unmistakable, sharp sound of the Inuit's whip.

So did Rune. He climbed out of the Inuit *qamutik,* sword swinging high.

If Anya hadn't been so upset that he might be dead, she would have laughed at his jerky, scattered movements, the way he wielded the blade over his head and battled the frozen air like a shaman beating a slippery drum, unable to break out of his drugged trance.

The dogs stopped barking, Chukchi and Inuit, obviously surprised and curious at Rune's actions.

Anya didn't move. She waited for Xander to jump out of the sled's basket behind Rune.

"By God, boy, you're alive after all," Zeke greeted Rune.

The miner took the words right out of Anya's thoughts.

"I reckoned for sure that thing gotcha and I'm damn glad it didn't." Zeke shook his head in astonishment.

"What thing?" Anya cringed at the miner's words, yet stayed focused on the *qamutik's* basket. Aware Rune had climbed out of the sled, she still waited for Xander. She willed him to show himself.

Rune stumbled past the dogs gathered round, jumbled ties and all, and finally reached Anya. He let the blade drop to the ground.

"You all right?" he asked in a whisper.

She didn't look at Rune but nodded her head in a slow yes.

Right away Rune caught the problem. He didn't see Xander among the dogs around him.

"What happened to Xander?" Rune wasn't sure if he wanted to know. The black and white husky meant a lot to him.

Anya looked at Rune and away from the sled, her soft features squeezed into a pained expression.

"I let him go. He wanted to go with you."

Rune took hold of Anya's frail shoulders, involuntarily digging his fingers deep into the fur layers of her parka to comfort her. He'd been thinking of Xander, but when he touched Anya, every part of him went to her. The moment he touched her, a jolt shot through him and sent shock waves up his arms and across his chest. His body warmed. His heart pumped, even hurt a little. His whole body tensed. He wasn't used to this kind of fierce upset, this kind of reaction in him to any girl. But he knew right away what it was, clear as day on this shadowy night.

No one had to tell him *he loved Anya.*

Hers was the face he wanted to see most; more than his family, more than the dogs he'd come to care for, and more than the draw of the adventuresome arctic oceans he'd traveled all his life. Three times now he'd all but died, then came back to life—*to Anya.* What if she hadn't been there, waiting? He didn't want to be anywhere else but with her. He ached to crush her against him now and kiss away her pain. His youthful passions raced all in a split second, catching him up in the impossible, fevered moment; in the time it takes for a heart to beat, giving life or taking it away.

It was the hardest thing he'd ever had to do, letting Anya go at this moment. But he did, and backed away from her as if burned. He never thought he could love anyone! Love was something for others, not him. He didn't think he was capable of it, or even wanted it. He didn't travel the oceans looking for love, but he'd found it in this slip of a stowaway girl. Now he had another secret to keep, afraid of what she might do if he told her he loved her, afraid she wouldn't feel the same.

He backed farther away from her, not ready to answer the questions he saw coming. What if he made a mistake in trying to answer them? He couldn't show his feelings to her. Any mistake now could be his last, or hers. Nothing must get in the way of his protecting her and the dogs; not even love . . . especially love. He had to keep his full concentration on the fight ahead. Anything less could kill. The risk to them all wasn't worth it. He had to keep his head in the fight and his heart frozen as the ice under his feet. He didn't have a choice.

When he spotted his blade on the nearby ground, he snatched it up and forced his thoughts away from Anya. To get the sword quickly out of sight, he ran it inside one of his mukluks. The metal still singed. It made him remember what happened, every detail.

The fire had been sudden, exploding up from the iced-over lake in a rage of flame and shadow, and had swiftly surrounded the two men Rune had gone to find. They weren't dead yet. Then the fire took on human shape. Rune could have sworn the burning mangle was *Frank Lundgren,* come back to life. It couldn't be, but there he was, trying to kill the two men, whipping at them, sparks flying everywhere.

Rune had just come over the rise and had tracked the men there. That's when the molten figure saw Rune, and came at him. Rune held his sword ready, both hands gripping its handle. When Frank Lundgren raised his whip in the air and then cracked it sparking and spitting at Rune, Rune's Viking sword first sliced the whip in half, then Frank Lundgren's ghostly shape. Embers spat at Rune after that, embers pathetically trying to stay aflame on the snowy ground.

Zeke Raney and Homer Jessup thought on what had just happened. They still couldn't believe what they'd witnessed!

The miners had lived on the Alaskan frontier a long time and never seen the like. It was as if the fires of hell had come after them. Neither man was particularly religious. They couldn't turn to God for help exactly, but both thought without even saying so that the boy had been sent from Above to save them. The moment they saw the fire had died and the boy seemed all right, Zeke and Homer climbed back up the snowy embankment toward the scene. Still clutching their rifles, they hadn't even had a chance to get a shot off at the thing.

"You all right, kid?" Zeke had called out as soon as he was within hearing range.

Rune noticed the men then, glad to see they were not dead but very much alive. Something still wasn't right, though. The embers at Rune's feet hadn't died out. *Demon sparks,* he thought.

"Don't come any closer," Rune had cautioned the miners.

"What—" Zeke didn't have time to say anything else. Fire shot up out of nowhere and lashed at the boy, then took off in the direction of their place.

"Get . . . out of . . . here," Rune managed to choke out, his chest suffocated in smoke.

"But—" Homer spoke up this time.

"*Go*. I'm good," Rune said in a better voice, when he wasn't better at all. Forcing himself to stay alert until the men got out of there, he lost consciousness the moment he saw they had gone.

The flock of ravens swooped low over the gathered wolves. They circled the wolves in the same manner the wolves protectively circled the dog, trying to keep it alive. When the wolves tightened around the dog, the ravens did the same. They sparked and clawed in the air, ready to kill. The skies turned to fire. The ravens hit the wolves, burning and charring at the pack to get at the Chukchi dog.

Xander tried to break free of the circle of wolves but they wouldn't let him, or leave him to the enemy overhead. Their instincts told them to protect the dog. Their feral impulses told them *the wolf and the dog must battle as one*. Their ancestors howled in the heavens, calling louder as each one of their own fell. Burnt fur polluted the air. The wolves were dying, one by one. Those still alive pressed into and over Xander to protect him, obedient to the call of the wild.

Forced to the ground, Xander fought against the press of wolves left and struggled to fight with them. He wanted to rip apart the predators that brought fire. Suddenly it ended. Xander was free to get up and fight! When he did, he saw no fight. He saw no wolves.

The wolves were dead, all of them.

The enemy birds of fire had flown.

Surrounded by an eerie silence, Xander sniffed the charred ground where the wolves had died. Their ashes singed and clung inside his nose and mouth. He couldn't find the leader. He whimpered in worry, then stood straight and alert, and circled in the mangle of scorched remains, keeping his watch-blue eyes wide open for any sign of the enemy birds of fire.

Alone now, he would wait.

Alone now, he mourned the deaths of his companions, the wolves.

His canine instincts led him to this behavior and motivation, one with the ashes at his feet.

Anya bent down and began disentangling the jumble of leather ties that kept her dogs caught up with the Eskimo Inuit dogs. She'd rather do anything than feel the chill of Rune's sudden disinterest in her. He'd pulled away just when she wanted him *not* to. She didn't know what she wanted of him, really. She just didn't want him to pull away when he did.

Catching herself in such thoughts, she cursed the girl in her and wished she'd become the true shaman woman she needed to be to help her dogs and her People . . . and *Xander* most of all. No sooner had she thought of him than she heard him call across the tundra! Her senses keen, she stopped what she was doing and closed her eyes to better concentrate on the welcome sound carried by the Directions.

Rune was saying something to her.

She ignored him.

The Inuit hunters tried to get her attention.

She ignored them.

The dogs barked louder than ever.

She ignored them all and listened only for Xander's unmistakable howling on the winds. He was *alive*. Thank you, Morning Dawn, for saving him, Anya prayed in silent earnest.

Hearing Anya's prayers, the Gatekeepers had been watching the struggles below on Native Earth: the dangers put to Anya, to Rune, to the wolves, to Xander, and to all the dogs. They'd watched the two humans who tried to help. The immediate danger quieted, but the Gatekeepers kept their watch eyes open for more. But soon others, not of Native Earth, beckoned to them. The Gatekeepers at once turned their masterful heads in the direction of the otherworldly cries.

Anya opened her eyes and stared hard out over the snow-covered horizon. The low light didn't hamper her vision; she was used to the Arctic's ways. Her breath caught in her chest the moment she saw him. Time stood still. Xander didn't run toward her? It scared her but she at once understood what he felt, pulled between two worlds as he must be—between the world of men and the world of beasts.

Which did he want? She held her breath and waited to see. If he ran off again, would she go with him or stay? Anya swallowed hard. It wasn't what she wanted that made the difference but what she *must* do. Her grandmother had said it. The Gatekeepers had commanded her, along with their Chukchi gods. Anya was born to Native Earth to protect the dogs so some might survive the relentless ice storm.

No, she could not chase after Xander, no matter how much it would hurt to let him go.

Her heart went numb, sensing his indecision. Even his low whimpers, she heard. His powerful body shone against the night sky as if captured there for all time. Such was the might and courage of the Chukchi dog, shining through in her beloved Xander now. She'd never been more proud or more afraid of which world he would choose. Just like him, she didn't like being alone.

Agonizing moments passed.

When he took off in a heartbeat, in the time it takes to begin life or end it, Anya froze—only to melt when Xander licked her cold hands with his warm muzzle. He'd come home. They were both home, together again. She dropped to her knees and circled his neck, and wrapped her arms in his thick fur, happy for the first time since they'd lost Zellie. The pain of Zellie's death remained and always would, but having Xander with her again was like having a part of Zellie, renewing both their spirits; hers and Xander's.

Relieved to see Xander back, Rune left Anya alone. Best anyway for both their sakes. He didn't trust himself yet around her. He didn't trust that he'd be able to let her go if he touched her again. His feelings were too new, too raw.

"Say, kid, I'm Zeke Raney and over there is Homer Jessup." Zeke waded through the dogs and reached Rune.

Rune had a smile for the miner. His kind face showed concern.

"Hey now," Zeke said to Flowers and Frost, trying to sidestep their ties.

Rune reached down and separated the ties, the two excited huskies licking his hands the whole time.

"They sure like you," Zeke joked.

Rune squatted down next to the huskies and gave each one a good hug, then stood back up.

"It's mutual," he said. "By the way, I'm Rune Johansson." Rune held out his hand for a shake, then took it back to pull off his fur mitt, before he offered it again.

Zeke pulled off his heavy glove and shook Rune's hand.

Just then one of the Inuit hunters shouted out something. It was the same hunter who'd helped Rune; who'd loaded his injured body onto his sled and brought him here. Rune gave the Eskimo a nod of thanks. He had no idea if any of the hunters had seen what happened—the dark magic.

"Anya," Rune said, compelled to turn to her for help.

Anya stood up and faced Rune.

Xander stayed at her side.

Rune sensed a change in the stalwart black and white husky. His watch-blue eyes held sadness and upset in them, yet he appeared, "more enduring . . . more ferocious . . . and more intelligent . . ." than before. Rune wished he knew what Xander had just been through. He had his suspicions, relieved all over again to see him come back safe.

"Anya, can you find out if the hunters saw anything? Why they brought me here?" Rune asked his questions of her, hoping she was all right to go and talk to the hunters. A smart girl, she likely knew some of the Eskimo tongue. He wouldn't ask her to talk to the Inuits unless this was important. It was life or death. Rune and Anya had to know every move their enemies made to better fight them. The hunters could give them life-saving information.

Anya nodded yes to Rune, then motioned for Xander to go with her.

Rune watched the two make their way past dogs and sleds, over to the hunter in question, worried about Anya and Xander's well-being and worried about what the Inuit might have to say.

"Rune," Zeke suddenly spoke up. "That's a fine name, like the Vikings."

Rune looked away from Anya and fixed on Zeke Raney. Odd the miner would know anything about Vikings. Miners on Alaska's frontier didn't know about anything but digging for gold, downing shots of whiskey, making Arbuckles coffee, trying to stay alive in the arctic north, and wanting to bet on sled dogs. They didn't know anything about the sea or Viking legend. At least that's what Rune had thought.

"How do you know about Vikings?" Rune accused more than asked.

Zeke chuckled.

Rune waited for his answer. He didn't smile at Zeke Raney.

"Son, some of us from the lower states know a thing or two besides mining and such," Zeke said, still chuckling. He looked over at Homer for a moment, and saw that his friend still walked around amid all the dead ravens. He didn't feel like laughing any longer. Yeah, Zeke wondered, too, what might have happened here. Exhaling sharply, he tried to keep his tone light. He felt sorry for the kid and didn't want to add to his current troubles. The kid had been through enough for one night. Hell, for that matter so had he.

"How do you know about Vikings?" Rune's tone raised, his suspicions over these men raised at the same time. Maybe they were a part of the trouble he and Anya and the dogs faced.

"Easy, son," Zeke said in a calm voice. The boy was on edge, for sure.

"Like I said, some of us in the lower states might have grown up on the frontier, but we had learning all the same. I'm not herding cattle now or even caribou, but going for the gold in these hills. That doesn't mean I've never had any schooling. Why, a friend of mine is General Palmer, himself, who platted out the city of Colorado Springs. And some of the ranchers in the same parts know about calculus and mathematics and read books in French after sundown when the work day is done.

"Folks have to fend for themselves, mostly. When they're hungry, they hunt. When they need shelter, they build it with their own hands. When they get sick, they either get better or die. That's life on the frontier in the lower states, and it isn't much different on your arctic frontier. Maybe there's not as much schooling here yet, but it'll come. Point is, Rune, I can read and I know about the Vikings. Your name tells the tale far as I'm concerned," Zeke finished, fresh out of any more explanation.

It was Rune's turn to exhale sharply. He tore off his other mitt and tossed them both away, then ran his hands through the frozen strands of his hair in exasperation. He wanted this awful day to end. He wanted to feel normal and trust people like he always had before. Zeke seemed trustworthy and honest enough.

Rune longed for somebody to lean on like a father. His own wasn't here. His own didn't trust him; that had been the problem all along.

Zeke watched the boy. The kid got to him. He wanted to help.

"Listen, son. I don't know what's going on here. It's beyond me. You and the girl are in trouble, I know that much. Strange things are happening, dangerous things. I'll help you if I can and so will Homer over there." Out of habit, Zeke scratched his graying beard, loosening the ice chips formed there, then flicked them away.

Rune couldn't tell Zeke what was going on, but he could use his help. He and Anya needed a place to stay through the arctic spring until the ice melted and he could get Fox Maule Ramsey to Siberia. For that he would need his father's help. In fact he was banking on the hope that his father would anchor outside Nome on his normal summer trade route, and would let Rune pay him the twenty-five thousand dollars he had from Ramsey and take the *Storm* to Anadyr.

His father might not trust him to captain a steamer, but he would understand the stiff payment to let him. His father could put a lot of trust in that amount of money. Rune intended to use one of Johansson and Son's ships. After all, he was the *Son*. He hoped that counted for something with his father and that his father would agree to Rune's proposal. Like Zeke Raney just said, "strange things are happening, dangerous things."

The Bering Sea crossing would be more dangerous than ever, given all that had happened. Rune knew what waited in the shadowy depths. He had to outsmart, outrun, and outdistance it, for the dogs on board to have any chance at staying alive. The sword at his side singed still. The single blade wouldn't be much help against the whole of the Bering Sea.

The gods of the Vikings might be at his back, but Rune knew

the winds of evil were set dead against him. In ancient times he might have made a trip to Uppsala, to make a sacrifice to the gods so his journey might be a safer one. But these were not the times of old. These times put the lives of all the dogs at risk. Rune had no intention of offering any of them up as a sacrifice. He'd offer himself first.

"Rune!" Anya roared in the Chukchi way, more as a man would than a woman. This was no time for whispers since Rune appeared to ignore her. Was he so disinterested in her he wouldn't even listen to her, to what she'd just found out from the Inuits? She had to remind herself this was all for the dogs; not for her and not for him. She and Rune were in this together, and she had to see it through *with* him. If that meant putting up with his lack of interest, then so be it!

She would never let him know her feelings for him went beyond being just friends. Maybe she really didn't find him handsome or tall or brave or affectionate with her dogs. Maybe she didn't really care he wasn't affectionate with her. She didn't need anybody anyway; only her dogs. Nana-tasha was gone. Vitya wasn't here. *So be it.*

"What, Anya? You don't have to shout." Rune finally looked at her and answered her. He made an attempt to smile but found he couldn't. Where a minute ago he hadn't been paying attention to her, he was now. He could kick himself for letting his mind wander.

Anya softened toward him a little when she saw his upset. She shouldn't forget they both were upset over things out of their control. Luckily she'd understood most of what the Inuit had said, relying on her own intellect and insight as a shaman. Growing up Chukchi, her village was far away from the village of the Eskimo, their language and culture, different.

"The hunter told me he was following caribou when he saw fire in the sky," she said to Rune. "The fire did not belong. It was not a good sign. The fire broke into pieces like shooting stars. The fires hit the ground and still burned. It was far off and chased the caribou away. He heard the howls of the wolf and then smelled burning animal flesh. He went to see. He and the others followed the signs and found you, dead, they thought.

"A black smoke covered you, then blew away when they got near you. It was not a good sign. They meant to leave you and return to their village. The night was too dark and the signs too dangerous. Then you moved. You were not dead. They wanted to leave you but instead brought you here, following the tracks," Anya finished.

She understood the hunters' fears. They didn't have to tell her how afraid they were of Rune and what they'd just witnessed. Being shaman, she'd wanted to ease their fears but she couldn't. No healing potion or spiritual trance would give them any comfort here.

Rune watched the Eskimos turn their sleds away and crack a guiding whip in the air over their dogs. He didn't have the words to thank them. They were soon out of sight but never out of mind. He wouldn't forget their kindness. They had to be as scared by all this as he was, and Anya, and the dogs . . . and Zeke Raney and Homer Jessup.

"Say, kids," Zeke broke the uncomfortable silence. "Suppose either one of you want to come on inside our place and warm up. Is anybody hungry?" The corners of his mouth crinkled into a smile, hard to spot under his icy beard. "Homer's already inside stirring up some grub."

Grub? Anya hadn't heard that word before. She warmed to the miner; his tone comforted as a father's might. Then again, what did she know of fathers? Grisha had never been a comfort to her. She pushed her Chukchi stepfather from her thoughts; Rune, too; at least her true feelings for him. She felt Xander's touch at her side. His presence brought all the comfort she needed for the moment. Was she even hungry? The dogs . . . they *had* to be.

"Do you have something for the dogs? I can go hunting or ice fishing if you don't," she quickly proposed.

"No need for you to go hunting," Zeke reassured, admiring the girl's wherewithal. "I'll scare something up for your dogs . . . Anya, is it?"

For the first time all day, she smiled.

"Yes, Anya."

"How do, young lady. Name's Zeke Raney," he offered, then touched his fur cap in introduction.

Her smile brightened.

"I'll help you, Zeke," Rune interrupted. He wanted something to do besides stare at Anya's enticing smile. He needed to keep his mind on the events of the day, not on his newfound feelings for Anya. The cabin and its surroundings had to be secured, at least Rune meant to try. A dog yard should be built. He'd seen some and would figure it out. If he messed up, Anya would help him get it right. None of this was over yet. They had to work together. He'd have to keep his feelings for her in check. He had no choice. Safety, hers and the dogs', came first.

The golem eased its breathing, content now to wait until summer when his spiritual forces would strengthen. Still trapped behind steel bars he wasn't free to do the killing himself. He didn't have to, since he'd gotten the spirits of the Raven god and *Hel* to strike against the dogs for him. Ah, but soon he could, when free. He already smelled the blood he would spill, and it revived his dark spirits. The wolves had been hit. The boy wasn't dead yet, but the golem meant to get him and the girl before this was all over. The golem reared its head in a vicious roar for all to hear, shaking the bars holding him in and the concrete beneath his heavy-booted feet.

"I bring the ice storm. Your life means nothing to me, nothing!"

The fit passed, the golem sank back against his cell wall. He lit a smoke, the tobacco almost as soothing as the knowledge he could kill so many, so fast, and soon. His power would know no bounds. Blowing circles of smoke into the dank air, the golem shot a finger through each one, imagining each killing strike. Once free and once in power, all would bend to him, or die. The plans were set in his mind. The last ones who would stand in rebellion against him were the Chukchi in far, northeast Siberia. It would be the last place in Russia to conquer and bring to its knees. The golem was good at that, spreading lies, setting people against one another, dividing, conquering, and then killing.

No kulaks can live!

This roar he kept to himself. The Chukchi would try to run from him. Their dogs made them kulaks, part of the elite, part of the envied. No one could have wealth and means in the Russia of the golem, *no one*. No Chukchi dog breeders will live. No Chukchi dog will live. The golem would not allow any people in Russia to keep separate and live away from collective farms. Individual thinking must die. No one group could be more important than the other and ruin the golem's plans for power in Russia. Until he got out of prison, the golem could not do the work of death himself. Dark spirits would keep after his enemies. He could rely on them. His power held dominion in the spirit world.

The girl, Anya—he knew of her *Spirit* and meant to crush it.

The boy, Rune—he will hang him upside down, dead in Uppsala, his life blood dripping out drop by painful drop.

The golem thought on.

One of the nine dogs, their leader, was dead. Eight are left. More will try to escape across the sea. They will not make it.

They will not create new life. The Chukchi are to be punished, now and forever, for daring his power. He threw the butt of his lit smoke to the ground and crushed its life out, just like he would the Chukchi and their dogs—and any others that challenged him.

The moment smelled sweet.

He slid down on the iron bunk in his cell, savoring every kill.

CHAPTER EIGHT

"In the new summer growing" ~ *the end of May, 1909*

Anya waited for Rune to return from Nome. Soon it would be "in the first summer" and the ice holding them to the land would break and leave the seas open for travel. Rune had shared his plans with her, to take one of his father's ships to Anadyr, and take Fox Maule Ramsey to the Markova Fair to bring back sled teams of Chukchi dogs. Anya had listened, scared for all of them. She couldn't help but go back to the moment in time when her arm brushed Rune's at the fair, over a year ago—a lifetime ago. Was she even the same person?

No, she was not.

Her coastal village in Siberia had been replaced by a log cabin on the Alaska frontier where she had to spend most every waking moment avoiding Rune's glacial-blue, penetrating eyes. His handsome, masterful look always made her squirm under her already-uncomfortable new clothes. She wore thick-cloth, scratchy underclothes beneath her seal-fur kerker. She'd started to put together a new parka made of caribou fur but would always prefer her old one, and her old ways, she'd discovered.

Life with the companionable miners, Zeke and Homer, was far different from life in her home village. She would never get used to their fried meat and hen eggs and beans. Everything was cooked too much. Fresh blood provided the best nutrition, but white men didn't agree. She couldn't convince the miners to eat the raw flesh from the hunt or the most succulent parts of the animals killed—the parts with the most blood in them. Then too, the miners didn't try to hunt the seal, the walrus, or the whale. Inland, they chased rabbits and ptarmigans and caribou and bear but never the wolf. She forbade them to harm even one. Chukchi never harmed a wolf. The wolf and the dog battled as one.

When a pack would draw near the dogs and the cabin, Zeke and Homer would go for their guns and Anya would stop them. The miners would always shake their heads at her and always relent. When a wolverine would approach, Anya held a much different opinion. Wolverines stalked in shadows, waiting to strike. Anya had to strike first to protect her dogs. She used the gun of the white man to scare off the nasty predators. She didn't relish going after the wolverine with her crude knife and her bare hands. If she did, most of the blood spilled would be hers. She might be a shaman, but she bled like every other human being on Native Earth.

There it was. She was a shaman . . . a shaman without a village to counsel. The reality stirred her souls, all of them. How many of her souls already lay dead at her feet? She'd lost count. Bits of her, she felt, were scattered on two coasts, one Siberian and the other Alaskan. Then who knows how many were lost in-between, drowned in the Bering Sea. A memory rushed in. Her head hurt. Her grandmother foretold the troubles, found out through divination and prophecy. The way would be difficult and the burden great.

You are the first of your kind on Native Earth, Nana-tasha had said. Anya rubbed her temples, trying to chase away the pain. She'd had the same pain before. The "burden" placed upon her had revealed itself more than once, clear as her reflection in any summer pool. She must protect the dogs. She must help them live so the Chukchi might survive the next generations. All depended on the dogs. The race for their lives wasn't over; that reality the clearest of all.

What was not clear to Anya was why the demon spirit after them had left them alone through the Alaskan spring. It had drawn away from this place and had left her and Rune and the dogs in relative peace. The miners hadn't been attacked again, either. They came and went from the gold mines on the lower ridges and returned safely each day. Zeke and Homer even stopped taking their rifles with them, no longer worried about wolves or any unexpected trouble. Anya tried to warn them to be ready with their guns. The miners would just smile and leave without their weapons. Not Anya. She kept her knife tucked safely inside the pocket of her kerker, in easy reach. She couldn't afford the luxury of letting her guard down. Neither could the dogs.

The past months had been taken up with running, resting, hunting, and most of all, healing inside and out. Rune and Anya had set up a functional dog yard, which afforded each dog its own tie and its own space. No dog houses were necessary for the venerable Chukchi dogs; especially with the warm months ahead. When the cold months would come again, in the season with the first light frost, Anya would have something made for them. They'd be well settled when the season of new snow arrived, each dog with its own yaranga, its own Chukchi home. But where would they be settled? Where would their lives take them when the new snows came? Anya didn't know; the Directions had kept silent.

Though none of the Siberian huskies took their watch eyes off the frontier horizon for long, housed in the comforting silhouette of the miner's cabin, they ate and slept in relative quiet. Their once-torn paws had toughened to the rugged landscape, their bodies too. Given time to run, to play, to hunt and roam freely, they never veered too far from the cabin and always stayed together. None left the pack. To do so meant death. They hadn't forgotten what happened to their leader when she left them. Stubbornly aware of the consequences when separated from the pack, each husky ran as one. Their canine instincts kept them together, kept them safe.

Xander stopped having fits, his body seemingly back to its full strength. Little Wolf would follow Xander around when he could, like a little brother that wanted to be just like him. So would Flowers but in answer to very different instincts. Her heat was coming on. Magic and Midday, the other females, did not show the same signs. They would lick themselves as if in heat, but their bodies stayed cold. Anya had feared this. Since the day the Raven flew against the females, she'd feared this. Deep inside her, she had the same fear—that she could never have children. Quickly she pushed this from her mind.

She wasn't important. The dogs were; especially the females.

The demon spirit that sent the Raven to fly against them knows this. It is another way to kill the Chukchi dog, not letting them have puppies! Anya cried inside for Midday and Magic and hoped with everything in her, the damage wasn't permanent. Midday, all white and pure as snow, innocent of this evil befallen her, whimpered low, then sank to the ground and curled up in a protective circle. Magic's copper-red and white fur sparkled in the spring sun despite her sad demeanor. The dog knew something was wrong. Anya could see it in Magic's eyes, the way they shuttered closed, then reopened, showing her upset. Once bright blue, her eyes shone gray, like the changed day. Magic curled up next to Midday, the pair quiet and still.

Anya went over to both huskies and crouched down to them. She ran her hand along their backs in turn, cooing over them as if children, her own. In truth she felt like their mother, their protector. Worrying over their sudden depressed behavior, she wished she had the magic drumbeat of the shamans to make them better. She only had words that might comfort.

"In time you will heal," she kept her voice in the Chukchi female whisper. "Our gods watch over us. The Gatekeepers protect us. Do not fear, little ones. Do not fear," she soothed, as much for herself as the dispirited huskies. Both dogs kept their eyes closed and kept still, not showing any response to her. Anya swallowed back the lump in her throat, then closed her eyes and imagined her Spirit, wondering if anything had happened to her counterpart in the spirit world of the Chukchi. She hoped Spirit was all right. She'd pray to the Morning Dawn for them all to heal from the Raven's claw.

At least Flowers showed signs of heat. Everything depended on Flowers, Anya realized. Flowers' pups would be the firstborn on the Alaskan frontier. Gasp! New fears rushed in. Anya's eyes flew open. The newborn pups will be marked for death the instant they breathe life! The cruel reality made Anya sick to her stomach, feeling the press of so many bad spirits that waited in arctic shadows for first blood.

Fighting panic Anya struggled to remember her grandmother's prophecy and divination. Nana-tasha said she, Anya, must become master over the bad spirits. She is the firstborn of her kind to Native Earth. She must prevail over the darkness coming. She must protect the Chukchi dog so some might live.

"I will become master, Nana-tasha," Anya whispered in determination, at the same time finding her knife. The blade warmed in her cold fingers. "I will fight for you and for Zellie and for the People. The Gatekeepers watch over us. Once won, the ancestors will speak of this battle in drums and trance, telling the tale over tundra and ice to those born and yet to be born."

A sound behind her made Anya turn. She let go of her knife the moment she saw Xander approach Flowers. Right away she knew. Xander and Flowers would mate. Xander would be the father of the firstborn Chukchi pups in Alaska. Her fingers re-circled her pocketed knife. She must keep it close. Their enemies would not like this.

Rune stepped outside the Board of Trade Saloon and loosened the neck of his parka. The late spring day had turned warm. He'd just heard the news inside that the *Storm* weighed anchor two miles out, off Nome's shore. The saloon buzzed with the news since a second ship of Johansson and Son Shipping moored alongside, the *Nordic*. Rune couldn't decide if this was good news or bad. It struck him as odd his father would bring two ships north right now. Maybe his father expected good trade, too much for one ship to handle. The *Nordic* obviously had been delivered to the Seattle Harbor, finally completed. Rune knew of its plans. What he didn't know was why the new ship sailed with the *Storm*.

Nervous about seeing his father after so long, he dreaded the meeting. It wasn't so much seeing his father that disturbed him, but what he had to ask—to captain the *Storm* to Siberia to transport dogs back to Nome. A simple business arrangement, that's all this should be. At least that's what Rune told himself. *Far* wouldn't turn down a twenty-five-thousand dollar payday. Besides, his father owed him—owed him a father's trust. Swallowing any upset, Rune shifted his attention back to the business at hand.

He had just left Fox Maule Ramsey inside race headquarters. The Scot was still intent on putting together teams of Siberian huskies for the next All Alaska Sweepstakes, set for the following April. Fox would need time once he returned to Nome, to put together dog drivers and train the Siberian dogs to run against the formidable, mixed Alaska malamutes. He was anxious to leave Nome. So was Rune, except for one thing. He wasn't anxious to leave Anya, or to leave her alone in the Alaska wild. The dogs, either. It churned inside him, what to do. Not once did he worry over what waited for him in the Bering Sea; he was too worried over Anya and the dogs.

Unaccustomed to the growing arctic sunshine, Rune shielded his eyes from the light. He stepped off the wood-planked walkway onto the muddy street, his mukluks quickly covered over in the melting slush. Every step toward the beach took effort, slowed by the deep mud and the thought of seeing his father again. The lighter boat was in view. He made himself look through the still-uncomfortable light. The boat used to ferry passengers and supplies to shore was full, so full he couldn't make out faces. The only face he could see clearly was in his mind's eye: *Anya's*. He would soon hop aboard a boat just like the one ahead, and leave her; not sure if he could.

A crowd picked up behind Rune, pushing him and his doubts onward.

Nome came to life with winter over, no longer isolated from the rest of the world by weather and ice. Doors shut to the outdoors sat part open now, with storekeepers, town offices, and local residents shoveling and sweeping their walkways clean enough for people to pass. The change in temperature from well below zero to fifty above meant a change in the rhythm of the whole frontier city. The ice off Nome's shores disappeared, allowing waves of travel and trade to resume.

Until now, the only way to get to Nome from Seattle was by dogsled, which took months. Not so with steamers able to navigate the open waters. Mail arrived via sled weekly with supplies easier to come by. Dogs barked, inside and outside dogs; those native to the North and those brought in from the lower states. Many breeds had arrived in Nome after the initial gold find of '98, since every dog counted for gold dust in their pockets to miners. It was the only way to get around and to get anything done, having dogs to work alongside.

Life on the muddy thoroughfares began anew with phone

communication and electric lights more certain in the milder weather. Horses neighed. Freight wagons rolled in. Children played. In a few instances, car motors cranked up. Men shouted. Mining had opened up, getting into full gear. The Pioneer Mining Company, the Arctic Mining Company, and the Anvil Gold Mine had switched from winter drift mining to summer mining, including dredging, and from shovel to hydraulics that washed the sluices clean so the gold dust might settle below. Some doubted the gold was still there. Many prospectors had deserted Nome. Their pockets were empty and they believed the gold rush was over. For many, it was. Thousands had moved on, yet thousands had stayed.

The Pioneer Mining Company alone, in one week's diggings, collected two hundred and sixty thousand dollars in gold dust the season before; proving skeptics wrong. Jafet Lindeberg, one of the original Lucky Swedes who first discovered gold on Anvil Creek, owned the successful operation. Any connection to him seemed golden. That's the word spread around the frontier city. Time would tell.

Rune wondered about the truth of the rumors about Jafet Lindeberg since Zeke and Homer worked for the Pioneer Mining Company and hadn't struck it rich yet. Anya and the dogs stayed in the hills with the hardworking miners who seemed content to "keep at it for as long as it takes." Zeke had been insistent he and Homer would strike their own gold one day. So, too, Rune and Anya would "keep at it for as long as it takes," Rune gritted to himself; not to strike gold but to strike down their enemies. What choice did they have? None.

"Rune! Rune!"

He looked up. The shouts were for him this time. His father found him. His first thought was to get this over with, the sooner the better.

Lars Johansson grabbed his son in a strong embrace.

Taken aback, Rune didn't return the hug. He hadn't expected the contact, even after so long an absence. He didn't think his father cared about him in any way except having another hand on board ship. His father never felt for him what he did for Inga, his spoiled sister.

Lars let go of his son, only to turn and pull Inga in front of him. A broad smile still covered his face.

Rune wasn't happy seeing Inga in the flesh; then, when his mother stepped alongside, his mood worsened.

"I've brought the whole family this time, son," Lars announced; his smile disappeared. "Your sister and your *Mor* wanted to come with me to find you," he lied. "I'm going to build a home for us here in Nome."

"A home for *us*?" Rune repeated; the sarcasm in his voice unmistakable. "Who do you mean by us?" He looked straight at his father, just as tall, and just as direct. People milled past their party, but Rune paid little notice. He waited for his father's reply. His sister had stepped aside and stood next to his mother now; their expensive fur muffs held waist high. Rune glanced at them. Neither said a word, their tight faces unreadable.

"Son," Lars began. "We are all happy you are all right. We've agreed it's best for us, for our whole family, to make a life together in Nome for the present."

"For the present," Rune parroted, still sarcastic. There was no way he believed his sister and his mother wanted to come here and leave their easy lives back in Seattle; even the extravagant travel suits they wore, no doubt were "special-made" for the journey. His father must have put them up to this, bribing them with promises of a gold mine or something. Ha. As if they needed more money. He looked first at his sister, then his mother. Neither one smiled. Neither one cared. The truth of it was he didn't care either. Not anymore. There was a time, but not anymore. What was this about, *Far* bringing them from their soft life in Seattle to the hard frontier? He looked back at his father and wanted to get the truth.

"Really, Rune," Margret Johansson blurted, stepping in-between the two men, shaking her finger at her son. "That's no way to greet us, to thank us for coming and finding you. We were so worried about you and come to find out, you haven't worried over us. Shame, Rune Johansson, shame," his mother lectured. "Look what we've sacrificed for you, exposing ourselves to this horrible, wild place just to help you. Look at my new boots, just look at them!" she complained, and pulled one of her suede-covered feet out of the slushy mud as proof.

"That's enough, Margret," Lars clipped and put his hand in the crook of her arm, tugging her out from between him and his son.

"*Ja,* mama is right, Rune," Inga echoed her mother. "You are ungrateful. We should have stayed home instead of coming here. You don't even care," she whined.

Rune didn't miss his sister's sly smile. How could he when he'd seen it the whole of his life. Inga was always up to something, but never the truth.

"Rune, let's—"

"*Far,* we have to talk," Rune said.

"*Ja,* when we get to the Nugget Inn and get settled, we will talk, son." Lars put a hand now to both Margret and Inga, then started the two along Front Street and away from the busy beach.

"*Nej, Far.* We have to talk now." Rune kept his voice calm but his body in the way of any progress his family tried to make. Ir-ritated by the arrival of his mother and sister, he knew they didn't have any "business" being here. But his father; Rune meant to cut a "business deal" with him. Too many lives depended on it.

Lars eyed his son as if for the first time.

Rune held his ground and his tongue.

"Let me get my *fru* and *dotter* to their quarters first, Rune," Lars said, his voice empty of any emotion.

Like his father, Rune didn't show any emotion. His father had said, "My *fru* and *dotter*," my wife and daughter and not your mother and sister. In that moment Rune thought his father knew and maybe understood how he felt about them. He read the cloudy upset in his father's once-clear blue eyes.

"Meet me back here at the Board of Trade Saloon. I'll wait," Rune said to his father, without a word of hello or goodbye to his mother or Inga. Regret gnawed at him, but not enough to change how he felt or what he said right now. A lifetime of hurt cut deep, too deep to heal in a few minutes of talk.

Lars gave Rune a gruff nod, then guided Margret and Inga down the street, toward the Nugget Inn.

Rune's jaw tensed as he watched them disappear in the crowd. No one had a goodbye for him. Fine, he didn't expect any. He couldn't worry over his family now any more than he could worry over loving Anya and not being able to tell her. His focus had to stay on the fight at hand. To do otherwise would be deadly. That thought made him reach inside his parka, at his back, to feel the edge of the Viking sword he carried.

It wasn't there!

He kept the easy, short blade stowed on him inside his clothing and never left it behind. Had he lost it? Had he forgotten it? Had he left it inside the saloon? No, he wouldn't have been so careless. Maybe it was *stolen* from him inside the saloon. Charging for the front door of the Board of Trade he'd search every inch of the saloon and every person inside if he had to, to find the sword of war and wisdom—the secret of the runes.

The Directions swirled past, sending a shiver through Anya. She stood still on the otherwise calm, clear day to better understand the sign. Gasp! It was *Rune*. He was in trouble. Her connection to him had grown so strong spiritually in their time together, she could feel his upset on the telling winds. Still upset herself, over what had befallen her female dogs, she might have missed the sign if not for Xander's sudden bark.

Anya stared hard into his intelligent watch eyes; their blue depths were consoling yet fearful. He had lost Zellie. He sensed the danger Rune faced. Anya knew he did. She wanted to go after Rune, but she didn't want to leave any of the dogs. A queer sensation suddenly struck, as if she could hear the great Bering Sea beckon to her on the winds. A second shiver shot through her. Was this the sign she'd been waiting for, to come out of hiding and into the open?

Just then the carved ivory husky at her neck warmed then turned hot against her cold skin. *Gitengev*. She heard *gitengev*. Only Vitya called her that. Did he beckon, too? Another sign she couldn't ignore.

Then when Spirit's call reached her, Anya's whole body felt arched to the winds, her reaction immediate, as if she'd become her husky counterpart from the world beyond, racing back and forth along the unexplained rupture in the Great Crag brought upon Native Earth. Alarm sounded on every heartbeat. Anya tried to stay calm, breathing in and out of the telltale air. She stood tall against the horizon.

Signs born out of mist and magic had spoken. Long asleep voices wakened in the spirit world.

It is time.

The Gatekeepers turned their masterful heads back to the Alaska wild, to Nome, to Anya and Rune, and to the dogs.

It is time.

Anya felt their watch-blue eyes turn to her, and thought she understood the Gatekeepers.

It is time.

Generations of shamans whispered through the winds, hand in hand with the spirits of the Chukchi, summoning her to battle. Drums of the ancestors echoed overhead, sending new traces of red, green, blue, and yellow light to race across the skies in warning. Their message pulsed in Anya's veins. The run for their lives wasn't over.

The dogs must race again.

The Great Crag widens . . . its drop-off forever.

Shadows haunt and bring the ice.

It begins again.

Anya had been summoned before by the Gatekeepers, but this time she picked up new urgency and new warning in their instinctive call; at once she heard generations of Chukchi dogs, long dead, come alive in mournful howls. News of the Great Crag startled her, of the rupture within. The Great Crag was a place of sacrifice, known only to shamans. The Gatekeepers signaled the sheer danger ahead. Ancestral drums joined the call. Anya slapped her hands over her ringing ears, momentarily deafened and disoriented. In moments she reasoned out the grave message.

The dogs are meant to fall into the ceremonial Great Crag, all sacrificed, all disappeared into icy darkness for all time.

Anya tried to keep steady and tried to remember she was born to become shaman for this task.

Confused about which world she walked now, spirit or human, she felt a strong pull in both directions. In which shape, in which form, could she do the most good? Danger for the Chukchi dog and the People loomed in both worlds. But did she have the same powers in both worlds? Could she come and go at will? She didn't think so. Best now to keep her shaman feet firmly on Native Earth with her knife from the gods in hand and the dogs close. It was the more certain way to help Rune, she decided.

She had to get to him in time and wasn't able to think something bad might happen before she did; forgetting her promise to forget her feelings for him. His Viking gods will protect him, she prayed, then quickly gathered all eight dogs together and had them in harness and sled formation in no time. Zeke and Homer were off in the mines. She didn't know how to write them a note or she would have. They were built of true kindness and brave of heart, both of them. Maybe their paths would cross again. She would wish for it.

"Mush!" she called to her team, and charged their sled down the melting snowy trail toward Nome, toward Rune.

The dogs took off immediately, in little need of any command from their guardian. One of their own was in danger.

"Looking for this?" the ugly Yukaghir snarled at Rune, at the same time he tossed the blade on the table where he sat, for the Viking boy to see. The hard metal hit the wood with a zing then settled, frozen still as deep ice. "Sings like a bird. Like a raven, don't it?" Mooglo taunted. His yellow smile was viperous like his eyes.

Rune fixed on his sword, then on the stranger who'd stolen it. The stranger looked out of place. He wasn't Eskimo. He wasn't white. He wasn't any frontiersman or miner. He wasn't like any native Rune had seen in Alaska or Siberia. He didn't look like any kind of human—

The unreal moment hung in the air between the two.

Rune stood on full guard, eyeing the stranger for what he was: a ghoul sent by serpents from *Hel*. The layers between this world and the next peeled away to reveal the ugly truth. Isolated from all the others crowded into the busy saloon—others safe in a world away from his current situation—Rune stood alone with this demon. Without his Viking sword in hand, he had to wait for the demon to make the first move. It wasn't going to be a fair fight no matter what.

Mooglo scraped his chair out, then took his time getting up, in no apparent hurry and with no apparent concerns. The whip wrapped around his shoulder, coiled like a snake ready to strike; each hide knot painstakingly crafted to draw blood.

Rune watched and waited. He tried not to breathe, the stench of death in the air choked.

"Take the sword," Mooglo hissed. He held his arms up and splayed his fingers as if innocent of any wrongdoing; his yellow smile gone.

Rune wasn't buying it. The thief wouldn't just give the secret of the runes over to him without a fight.

"Why?" Rune heard himself ask the question before he could call it back, as if this were some kind of normal exchange.

Mooglo sneered and dropped his hands to his sides. He turned to leave, hesitated, and then turned back to Rune.

"Because I can steal it again," he rasped, "when I want and where I want."

The demon held all the power of the dark days ahead in that rasp, Rune knew. Feeling helpless to do anything but lean in and take up his sword, Rune kept his eyes on the evil before him. He tightened his fingers around the sure handle of the blade, then watched the dangerous figure disappear into the suddenly-come-alive saloon crowd.

The truth of the moment weighed heavy on Rune. That his sword could be so easily stolen unnerved him. What protection would he have against such an able thief? Why didn't he kill Rune when he could easily have done so? Rune tucked his sword inside his parka, out of sight of any possible onlookers, only now aware of others inside the saloon. He took a seat to wait for his father's promised arrival. The wait would be hard. No matter how much time Rune had to think on it, he might have escaped death, but he'd just been outsmarted by the enemy. It could all end any time for Anya and her dogs with such a formidable enemy; the passage back and forth across the Bering Sea made all the more treacherous by this unexpected encounter.

"Rune," Lars Johansson broke into his son's heavy concentration.

"Far." Rune meant to get up but his body wouldn't obey, weighted down by worry.

Lars took a seat at the table across from Rune, reminded right away of his son's Viking heritage, blond good looks, weathered strength and all. He'd missed their days together at sea. He didn't realize just how much until now. His son looked all right, but Lars could tell he was not. Something ate away at him. Rune looked older than his seventeen years. The longer he stared at his son's unreadable expression, the more he worried for him.

Did Rune have the same nightmares he did, warning against the sea serpent of old? Did dark elves haunt Rune the same as they did him, warning what will happen if Rune takes to the sea again? Lars couldn't and wouldn't speak of this to Rune. It was only nightmares and dark elves that haunted and taunted; nothing more. It wasn't real . . . yet Lars worried for his son. Coming to Nome and bringing the family was the right thing to do at this time, and the only idea Lars could come up with to keep his son off treacherous waters.

"How are you, son?"

Rune breathed mechanically, his expression unchanged. It took effort to focus on his father and not on the ugliness he'd just experienced.

"Good," he said.

"Good." Lars affirmed with a nod.

Silence fell between the two.

Rune didn't know where to start. He had to get his father to agree to let him captain the *Storm* across the Bering Sea to Anadyr. *He* had to captain and not his father. The task was Rune's, not his father's. Rune was not about to challenge the Viking gods at present, with so many lives at stake—Anya's most of all.

"What happened to the little Siberian girl?"

Thrown by the question, Rune straightened in his chair, buying time.

"Did Boris Ivanov get to race his dogs?" Lars smiled at his own mention of the Russian fur trader, remembering how bumbling he was around the adept Siberian huskies; the dogs more skilled and able than the man who traded for them. "There were nine Chukchi dogs as I recall."

"Eight . . . eight now," Rune spoke low.

"I'm sorry, son. What happened?"

Rune's shoulders slumped. His energy for this conversation drained him, but he had to have it. The choice wasn't his.

"Boris Ivanov had his race. The leader dog died because of it. So did Boris . . . but not Anya and not the rest of the dogs . . . not yet anyway," Rune said. He had more to say but he couldn't find the right words to explain any of this to his father. He couldn't tell his father much other than the basics he just had. The secret of the runes must stay secret for the time being; especially from his father.

CHAPTER NINE

Nome was in view. Anya longed to be coming up on her coastal village in Siberia instead of this frontier city in the Alaska District. She longed for the time when Zellie and Xander ran as pups at her feet, when their lives were filled with promise, where the width of tundra and ice beckoned them to run free on arctic winds. Instead, Zellie was dead and Xander's life was on the line, along with the rest of the Chukchi dogs. Whatever fate they met would be Anya's. She meant to cross into the hereafter guiding their sled. Zellie would be waiting.

"Ainngai!" a man called out to Anya.

He was Eskimo, Inuit.

"Easy." She signaled her dogs to slow, then stop. "Whoa." The dogs didn't stir at the man's hurried approach, not threatened. She relaxed a little, yet kept her eyes on him and her knife close.

"Ainngai," Chinook said again, winded.

Anya nodded her hello. Right away she thought of Grisha. This Eskimo looked close in age and appearance. She thought better of extending any friendly greeting beyond a nod.

"Kringmerk nakkertok," Chinook said, pointing right away to the Siberian husky team.

"English," Anya instructed. She knew the Eskimo said the "dogs were fast," suspicious of why. Maybe he'd seen them race. The ancestors gifted her with understanding English in this place and she would use it, even with other tribesmen. It felt safer.

"Yes, English," the aging Eskimo agreed, his broken smile warm. "I am Chinook."

"Anya," she answered warily, glad he could speak the white man's tongue.

"*Alianaiq.* Good to meet you," Chinook said, "your dogs, too."

"Did you see them race?"

Chinook nodded his head in a definite yes.

"My whole village saw them, and many other villages. They are fast, your little huskies," he underscored.

"Yes," she reluctantly agreed; her eye still on where this talk would go. It had been months since the race. She and the dogs had been isolated away in the mountains. She didn't think anybody but the Scot, Fox Maule Ramsey, had paid close attention to their finish. She didn't think their finish mattered to others. Evidently, it did.

Chinook eyed Anya carefully now, as if sensing the spirits around her—bad spirits.

"Where is the boy, Rune?" he suddenly asked.

Anya froze, alert to danger.

"How do you know him?" she accused with her question.

Chinook took a step back and put his hands up in submission.

"I run our village trade store in Nome. Rune came for meat and fish. I know him from then," Chinook explained. "I run our village dog races and Rune and I spoke of your dogs."

Anya let out the breath she'd been holding. Xander and the dogs seemed just fine with this Eskimo so close. Still, talk of Rune unnerved her.

"Have you seen him?" She blurted her question, anxious for any news of Rune.

Chinook looked into the girl's innocent face, apparently sensing the same danger around her he had around the boy, the same bad spirits. He shook his head in a no and said nothing.

Anya swallowed back her fears for Rune and put her feet on the sled runners and her hands on the handlebar, ready to call "mush."

"When time comes, can I have two of your pups?" Chinook hurried with his purpose. "I want to breed your dogs with mine. They will be faster than the wolf."

"No!" Anya's reaction was visceral, immediate. "The Chukchi dog will not breed away from our traditions. *Never!*" A thousand times over she'd told herself the Chukchi spirit will not be broken. Chukchi dogs will not be bred out, mixed with traditions to weaken the People. Their very survival was at stake. "Mush!" Anya abruptly shouted, putting one foot down on the slushy path to help pedal a quick start. She needed to find Rune. She didn't have another word or another look for the Eskimo and realized he was a threat after all.

"Your mother and your sister send their love—"

"*Nej.* No, they don't," Rune challenged his father. "Don't lie to me and I won't lie to you."

Lars leaned back in his chair, his tired eyes still on his son. Long moments passed.

"Why did you bring them? The truth," Rune demanded.

The saloon noise picked up around them with more miners, shipmates, businessmen, and travelers arriving in Nome, thirsty for gold or anything to do with it. The first and best stop always meant the Board of Trade Saloon. Others, like the Discovery and the Nugget, were just as busy in the inviting summertime weather. There wasn't a table empty nearby the Johanssons. Whiskey poured full. Faro cards shuffled. Lit cigars, pipes, and cigarettes sent smoke into the air over every customer. A piano played. The saloon doors swung in and out with the hum of traffic.

"You boys want to buy me a drink?" A fancy woman sidled up to their table, her voice low and her dress lower, showing more bosom than material. Pretty with her dark hair coiled in a soft topknot and a touch of rouge to her cheeks and lips, she had eyes for both Rune and Lars.

Lars put his hand up to her in a flat no.

"Maybe later," she purred, then turned to the next table.

"Why?" Rune stayed with his question, his jaw set.

Lars rubbed his face hard, then put his hands on the table and his eyes square on his son.

"Our family lives too far apart. I want us together under one roof, and right now that's in Nome. Our ships will sail on without us this time, Rune. We will stay on land and make a home together, *all* of us."

"No!" Rune shot up from his chair. "I won't do that. I can't."

"Sit down, son," Lars asked more than ordered. "Please."

Rune lowered into his chair and blew out what breath he had in him. He recovered his composure.

"This talk is about the truth, *Far.* So here it is. I need to hire out the *Storm* from you and captain it across the Bering Sea to Anadyr to bring back more dogs. I have the money and the course mapped out. I need to leave as soon as the ice lets me." Rune cut himself off from telling his father more. He wasn't lying; he just couldn't tell the whole truth.

"No, Rune," Lars commanded. "No."

"I have the money. I'm in the trade business, a part of Johansson and Son, just like you. I know how to captain a ship, just like you. You need to trust me to do this," Rune pressed, his voice a little shaky. His father's trust was all he'd ever wanted, that and his love.

"Rune, this talk is over." Lars pushed back from the table

and got up. "We are all staying on land: you, me, your mother, and your sister. We are going to live in Nome. That's final. No more talk of going to Anadyr again. Understood?"

Rune slumped in his chair and looked away from his father. He understood all right. His father didn't trust him, didn't love him, and only wanted to keep ordering him around like a deck-hand, a greenhorn at that. Rune straightened his spine. This wasn't about him, but Anya; about protecting her and her dogs and bringing more Siberian huskies to Nome, to race next year. The Viking sword tucked at his back singed against his skin in warning. Until now Rune didn't know exactly why it was so important for Fox Maule Ramsey to succeed in his efforts.

Now he did.

The message steeled down his spine. Rune clenched his fingers into tight fists, the message of war in one hand and wisdom in the other, clear. When he harnessed his thoughts enough to focus again on his father, his father had left. Just as well. Rune cleared away from the table and headed out the doors of the Board of Trade Saloon. He needed to get in the open where he could think, and figure a way out of this—out of Nome and across the Bering Sea to Anadyr.

Anya ran out of snow. Her feet sank into the mud and slush. The dogs would keep going no matter how hard but she called "Whoa." No point in taking any chance on injury. She'd had this sinking feeling before, unnerved by the memory. She could still see the whips disappear in the mud, down, down, down, then gone. Her arm tingled from the recall, the layers between worlds fragile with so many spirits, good and bad, working away at them. Eventually spirits do break through. She was proof enough . . . *and Rune.* He communicated with the dead, too.

Her heart leapt into her throat. She was afraid for Rune.

The dogs barked, restless.

Anya studied the mask of each one, beginning and ending with Xander. The intensity in his trusted blue eyes reached out. He didn't want to stop here. He whined in soft barks and pulled against his harness. Next to him, Midnight behaved the same. So did the rest. Was it fear or excitement stirring them? Anya raced up to Magic and Mushroom at the front of the sled, then took hold of the dogs' neckline, quickly guiding them off trail into still-deep snow where they could make some headway. Whatever fate lay ahead in Nome, Rune would be there. Anya hurried her team on, unwilling to think the obvious—whether Rune would be dead or alive when she did.

It was Lars who spotted her first; not believing the little Siberian girl bumped her way through the hurried crowd with her dogs held alongside. He hadn't made it back to the Nugget Inn after his tough conversation with Rune before he saw Anya. Not so easy to spot, it was lucky to see her in the throng. Once met, he remembered wishing his Inga was more like the brave girl coming his way. His insides grated at the comparison. His daughter lived a soft life, while this girl didn't know the meaning of softness. Fatherly instincts took over. He stepped off the wood plank walkway onto the street and toward the child.

"Anya!" Rune shouted over the crowd.

Alive, she could tell herself now. Rune is alive.

"What are you doing?" Rune scolded the moment he came up.

"What am I doing?" she repeated in disbelief. "I came to see if you were dead or alive. I guess you're alive." She didn't try to hide her upset. He wasn't even glad to see her.

Despite their ties to Anya, the dogs crowded around Rune.

She wanted to yank them away but didn't. She wanted to ignore how much she'd missed Rune's impossible blond good looks, his bluest of blue eyes, and his body surely made by the gods, but she couldn't.

"Children," Lars said the moment he reached them.

Anya and Rune had the same look of surprise on their faces. The same thought, too. They couldn't talk now. They needed to keep whatever was between them secret.

"I'm not a child anymore," Rune said, standing even with his father.

"No, I suppose not." Lars had to admit, seeing how much his son had changed in a year. But in his heart of hearts, he knew Rune would always be his little boy, the one he'd held in his arms as a babe, the one he loved and wanted to protect from the dark elves of his nightmares. He knew Rune had the skills to navigate a ship across the sea, but did he have the skills to fight what waited for him beneath the dark waters? No. No man did, Lars knew. The only way for Rune to stay safe was to stay on land with his family. It suddenly dawned on Lars how to keep Rune home.

"Anya," Lars greeted her personally. "It is nice to see you and your dogs. I do not think your time has been easy since we last met." He paused. "Is this language good, to speak English? Do you understand me?"

Anya glanced up at Lars Johansson when she wanted to confront Rune.

"Yes," she answered the kindly sea captain, her mind elsewhere.

"You are a smart girl. I remember," Lars said with a smile. "Do you and your dogs have a place to live?" He jumped in with the question before Rune could stop him. "I have come to Nome to make a home for Rune and you are welcome in it, to stay as long as you like. You will be safe with us." This last slipped out. Lars meant to stay away from such topics. He wasn't going to share his nightmares with the children.

"She's native, *Far.* She doesn't want to live with the white man," Rune blurted. The dogs bumped close and held him to the spot.

"Rune," Anya reflexively chastised, her tone disapproving of his lie. She didn't have anything against white men. She looked at Captain Johansson, her full attention on him. "That's kind of you but—"

"Good, then it's settled," Lars pronounced, then put one commanding hand to his son's shoulder and the other to Anya's. "The dogs can't go inside the Nugget Inn, but perhaps out back will provide sufficient space for them tonight. I will make sure for you, Anya. Tomorrow we will go to our new home. I have just the place in mind. You will see. Come now," he ordered, then abruptly turned. "Follow me."

Anya and Rune exchanged exasperated looks. They hadn't been able to talk privately yet and they had no idea how to get out of their current predicament. The dogs wanted to follow Lars. Rune and Anya sorted their ties, letting the dogs take the lead. Though the Nugget Inn wasn't far, the divide between Rune and his father widened. Anya could feel the winds whisper sadly by, unclear of their Direction.

"How ugly," Inga snapped out the moment her father introduced the girl standing by her brother in the hallway of the Nugget Inn.

"Inga!" Lars reprimanded. "Go back in your room and come out when you've found your manners."

"I will not," Inga whined, then eyed the new girl up and down. "Her clothes are ugly. She's not white like us."

Margret Johansson entered the hallway from her room, no doubt hearing the commotion. She went to her daughter's side rather than her husband's.

"Lars, why do you speak to our child, so?" Margret criticized.

"And just who is this with you, Rune?" She finally acknowledged her son and the girl next to him.

Rune glared at his mother, then back at his sister, more ashamed than angry.

Anya watched Rune's face change, seeing he didn't like his mother or his sister very much, once she realized who they were. Unwittingly she edged closer to Rune and away from his family.

"*Her name is Anya*, Margret. She's Rune's friend, and she's going to live with us in Nome," Lars stated, his tone agitated.

"No!" Inga shouted. "I didn't want to come here and I don't want this stranger living—"

"Enough, *dotter*," Lars warned, interrupting her protests. "How about you, Margret?" he dared his wife to go against him in this.

"Fine," his wife said, her jaw clenched in defeat.

Anya could tell it wasn't "fine" with the mother or the sister. Well it wasn't "fine" with her, either. The sooner she could get herself out of this predicament, the better. She edged closer to Rune, worried about how she could do it.

Inga ran inside her room and slammed the door behind her.

Margret had an insincere smile for Anya and frowned at Rune before she disappeared inside her own room.

"Anya, your room is here." Lars showed her to number eight, his voice strained with obvious embarrassment over Inga and Margret.

Anya held fast and didn't go inside.

"Rune, you go here," Lars said tiredly and took hold of his son's elbow to guide the way.

Shaking off his father's hold, Rune stared blankly at his assigned room number. The shiny brass "9" had been up-righted since his last visit. He never saw it overturn and fall since he'd slammed the door behind, when he'd left in such a hurry to find Anya and her dogs.

Nine times the runes turn.

Nine serpents you must slay.

The birthmark at his neck prickled in warning. Rune instantly remembered the words of the Viking gods to him. *Nine* dogs came from Siberia—*a magic number.* Rune felt the magical connection down to his toes, reflexively shifting his footing. Dark magic pursued. He must stay on his Viking guard.

"Thank you, Captain," Anya broke into the moment, "but I'm staying out back with my dogs. There's plenty of room and I'll sleep better with them."

"No, child, it's not a good idea." Lars took hold of her elbow and tried to guide her to number eight.

"No," Anya protested and held her ground.

Fifteen-year-old girls all sounded the same to Lars about now; all rebellious and wanting their way.

"I will be fine, Captain," Anya quietly intoned. "You will see." When she started down the hallway Rune stopped her this time.

"Will you, Anya, really . . . I mean, be fine?"

"Yes." On impulse, she wanted to touch his arm to help reassure him but dared not.

"Both of you listen to me." Lars shook his head at them and blocked the stairs. "You're not sleeping outside on a bed of straw, either one of you. You're staying inside, here with us."

"*Far,* you might as well give back the money for our rooms. Anya and I are staying with the dogs. We have our reasons. Besides, we've been taking care of ourselves for a long time. You don't need to worry," Rune said, not believing his own patience with his father in this.

Oh, but I do, son, Lars wanted to say but didn't. It was worry that brought him to Nome and worry that kept him from allowing Rune to go to sea. The dark elves made sure of that! Lars bit back his upset, believing their Viking heritage more a curse than any proud tradition. The lines between what was real and unreal blurred. The Midgard serpent might be real and might be waiting for his son. Then again, he might be wrong and just losing his hold on reality with so much time at sea, a lifetime in fact. He exhaled heavily and looked into the faces of the brave children in front of him, one his son and the other a girl he wished he could call daughter.

"For this one night, all right. Stay outside if you wish. Tomorrow we will make ready to live in our new home . . . *inside*," he underscored, and smiled uncomfortably. "We eat first." He suddenly thought about their empty stomachs. "You must be hungry."

"*Far*, it's all right. 'Fine,' remember," Rune said. It was his turn to smile uncomfortably. "Anya and I will feed the dogs like always and then we'll eat . . . with you if you want." Rune ignored Anya's jab at him.

"Good. Good." Lars nodded his approval. "We will eat together tonight, the whole family. It will be good."

No, it will not be, Rune and Anya thought at the same time, their worries over another encounter with "the whole family" matching each other. Anya's worries went a little beyond Rune's. She'd never eaten "out" with anybody but Zeke and Homer, the only other white men she knew. They'd eaten in their cabin together. That was fine except she never liked their food. She would have more on her plate tonight than worry over what was on it, and dreaded seeing Margret and Inga again. Her appetite for their company was gone before it started. They could never live among the Chukchi. They would never be accepted. The Chukchi did not invite the grudging or the greedy to share their fire, their food, or their home. *Fine!* Anya didn't want to share one with Margret or Inga, either. She never wanted to be anything like them.

★ ★ ★ ★ ★

Staked out back of the Nugget Inn, the dogs danced unevenly in place, restless over the unaccustomed sights and sounds of the frontier city. None circled down on the provided straw to sleep. When their guardians returned they would sleep. Not until. They were tied. They could see dogs run free nearby. On extra alert, Xander tried to shelter Flowers from any dogs coming close. His senses were tuned to hers. Generations of Chukchi breeding tied them to each other.

The hole in Xander's life had begun to fill. He understood the mournful call of the ancestors and knew he'd never return to his arctic home again but must live in this new place, without Zellie. Each day began and ended without her. He waited for her, looking out over the horizon at the appointed times, but she never came back. Instinct pounded the message home when his daily watch for her did not. Alone but not lonely anymore, he brushed closer to Flowers.

"Well son of a gun. What do we have here, boys?" A suspicious stranger came up on the dogs, rounding the alleyway corner behind the Nugget Inn. Four men followed; a mix of frontiersmen and miners; all already in their cups. One held up a bottle of whiskey, taking a swig nearby Xander.

Xander growled and bared his teeth.

"Aaaahhh . . ." the drunkard sneered back. "I got myself a whip, fella. Don't be a-growling at me." He downed another swig of whiskey. Cough. Cough.

Xander had already spotted the whip, ready for it. He growled again.

This time Midnight and Little Wolf growled. Frost and Mushroom barked. Magic and Midday stood their ground.

"You fellas are all tied and you're all gonna get what's coming to you if you don't shut your yaps," the same drunkard warned. "Pretty little things, ain't you?" he said, then laughed.

"Maybe you won't be so pretty when we're done with you." He went for his whip.

"Hold on there, Moody." The intervening fur trapper wasn't drunk like his friend. "No call for any of that. These dogs don't look big enough to put up a fight anyway. Let's go. Come on."

Moody took another slug of whiskey. He didn't look like he wanted to go anywhere.

The other three men moved in closer. They itched for a fight. Drinking and dog fighting were why they came to town most nights. Drunk or sober, didn't make any difference. A good fight did.

"They look like rats, not dogs," one of the men jeered.

"They're big enough for a fight," Moody spat. "Go on, get 'em," he ordered but stepped back himself to take another swig.

No one followed his order.

"Damn you," Moody cussed, and drew out his whip, then looked straight at Xander. The instant he tried to strike, Xander caught the whip in his mouth along with his attacker's hand.

"Get your pistol! Shoot this g-damn rat!"

Xander didn't let go, shaking his prey back and forth like he'd caught a wild salmon for dinner.

One of the men drew a gun.

Anya had her knife at the man's throat before he could use the gun, surprise and sobriety on her side.

Sword clenched in one hand, Rune pulled Xander away with the other and faced the man who tried to whip him.

"You kids got no business letting this killer dog in town," Moody warned, and stared hard at the blade pointed at him. His hand bled and his whip had torn in two. "That damn rat dog could have done me in. I'll get the law on you."

"Go ahead," Rune said, not letting his guard down.

Anya felt the man swallow against her knife, ready to stick it in him if he tried anything with his gun. When he dropped his pistol, she took down her knife. Surprise was still on her side, she knew. He was bigger and stronger than she was . . . just not as willing to act. And, he was drunk. The moment she could, she went over to Xander and ran her hand along his back.

"Clear out of here," Rune told them all. "Don't come back and don't come near these dogs again."

Moody lingered while the rest backed away. They stumbled down the alleyway and were soon out of sight.

"You think this is over, kid. It ain't. You'll see, you and your dogs," Moody threatened, wiping his bloody hand against his buckskin shirt. He threw his empty whiskey bottle against the closest wall, laughing when it smashed into jagged pieces.

The dogs scrambled away from the icy maelstrom.

"Clear out," Rune ordered again.

This time Moody did. Bloody bits of glass trailed behind him.

Anya thought of the ugly Yukaghir in Anadyr and the bloody trail he left on her hand, and shivered; this mean drunk reminding her of Mooglo. This whole incident gave her the shivers. New dangers awaited them in Nome, mortal dangers. She hadn't thought about that until now, not in so many words, that anything would come after them but their enemies from the spirit world.

"Rune, I'm not going to eat. I'm keeping watch tonight," she said, her eyes on the trail of broken glass.

"I'll stay with you." He kept his eyes on Anya.

One by one the dogs settled into sleepy circles on the straw. Their guardians had returned. Their guardians would keep watch. The last to close his eyes, Xander hunkered down but would not sleep. His watch was not over. He'd tasted the blood of the enemy. He would remember the scent and not forget the whip. Out of habit he opened his eyes and sat up, scanning his surroundings, still waiting for Zellie to return. When she did not, he settled back down in a low whine.

Anya watched him, her heart as broken as his. She wondered if either would ever mend. Right now she didn't think so.

Fox Maule Ramsey bade goodbye to his two uncles and made ready to meet the lad, Rune Johansson, at the lighter boat dock. He'd packed what gear he thought he'd need, leaving the rest up to the lad. Not once did he have second thoughts about Rune's skills in captaining a steamer across the Bering Sea. Admittedly he worried the lad might not get a steamer. He never once worried about the money he'd given the lad. Fox knew of Johansson and Son Shipping but still doubted Rune would get his father to agree. In truth Fox had thought to approach Lars Johansson if he had to, not trying to convince him about his son, but to take him to Anadyr, himself. Not behind the lad's back.

A week ago when Fox met up with Rune at the Board of Trade Saloon, Rune hadn't talked to his father yet, much less secured their needed steamer. Fox had given Rune a hard time about this, jittery to leave Nome before bad weather returned. He didn't relish any journey on rough seas. Summer was bad enough, but winter would make travel impossible. Then again he had a good feeling about the lad or else he wouldn't have trusted him with so much money. Fox wanted the "prize money" from the next All Alaska Sweepstakes, not because of needing gold in his pocket, but because he needed to race Siberian husky teams for a "win."

Three teams would get him a win. He planned to bring back no less than sixty Chukchi dogs from the Markova Fair. Out of that number he would get them trained up over the winter ready to race the next year. Fox had in mind one other person who would dog drive besides him: John Johnson, a local musher. Fox needed to find one more. Expert mushers were hard to come by. Scotty Allen was the best right now on the trail. Fox wanted to best him. Three teams of fast Siberian huskies should do just that.

Fox had come to the District of Alaska to help mine the family gold. He never thought to become a dog driver and catch the fever for racing. When he saw the Siberian team cross the finish, he had to find out about the unlikely huskies. Like most before the race, he thought size mattered and that larger, more-muscled husky mixes would outrun them. Rune's team might not have won, but their brave finish sold Fox on them, one hundred percent.

Fox closed the door of his quarters at Ramsey Mining and took the trail down into Nome. The edge of the Bering Sea wasn't far. Whatever Rune had said to his father in the ensuing week must have worked or Fox wouldn't have gotten the message to set sail. Rune obviously had an agreement with Johansson and Son Shipping to captain one of their steamers, and Fox had an agreement with Rune and Anya, to help him bring back the remarkable Chukchi sled dog.

Just in time, Fox thought. Like most on the Alaska frontier, he never trusted the weather to hold steady no matter the promised season. It could change in a heartbeat, in the time it takes to give life or take it away.

CHAPTER TEN

"Take the money." Rune slid the promised twenty-five thousand dollars along the oak roll-top to his father. "It's short one hundred dollars."

Lars looked at his son and not the money shoved his way. This had gone too far. He and Rune had bucked horns ever since he'd brought the family to Nome a week ago. A lifetime ago, it felt like. They lived in a fine house now recently vacated by Jafet Lindeberg, the Pioneer Mining Company magnate. Good fortune, indeed, to find such a house on such short notice, Lars had thought. Fortunes can change.

The house was fine enough for Nome's standards but evidently not enough for Margret and Inga's. They'd done nothing but complain since day one; Rune, too, but not about the house. The only one who kept silent was Anya. She never left her dogs except to come inside for a bite of food. Lars meant to do something about that; the girl couldn't sleep outside. It wasn't safe. There's that word again: safe.

What he'd agreed to let his son do wasn't safe. He didn't have a choice. Rune had him against the timbers. If Lars didn't agree to let him leave for Anadyr, alone, Rune was finished with him and the family. "This is something I have to do. I don't have a choice," Rune had said. "It's not about me. If I don't go, it's over."

His son's words had hit hard. Lars knew exactly what Rune meant by, "It's over." Rune wasn't being childish, but honest.

When Lars pressed Rune for more, his son looked him straight in the eye yet kept silent. The time for talk was over. Reluctant to agree to Rune's travel and trade for dogs across the Bering Sea, and still afraid Rune would leave and never come back, Lars had been more afraid of his family breaking in two. Already fractured, Rune's leaving would be his own finish, Lars realized. He'd never in all his years at sea been so pulled apart. He loved his son. He didn't want to lose him, or his love. In the end Lars didn't think he could risk this most of all.

"I have to get going. Take the money, *Far,*" Rune said again, still standing next to his father's desk.

"No," Lars refused and slid the money back to Rune. "You will need it to outfit the *Nordic.*"

"What, you don't trust me with the *Storm*?"

"This isn't about trust, Rune. It's about threats, yours," Lars leveled. "I don't like being forced into anything."

"Oh come on, *Far.*" Rune threw up his hands. "When have you ever cared what I want? You've forced me into things my whole life. I'm a good student, that's all."

"Enough!" Lars roared, then got up from his leather chair. He would lose his son now anyway, putting him at the mercy of the serpents in his nightmares. Here he wanted to be the best father he could to his son; turned out, he was the worst. "I will ride the *Storm* to Uppsala," he muttered under his breath.

Rune didn't catch what his father said. He waited a few moments, then collected the money off the table, and slipped it inside his sea jacket. The *Nordic* was a larger ship and would make the journey easier with so many dogs on board. He'd already taken the lighter boat to inspect both ships, curious to see the newest in the Johansson fleet. The *Nordic* shouldn't be a problem for him; the same workings on both.

His father was upset, angry at him. Rune didn't like having to do this to his father and have this disagreement, but he had to get a ship, get Fox Maule Ramsey, and get out of there. The weather wouldn't last. He started for the door, then turned back around to his father.

"Anya and her dogs . . . will you watch over them and keep them safe while I'm gone? I know it's a lot to ask. I need your help, *Far.*"

"*Ja, Run`a,*" his father answered, his mind elsewhere, back in times of old. He didn't hear the catch in his son's voice, the boy in Rune needing his father.

"Good then. I'll be going then," he said to his father's back.

Lars stood at the window and looked outside. He couldn't watch his son leave.

"I'll be back before the next snows," Rune told Anya. "I don't plan on running late and I don't plan on running into any problems."

Anya instinctively edged closer to Xander; the black and white husky already stood near. The rest of the dogs collected behind them, sensing the same danger.

"I don't plan on problems, either," Anya said, whispering in the Chukchi way. Through the next seasons of summer-into-fall, she would do her best to keep the Morning Dawn and all the gods of her People as close to her as the dogs were now. She would rely on the Directions to keep the Gatekeepers near. They would not fail her. And so she must not fail them. She was shaman. She was Spirit. She was born for this task, ready to sacrifice her life for it.

"You should be safe here with my father."

"Yes," Anya whispered still.

Both knew their words were empty, given the fight they were in. The bad spirits that had broken into their world on Native Earth could easily break into any house; no matter how thick the walls or strong the arms protecting them; no matter which arctic frontier, either side of the Bering Sea. No place was safe. Demon spirits didn't fight fair. Anya and Rune would have to become ". . . quicker of movement . . . swifter of foot, craftier, deadlier, more lithe, more lean with ironlike muscle and sinew, more enduring, more cruel more ferocious, and more intelligent . . ." to survive this hostile environment. The enemy waited in the ice, widening its cracks and crevasses, waiting for them to fall in . . . just the way they got Zellie and Boris Ivanov.

Anya and Rune didn't talk about it. They didn't have to. Their best weapon against such an enemy was to listen to the spirits of their ancestors and obey the call. Both knew they couldn't do this alone. They needed each other as much as they needed the gods on their side. They didn't talk about that, either. They didn't have to.

"You might see Grisha, my stepfather, at the Markova Fair, Rune," Anya spoke just above a whisper. "Say the name to the dog traders and one will answer. That one will be Grisha. Tell him . . . tell him . . ." Her soft voice trailed. Old hurts surfaced. "Tell him nothing. I only want to know if you see him." She hated that she still cared for her Chukchi stepfather. He never cared about her like a father. She shouldn't care about him like a daughter. That she still did cut deep. Anya pulled Vitya's necklace out from beneath her clothing and grasped it tightly in her shaky fingers, unaware she'd done so.

Rune watched Anya's soft expression turn hard. He wished he could change it back, and he wished he didn't have to leave her. He knew now what it felt like to love someone.

"What's that?"

Anya frowned at Rune's question, puzzled over it. She grasped Vitya's necklace tighter.

"What's that in your hand?"

"Oh," she said, and realized her mistake. "It's just a gift from a friend." Until this moment, she'd kept the husky carving hidden from Rune. It shouldn't make any difference if he saw it or not . . . but it did. She felt funny, exposed even. Quickly, she tucked the necklace back inside her clothing, well out of Rune's sight.

Rune didn't say anything but watched her careful movements. What "friend" gave her such a gift? He was jealous. He didn't like it and didn't have time for it. Regret poured over him. He wished he'd never gotten Anya any gift.

"Uh," he stuttered out. "I left something for you in your room." Dammit, he cursed to himself again. Why did he have to say that! She would have found the present on her own. He never meant to say anything about it. "It's not much," he mumbled.

Anya's heart skipped a beat. Maybe Rune did think of her sometimes . . . as more than a friend.

"Thank—"

"I have to go," Rune stopped her. "Just stay close to my father's house, you and the dogs. It's the safest place for you. Promise me, Anya."

She mutely nodded her head in a yes. He can't leave yet. He just can't. Then she remembered.

"Rune, I must tell you about Flowers—"

He'd already turned away from her, out of earshot.

The golem heard her well enough.

This time he didn't roar in his iron cage. He didn't have to. The ice had begun to move with summer's melt. He would bring the storm. No *kulaks* can live. He would make sure of it.

"Whips, or no whips?"

Albert Fink pounded his gavel to quiet the room. As president of the Nome Kennel Club he'd no sooner called their summer meeting to order when arguments broke out among the members whether or not to allow whips in the next All Alaska Sweepstakes. Last year they'd listened to the only female in their membership and agreed to forbid the use of whips in the all-important race. Many had second thoughts since the running of last year's race. Whips were used to guide teams despite race rules, used by all except the rookie driver of the Siberian husky team.

No one was censured for it, but no dog driver had abused their animals save one, Frank Lundgren.

He hadn't been spotted in or around Nome since the race. Good riddance to bad blood. Most dog drivers, white and Eskimo alike, used whips in guiding their teams, not to harm them but to command them. Frank Lundgren used his whip to beat his dogs down, nearly killing them. Every man and woman gathered at the meeting wished the poor-excuse-for-a-dog driver a taste of his own medicine. Little did they know; their wishes had more than come true.

"Let's see the show of hands for whips," Albert called over the noisy conversation. He pounded the gavel a second time, then a third. This time the conversation on this subject was over before it started, he could tell. Some would never agree, the female members, especially. There were two more women in their club now, and while he respected their opinions, he didn't agree. Not yet. In time he might have to, if this year's vote didn't go his way.

"Dog drivers need their whips!" someone shouted to the club Chair.

"The dogs expect them for command!" someone else followed.

"One bad apple spoils the barrel!" A female voice could be heard over the din.

Hester Bloom again, Albert silently lamented.

The crowd quieted down, enough to at least listen to "the

other side."

Hester got up, and stood at her seat.

"Look what happened last year with the second finish team," she lectured. "That dog driver finished his own team all right, practically killed them. None of us stopped it. We should have. Shame on—"

"All the telegraph lines went down, Hester. The storm came up so sudden, we couldn't follow the three teams that stayed in the race. The checkers couldn't check like they were supposed to," one of the members nearby interrupted with his challenge.

"Yeah, it wasn't the club's fault," another added.

"Besides, we all know most mushers don't do to dogs what that Frank Lundgren fella did," someone else chimed in.

"Excuses," Hester answered back. "All you have are excuses for the cruelty inflicted on the dogs last year and the cruelty that will surely be inflicted in race years to come if we don't do something about it," she fumed.

"Sit down and settle down, Hester," Albert politely ordered. She was probably right. Time would tell. Right now wasn't "that time." Avoiding Hester's frozen stare, he called again for a vote.

Whips it would be.

"Xander, what's wrong, boy?" Anya knelt down to him, afraid he was headed into a fit.

The usually watchful husky shut his eyes and moaned in a low bark but didn't move otherwise. He smelled the burn of the wolves that had protected him. He felt the flap of circling ravens. The air burned hot around him, full of new dangers sensed. He heard waves crash and roar and knew the sound, not from his good memories of another life, but from bad things in this dangerous place. The waters could hurt, like the whip. They could coil, then lash out.

A guardian left for the water.

Xander's keen instincts alerted him to Rune's direction. He opened his watch-blue eyes, and would every morning and every night, watching and waiting for his guardian to return, just like he waited still for Zellie. His husky ways, ingrained in him since birth, would not change. His loyalty to his pack and those that ran with him ever guided his head and heart through the storm—born and bred a Chukchi dog, intelligent, enduring, and gentle by nature. Because he was intelligent and enduring, he knew instinctively to answer the call of the wild now and not listen to gentle whispers on the winds of days gone by.

This was a new day and a new place, a hostile place. He must watch for circling ravens and coiled whips and snarling waves and not let them strike his pack—at the newborn pups most of all. Like the wolf, Xander chose a mate, one he would keep for life. The drive to create life and protect that life surged through him, the canine imprint centuries old.

But new dangers forced his attention. He must ever watch for ravens, for whips, for waves, for cracks in the ice and the shadows that hid inside.

"Xander, it's all right," Anya tried to soothe. Glad he hadn't collapsed into another fit, she knew something upset him. Upset over everything that had happened so far, herself, she could guess what stirred Xander. At present, it might be Flowers and the piebald husky's obvious pregnancy.

Flowers had a coat of many flowers, Anya thought approvingly, with soft splotches of copper-red, black, and gray over a field of white fur. Her mask wasn't typical of her Chukchi pack, being all copper-red with a freckled nose, then a white coat along her mouth and chin. Instead of her mismatched eyes taking away from her look, Anya thought them stunning with one soft brown and the other soft blue. Zellie's eyes hadn't matched either. Flowers's eyes showed similar strength and mark of

Chukchi breeding. Flowers resembled a white foxy girl, Anya decided. Her pups would be equally unique.

Anya's spirits took a sudden dive, as Xander's had moments before; worrying so over Flowers and whether or not her pups would survive. It was hard enough for a litter to survive in the Arctic where any change in temperature or smell or nature could mean life or death, much less here where *only* change waited . . . stalking in shadows . . . hidden in unknown crags and crevasses . . . and threatening to pull them down below the ice.

Anya suddenly thought of Rune.

The same ice waited for him.

The next passage of summer seasons wouldn't go smoothly.

Anya ran her fingers through the thick fur of Xander's back in gentle strokes and took what comfort she could from his nearness.

"What's that thing you have on?" Inga asked with a sneer.

Anya had just passed through the spacious parlor of the Johansson house on her way to the kitchen and then outside to the dogs. Too late, she realized she should have gone out the front door. For days she'd managed *not* to run into anybody living in the house, at least not long enough to have any kind of conversation. The captain wanted to talk to her, she could tell, but then he would pass by and say nothing. As for Rune's mother and his sister, she had no interest in any such talk; with Inga least of all.

"You look silly," Inga chided, getting up from the velvet settee and scurrying over to get in Anya's way. "I guess this is what you people wear."

Anya didn't like what Inga said and she didn't like Inga. No point in talking to her, period. Anya slipped past her.

"Just wait until I tell mother what a mean girl you are!" Inga shouted at Anya's back.

Anya had already cleared the parlor and was out the back door, not paying any mind to Inga's insults. She wasn't going to let any mean girl upset her, even if she were Rune's sister. She longed to get out of the Johansson house entirely, but she'd promised Rune she'd stay; she and the dogs. Safer than some places for them, she had to stay for Flowers's sake. Her time for whelping would come before Rune returned. On even higher alert now, Anya was scared for Flowers and her unborn pups.

"There's my girl," Anya cooed over Flowers, once she'd reached her in the dog yard, set well away from the large log and stone house. Anya thought of her home village. She preferred her village yarangas made of walrus hide to the captain's home.

Once inside the yaranga, she would crawl inside the polog, the fur-lined box meant for family sleeping. Usually the coziest of places, the polog turned uncomfortable as she grew older and had to sleep so near Grisha and his wife and sons. No, it wasn't cozy anymore. But neither was this place, this house with Rune's mother and sister. Anya didn't sleep in the same room with them, but she was uncomfortable sleeping under the same roof. She made sure to slip out of the house unnoticed and bed down with Xander, sharing his straw. A better, safer place for her, she knew.

Xander whimpered behind her, tied at his stake.

Anya turned to him, then took out her knife and quickly freed him. The other dogs didn't stir, but watched. She left them tied. The captain said she must not let her dogs free. They would run off or be stolen or killed by something in the wild. He didn't have to warn her of that! If freed now, her dogs would not run unless told to "mush." If she had to give that signal, she would, and go with them. The Gatekeepers would tell her when. The Gatekeepers watched over them. She crouched down to

Flowers and Xander, the big black and white husky having curled up next to his mate. Anya eased a little inside at the cozy sight, enough to think about something else for the moment: about the pretty dress she wore, the one Rune had given her.

The creamy buckskin, summer dress could be caribou or reindeer, worked into the softest of hides. The long-sleeved, scoop-necked garment reached just over her mukluks, and was brightly embroidered and beaded along its edges. Anya felt like a princess, a bride, like the most important of females in her Chukchi village. More than that, she felt like her beloved grandmother, Nana-tasha. Grisha had given his mother a dress like this to show her important place in their village. In life, Nana-tasha was the mother of one of the elite, a dog breeder. Anya's insides tugged. She wasn't any of those things. For Rune to give her such a present made her feel funny, all jumbled inside like a bunch of hide ties that refused to uncoil.

She wasn't any bride, much less Rune's!

Anya scrambled to a stand, then straightened the folds of her gift from Rune. She was shaman. She wasn't any bride. She was born to Native Earth to save the dogs, not to be any bride; especially to Rune Johansson! They were worlds apart anyway. It wouldn't be any kind of match. Vitya would be her match if she were ever to marry. That seemed the most right and acceptable to the ancestors of the People. Not any Viking warrior, no matter how handsome, or how blue his eyes, or how strong his powerful body, or how able to fight he'd proved to be—no matter how he made her *feel* all over when she thought of him.

Unwittingly she took out the ivory husky carving from inside her new dress, her long ago gift from Vitya. It suddenly weighed heavily around her neck although it never had before. The moment she realized what she was doing, her fingers burned from its touch. The sign startled her. She let go of the necklace but not before she slipped it back inside her dress. The sign meant nothing. It wasn't good or bad, she told herself. She refused to think of Vitya and Rune together and absolutely refused to think a sign from either of them meant anything at all! She didn't have time for this upset and stirred feeling over either one of them!

She had half a mind to toss away the necklace and Rune's gift to her, too. But she thought better of it. She might be shaman, but she needed help to save the dogs, help from Rune and any help Vitya might send. The practical side of her took over. She thought of Spirit, in the world beyond, waiting to help them. Anya held out her hands, examining them for any sign of change into her Spirit. When she got the signal, she would run with Spirit in the race for all their lives.

It wasn't over.

Whispers on the arctic winds blew past, their message clear and present.

It begins again.

Rune heard the same message, only in a much different way. The waters turned rough. The waves came out of nowhere, thudding against the *Nordic,* gnashing at its hull, the feared sound unmistakable. A storm brewed out over the Bering Sea, with Rune suddenly in the thick of it. The summer cyclone caught up with him. No place on the ship was safe; especially the wheelhouse. Its frame rattled. Its windows cracked. Strong gusts had the *Nordic* surrounded, spinning the steamer off course. Rune held fast to the wheel with one hand and pulled the ship's alarm with the other. The bell sounded to the crew, already battening down hatches and lashing everything tight, slipping and sliding their way port and starboard to secure the ship.

Rune didn't panic. He'd been hit by cyclones before. It wasn't unusual for these storms to come up in summer. What struck

Rune was the force of this one. It felt like a winter storm, the strength of it. Summer cyclones didn't churn the ocean or the ice like this. Swaths of the arctic ice pack could break off in such wind and waves and come at them out of nowhere. Rune tried not to panic, but to convince himself of the unlikelihood of this happening.

Even so, he strained to see through the storm for any sign of the hated "white stripe" closing in. If the ice came at them now, the *Nordic* didn't have a chance. Rune wasn't ready for this. Cursing himself, he should have been ready. Entrusted with the lives of all on board, he should have known what the serpent might cause. But whether caused by the ancient enemy of the Vikings or natural forces of nature, Rune still had to fight the storm.

The wheelhouse heated warm; so warm Rune halfway expected the fires of *Hel* to burn in all the churned-up water of the Bering Sea. He halfway expected to see the face of the thief who stole his sword appear in the waves that slapped against the ship. The arctic melting season never showed its hand like this. The signs were not good, no matter how Rune read them.

Right now he had trouble seeing through the storm, thrown off his direction. The day grew too dark, the seas unforgiving. He worried for his crew; that they and Fox Ramsey would go down with him and the *Nordic*, swallowed by the storm. Doing his utmost to hold onto the steerage and keep the ship righted, saltwater pelting him without letup, he saw Anya's face before him, only hers. Her smile lit the darkness. His love for her showed him the way.

The sunstone of the Vikings burned in his hand and put him back on course for the Gulf of Anadyr. A Viking warrior, he raged against the storm, but not with the sword of war. The sword of wisdom guided him. He was a sailor, a navigator, and he knew the sea. He must trust in his knowledge and his ability to captain the ship to safety. His crew was a good one. He'd made sure of that before he left Nome. Fox Ramsey knew to stay below during bad weather. Rune had told him enough times. The *Nordic* was shipshape, brand new. Most of all, there was no ice in sight from any direction he could see. Dark skies had turned twilight gray, allowing enough light for a visual of the watery horizon. No "white stripe" laid siege on them.

Rune held fast to the ship's wheel, intent on riding out the storm, willing the obstinate cyclone to weaken first. It did, but not for ten hours. They felt like ten thousand to Rune. When the winds finally died and the temperature of the sea and the air dropped to normal, all on board the *Nordic* had stayed safe. Rune relaxed his fingers on the wheel but not his guard. He would keep a better watch for storms between this point and Anadyr.

Vitya started up his sled, the final team he would take to the Markova Fair for trade. He'd said his goodbyes to his family, promising to send the profits earned back to them by a fellow tribesman. He trusted the friend, as he did most all in their village; all but Grisha and the shamans. While Vitya hadn't told his family he planned on finding Anya, wherever that might take him, he told them he would stay in Anadyr for a time and they must not worry. When he returned to the village, his family would be gone, Vitya's father said. He could find them in one of the reindeer villages, always on the move, always following the vital herds. The hunt would change from the sea to the land. That was all, his father assured. The family would be well. There was nothing to fear in their new life.

Vitya wondered at the truth of his father's words; if there was anything to fear at present. He wondered about his own life and where it might take him, searching for the girl he loved.

The unfamiliar cyclone had come in from Siberia, Nome
Eskimos rumored. The storm pushed the walrus away from
their feeding grounds. Ten thousand walrus crowded shoulder
to shoulder now on the nearby barrier islands off Port Lay and
Point Hope north of Nome, forced there by the moving, melting ice. The Inupiat villagers would not hunt down the trapped
walrus or do anything to start a stampede, the young pups the
most vulnerable of all. The polar bear must be kept away.

Something was wrong in the oceans.

The depended-on ice was moving, melting. Something tried
to kill the herds, to scatter them and scare them to shore in
their hunt for food. Female walrus give birth on the ice, then
dive into the shallow depths on the continental shelf for clams,
worms, and snails. Feeding grounds were in shallow waters, not
the Deep. It was always the way of the walrus but something
was after them. Warm winds and waves blew over trusted ice
fields, moving them, melting them, the Eskimos feared. The ten
thousand trapped walrus would have to find the ice again, but
the ice moved away to waters in oceans ten thousand feet deep
where they could no longer hunt and survive!

Anya had been to Chinook's village trade store only because
she had to. She needed fish and jerked beef for the dogs and the
Eskimo provided it to her, as a favor and on the possible chance
she might give him Chukchi pups to breed. Not chancing taking her dogs with her to hunt herself, especially Flowers, she
didn't want to leave them alone for long, either. The captain
said he would feed the dogs, but she'd refused his help. It wasn't
that she didn't trust him; she didn't want to depend on him. It
was his wife and daughter she didn't trust.

Better to keep separate from them when she could. Then too,
Anya was as stubborn as her dogs. It was in her nature, like
theirs. Rune had gotten food from Chinook and so would she,

for the moment. Always truthful with the native "dog trader," as she thought of him, she never tried to fool Chinook. She never promised him pups, instead she promised to pay him back in kind. When she could, she would hunt and fish and replenish his supplies. Chinook would puff on his pipe and nod, seeming to agree; the only exchange on her frequent trips to his village store.

This trip was different. She'd stayed to listen to the exchange between village customers, talking of ice moving and melting and of the mighty walrus brought down by the feared warming in the oceans and seas.

"Something was after them," one villager put it.

"The young will die first," another Eskimo foretold.

Chills shot through Anya at the talk of warming waters. All life in the Arctic depended on the ice. The ice was moving when it should not, even in this season of summer. Anya knew without thinking it, the ice storm had hit again. Not any usual storm but the disfigured, deformed, deadly ice storm, broken away from Native Earth, cutting down all in its path. It hit again, this time with a vengeance even more cruel than before.

Something is coming. Someone is there.

First the walrus pups, then Flowers. The pregnant female husky was trapped on the same barrier island as the walrus, it felt to Anya. So were all the Chukchi dogs. Soon more dogs would come here, caught in the same life and death trap. How could she or Rune fight such an enemy—an enemy hiding in icy shadows and dark crevasses that waited to strike the innocent? Wrestling renewed fears, Anya tried to remember her grandmother's words and trust in the reason she was born to Native Earth: to save the dogs. She was shaman. She was Spirit. The Gatekeepers kept their watch over them all, Rune, too.

Rune!

He was out there now over the same melting oceans and seas.

He had to come back safe. He *had* to.

CHAPTER ELEVEN

"I can't write," Anya quietly admitted to Margret Johansson. This time Anya hadn't been able to slip through the family parlor without being noticed. Rune's mother and his sister had stood up the moment they'd spotted her. Margret had a paper in her hands and proceeded to put it under Anya's nose.

"Humph," Margret said in disapproval. Still, she kept the paper and pen held out to Anya.

Inga put her hand over her mouth, snickering through it, at Anya.

The gods had already gifted Anya with many things. She didn't mind that she couldn't read and write English, even at this uncomfortable moment. A bad feeling shot through her. It got worse the longer she stood before the Johanssons. She wished the captain were here. She trusted him. She didn't trust these two.

"Your mark will do," Margret lectured impatiently. She put the paper down on the nearby table and motioned for Anya to take the pen from her and sign.

Anya didn't come from a world of paper and pens. She had no idea what any of it meant other than to keep tally of things like counting the number of seal holes spotted in the ice or the number in reindeer herds or maybe the numbers in dog trades. This, she didn't like and never would. Except the dog trades Rune and Fox Maule Ramsey were after mattered. If they didn't bring back enough Chukchi dogs to race in the next All Alaska

191

Sweepstakes, if they didn't get a good number in trade at the Markova Fair, all could be lost. Everything depended on good dog trades and a good race.

But then Anya thought about the trades she'd witnessed. When her beloved Zellie had been traded away, she didn't remember any paper. When she'd been traded to the ugly Mooglo, she didn't remember any paper. So paper must have nothing to do with dog trades. That thought made her feel a little better. This couldn't be about dog trades. Still, this was all wrong, what Margret tried to get her to do, to put her mark down for no good reason.

"Just where do you think you're going, young lady!" Margret Johansson shouted at Anya's back. "Do *not* leave this room without placing your mark on this paper."

Anya stopped in the doorway of the parlor but didn't turn around. Her hand hurt; the same one that carried Mooglo's ugly mark. The evil Yukaghir had left his mark on her, all right. The yellowy scar reminded her of decayed meat, left out in the open too long. Her hand looked normal enough to most, but not to her. She saw rupture and decay. She saw the mark of evil. Whips made such a mark, on dogs, worst of all.

"Well then, I'll just have to tell Rune you don't care what happens to him; that you don't care if he has a roof over his head when he returns," Margret threatened.

Anya gave Margret her attention but not her trust. Inga, either. She turned around and stepped back into the parlor. The mention of Rune drew her in.

"Good," Margret said, her tone all business. "Now you're being sensible."

"What am I being sensible about?" Anya eyed the two warily.

"For pity's sake, Anya, this is just a paper giving Rune ownership of this house and its property. Inga and I will be returning to Seattle and my husband will be on one of his ships, which will leave this house vacant and unattended. It's all for Rune. You wouldn't deny him that, would you?" she whined to Anya.

"What do I have to do with this? Why do you need my mark?"

Margret caught Inga's eye before answering.

They were up to something, Anya suspected. Yet, this *was* Rune's mother. She must care for Rune, she must love him enough to want him to have good shelter, a roof over his head, when she leaves. Anya thought of her own mother, of Tynga, of the mother who died giving birth to her—of the mother she never knew. She would carry the guilt for her mother's death always. Anya's shaman instincts blunted at the emotion of it, less sharp when she thought of what might have been. She'd never known a mother's love. Rune should.

"Why, *my* mark?" she repeated, this time less fervent.

Margret cleared her throat.

"You are living in this house. We all must sign this. See, I'll sign here," Margret set the paper flat on the table and penned her signature. Once done, she handed the fountain pen to Anya.

Anya numbly took the writing implement from Rune's mother and numbly made an X where she was told. Rune could rest easy, once he returned from Anadyr, in this house. His family lived here. The house would provide needed shelter from the storms ever coming at him. He was guardian. He was Viking. He deserved a fitting refuge. So caught up in thoughts of Rune when she exited the parlor, Anya didn't see the victorious look on Inga's face or hear the mean girl snicker.

The Gulf of Anadyr was ice free. Rune breathed a sigh of relief. The last time he'd arrived with his father on the *Storm*, the ice had kept their steamer from any close approach to the Siberian shore. They'd had to make the rest of the way over ice by fixing runners to the bottom of their lighter boat. Not this time. Now Rune could off-load their lighter boat and needed supplies, taking them up the Anadyr River with little trouble. The dogs could be run back overland then loaded onto the *Nordic*'s wide decks in no time. Time was something Rune never felt he had on his side, anywhere in arctic waters; especially now.

He had someone to get back to, someone he loved.

The ice could come between him and Anya any time. Currently late summer into fall, the danger of ice loomed in his thoughts, and he worried over storms ahead. The sooner he could get Fox Maule Ramsey to the Markova Fair to secure his teams of Chukchi dogs, then transport them safely back across the Bering Sea, the sooner he could see Anya again.

He had trouble remembering if anything else in his life mattered except gazing into her sooty-brown, dark-lashed eyes, feeling their mischief and sparkle touch him, warm him, and tease with the promise of love. Anya tried to keep this hidden, but he saw in those seal-brown pools what he needed to see. His throat tightened. There was so much he wanted to say to Anya but couldn't; not yet, not until she and the dogs were truly safe. He had to keep his focus on the danger they faced, only that. Still, he burned hot inside thinking of the moment he would be free to love her.

"There *ye* are, lad," Fox Ramsey acknowledged when he found Rune in the wheelhouse. "A wee bit of a climb, too," he joked at the same time, taking a few needed breaths. He'd obviously been in a hurry.

"*Hallo*, Fox," Rune said, doing his best to redirect his attention to the business at hand. The Scot had done well on the journey thus far. He'd measured up to the venture, rough seas and all. Rune had a grudging respect for the miner and dog driver. Fox had no idea what really brought on the sudden cyclone. Rune did. He wasn't about to tell the Scot, not on your life.

"*D'ye ken* how long before we get to the fair. I'm that anxious to see the *dugs noo.*"

Rune brightened at Fox's excitement over their arrival in Siberia. It helped take his mind off how much he missed Anya. Besides Fox, Rune had his crew to consider, which ones he needed to stay on board and which had to come with them. The crew, like Fox, had proved themselves during the stormy passage across the Bering Sea. Skilled at giving and taking direction, they worked tirelessly. A few had worked with sled dogs. He could rely on his crew to help keep the sled teams fit and cared for on the passage back to Nome, no matter that it would be a task new to many of them. The polar explorers couldn't find better men, Rune supposed.

The Arctic was a different place, on land or sea. If a man didn't measure up on shipboard or behind a sled, he'd best leave the North or risk quick death. If a body didn't want challenge, better to live somewhere else. Of course, before he met Anya, Rune never put much importance on sled dog driving. He did nowadays.

"With the winds at our back, we ought to make Markova in a day's time," Rune advised Fox, accustomed to thinking in nautical terms. "I'll be ready to leave in an hour, with the men and supplies needed, and our lighter boat in the water. Keep some of that Russian you know handy, Fox. We'll need it if I can't find a translator."

"*Aye*, lad. *Nee* a problem. I will *nae* be late and will bide on the gangplank for *ye*. *Guid cheerio the noo*," Fox said enthusiastically, then left the wheelhouse and scrambled down the appointed stairs, below deck toward his quarters.

Rune was left wondering if he'd just understood the Scot. Fox's accent was a challenge. As long as the Siberians, native and white alike, understood him, that's what mattered most. Maybe Rune would get lucky and find an English translator; maybe not. Either way, he'd figure it out. He didn't have a choice.

★ ★ ★ ★ ★

Anya walked to the edges of the Great Crag, at least in her mind's eye. She'd never been there before, to that holy place where sacrifices were made to the gods. In Siberia, in her village, she sought such a hiding place, a secret place where no one would follow. There were many such crags and climbs overlooking the edges of arctic oceans and seas. As a child she'd found them to hide. But the Great Crag was an unknown place, known only to shamans.

Anya's eyes flew open. *She* was shaman. *She* was Spirit. What did this sign mean? She looked up at the skies and almost expected to see ravens loom in black circles overhead, ready to strike. The Raven god and bad spirits must have broken into her thoughts and sent her to the Great Crag . . . where death waited.

Only silence and blue sky gathered overhead, nothing else.

Anya thought of Nana-tasha's words to her a lifetime ago, when she spoke of divination and prophecy in dreams. Calmed by this beloved memory of her grandmother, Anya realized the truth of her words. Anya was the first of her kind born to Native Earth. She didn't need a trance or potent mushrooms to foretell things to come. She didn't need a medium to talk to spirits. She *was* Spirit.

Right now Anya stood at the very edges of the world between human and spirit—where only shamans could. She could see the Dark waiting beneath the Great Crag for its next sacrifice. The Dark did not belong in the world of Chukchi spirits. *Something* sent it there to wait. Anya's eyes closed of their own volition as she willed the divined dream of shamans come to her.

First she saw a face, a man's face. It wasn't clear but blurred. He was a dog driver, fallen. His dogs all fallen with him. She couldn't see each of the dogs individually but could see they were Chukchi. She felt their panic, all of them. Her heart pounded. The drums of the ancestors beat hard in her aching chest. Blood poured down the steep slope only to empty into the dark unknown below. The crevasse ended in death. The ice opened up and drank the blood of its victims! The dog driver clawed the icy slope trying to hold on to life. The dogs pawed and tore at the unforgiving ground for any kind of foothold. Their desperate efforts left uneven imprints of red wherever they touched. The Gatekeepers howled from the heavens, mourning the certain death of their breed and its all-important guardian.

Gasp!

Anya opened her eyes to the reality of the prophecy. Her heart still drummed. Her eyes watered. Stinging tears trickled down her already sweat-covered face. She mechanically wiped the damp away but couldn't clear the upsetting divination so easily. If only she could put a face to the dog driver, to the unknown guardian just lost. The figure was male but it wasn't Rune. Were there others coming to the fight? If only she could know. If only she could prevent the dogs from dying, the dogs and the faceless guardian. So many were dead! She'd never felt so powerless despite her power of divination in knowing what the enemy had in store for the Chukchi. The Great Crag meant the End. How could any shaman stop such a force? They could not.

When the time of the prophecy came to be, time would be up.

Fighting the urge to drop face down onto the ground in prayer and call on the Morning Dawn, the Creator god, the Earth god, and Chukchi gods in all Directions for help, Anya did not. She didn't have to. The gods were already with her. They waited with her beneath the Great Crag, numb in the shadows of death to come, listening along with her to the mournful cries of the Gatekeepers.

"Veet-ya," Rune tried to pronounce the dog trader's name, since Fox Ramsey wanted every dog the native Chukchi brought to the Markova Fair; twenty in all. The Scot had no sooner spotted the still-harnessed team than he went over to them, examined each one, and then made his quick decision for them. The team sat among a sea of dogs, yet Fox selected this team and this trader for his first bargain. The trade hadn't been easy with the native Chukchi speaking no English and Rune and Fox no Chukchi. Luckily they'd found a translator who agreed to help, a native who knew some English and Russian words, enough to get a trade done at the busy fair.

Rune scanned the crowd of dogs and men, remembering his last time here. His father had sent him back to the *Storm* to ready the ship for "live cargo" to Nome. When Rune learned he'd be helping ferry Chukchi dogs across the Bering Sea, he remembered how mad he was, at his father and the dogs—at his father because he didn't trust Rune to stay in Markova and help, and at the dogs because he was a sailor, not any kind of musher.

That seemed a lifetime ago. He was seventeen now.

That seemed a world ago. He was a warrior now, called on by the gods of the Vikings.

No longer a boy in search of adventure in unknown arctic waters, he was a man set on a course in nothing but the unknown. He'd found adventure all right. He spoke to ghosts and would soon become one himself if the forces against him won out! Straightening his spine, he rubbed the back of his neck where he wore the secret of the runes. The connection, he'd come to believe, would help him keep Anya safe, Anya and her dogs.

His birthmark held a secret tie to Anya, as if they'd been born before and lived in another time. Rune shook off the impossible notion. They lived in *this* dangerous time, *this* dangerous place, called on by their ancient gods to save the Chukchi dogs. From what, Rune still didn't know. He was determined to help, no matter the price to himself. But he feared for Anya and her dogs, the ones here in Markova, too. He had a bad feeling about this place the longer he stared out over the dogs and the tribes come to trade them . . . telling him he needed to remember what he saw because it would soon be gone. The only place he would find it again would be in distant memories, nowhere else.

"Lad," Fox eagerly directed to Rune, "are these not *bonnie dugs*! They are *braw*, every one!"

Pulled back to the moment, Rune welcomed the interruption his ghostly thoughts had taken.

"*Ja* they are," he agreed with Fox. All of the dogs looked shipshape. They were a mix of colors and husky masks, but he saw no mix with other breeds. The distinct Siberian breed was truly "*braw* and *bonnie*." He looked again at the dog trader.

"Veet-ya is it?"

The young Chukchi nodded yes, apparently understanding Rune.

Rune noticed the Chukchi dog trader must be his same age or close to it. Evenly matched in height, Rune instantly felt a rivalry with him. He shook this suspicion off. His emotions had no place here. This was business, important business. He grunted a "*hallo*" to the Chukchi trader, then put his full attention to Fox and the needed dogs. The Scot had just asked him to stay with this trade while he sought others. Fox wanted at least forty more dogs; even more if he could find them. The translator hinted that many of the dogs were all traded up and would leave soon for tundra and coastal villages all over Siberia.

Though it was difficult to know for sure, the translator answered Fox's question about where else the already-traded dogs might be going.

Had any traders come across the oceans and seas looking for dogs?

The translator didn't think so and told Fox he was the only one. Rune read the relief on the Scot's face at this news. Fox wanted the only Siberian husky teams to race in the next All Alaska Sweepstakes, the reason obvious.

"You can go now," Rune told Vitya. With the trade done and Rune knowing how to care for the dogs, he didn't need the dog trader to stay. When the trader stood steadfast, his arms locked across his chest, and didn't move an inch; Rune motioned him away in a friendly manner. He tried to convey to the obstinate "Veet-ya" that the deal was over and he could leave.

Vitya shook his head back and forth in a no, and trenched his native mukluks deeper in the slush. This might be his only chance to find Anya, going across the great sea with his traded dog team. He'd been in Markova for days and had found no word of what had happened to his Anya. The only thing he'd learned was that one trade the year before—the trade taking some of Grisha's dogs—had gone across the great sea into the unknown. He meant to follow Anya anywhere, even into the unknown.

Convinced he was right about where she'd gone, he needed to convince these white foreigners to take him with them on their steaming boat, a baidarka that must be big enough for such a journey. He'd seen whaling ships before, far off on the horizon, but they'd never come in close enough for him to have a careful look. He looked forward to it; especially since the white man's baidarka would take him to Anya. She was out there in the unknown. He would find her.

Rune crossed his arms in front, same as the Chukchi. Rune

realized he wouldn't get anywhere with Vitya until Fox returned with the translator. The stubborn Chukchi reminded him of the Chukchi dogs, just as willful. Anya's dogs had the same streak through them; so did she. He smiled inwardly when he thought of Anya. Maybe Vitya wasn't such a bad guy. After all, he was Chukchi.

Vitya's team started to whine, even bark in some instances.

Both young men alerted to them.

Angry shouts came across the sea of dogs and men. Soldiers on horseback tore through the multitude, their sabers drawn in an obvious attempt to scatter the crowd and break up the trade fair. The troops had been alerted by watchers in villages near Anadyr, locals selected by Moscow for just such a purpose: to spy, to report all goings-on. None were native. Driven by hunger and fear, select Russian peasants reported on their own, likely thinking they had little to lose and everything to gain. Then again, there were a few who did not worry over their fellow countrymen, but over control in their towns and villages, power the motivator over hunger and fear. Some were *kulak,* having means noteworthy to Moscow. Best they take care. The golem is never far.

Rune and Vitya instinctively worked together to protect their dogs. Each took a side of the large team to shore up the lines. If anyone came at them, they needed to keep the dogs safe. Rune wanted to pull out his Viking sword, but his gut feeling said no. Forced to trust this, he held off. Wisdom had to rule over war. The cacophony of huskies howling and men shouting sent a swarm of dark clouds across the clear arctic sky, marking the blue heavens with red.

Rune and Vitya eyed each other, their understanding of the situation immediate. An attack was underway. The sounds were unmistakable. Rune and Vitya braced for a fight.

But none came their way?

The howls abruptly silenced. No men called out. An eerie quiet settled over the gray afternoon. Snowflakes dusted the air. A strange chill loomed but nothing looked out of the ordinary. Maybe there was never any attack?

Ah, but there was. Soldiers left their red mark on the Markova Fair, their message as cold as the turned day. A man from the Even tribe and his team of sixteen dogs lay slaughtered on the bloody ground where they fell. There was no warning! It happened so fast no one could do anything but watch the horror unfold. Lives had been taken, but for what? Fear shot through the annual gathering. It wasn't the first time, but this time was different. This time the sabers didn't just scare, but *killed*. Caught by surprise, native tribesmen from all parts of the region turned to each other for safety and for answers. Why this attack and why at this time? The tense air buzzed in upset. No one had answers, only more questions.

The moment Rune assured himself Vitya's team was secure, he took off in the maze of dogs and men to find Fox Ramsey. The Scot could be down. He could be dead. Drawn to the area where he thought the attack happened, Rune hurried there. In a run, he did his best to spot Fox's plaid tartan colors in the crowd. He hoped he'd find him alive. A line of men suddenly stopped Rune, a thick line of men crowded around the fallen Even and his dogs.

No one approached the dead. Rune shoved through the circle. Maybe some could be saved, not yet cut down to stay. He put a warm hand to each cold body, beginning with the native Even. The man had been shot, not run through with a saber. The man's eyes were scared open. Rune gently pressed them closed. Each husky he checked was the same, with their eyes open and their bodies stiff. All shot looking into the shadow of their death. Gently as he could, Rune put a shaky hand to each of their masks and wished them peace in death, wishing them to Valhalla for a long afterlife. They'd all been executed, a bullet to their heads. The mark of the gods at Rune's neck burned in mourning for these innocents.

It made no sense, these killings.

Then again, it did.

Whatever pursued Anya and her dogs, trying to kill them . . . did this. The cold hand of death had a far reach, too far for Rune to slay every serpent. That's why his instincts told him to hold back and not raise his sword in answer to the soldiers. He had to choose his battles. *Nine serpents he must slay. The wolf and the dog battle as one.* These dogs before him now, he could not save. Awash in grief over the dead man from the Even tribe and the man's dead dogs, he couldn't find the strength to stand.

He wanted to get up and gather the murdered huskies and their master in a funeral pyre and burn them, honoring them in death for all the brave life lived. He wanted to set them out to sea for their journey to Valhalla. No one in the circle around him would allow that, no doubt suspicious of any kind of ancient Viking tradition. Wrestling with his upset, Rune struggled to remember why he came to this Markova Fair and the promise he had to fulfill—to return to Nome with a ship of dogs, Chukchi dogs.

"Lad! Lad!" Fox broke through the circle of men still hunched around Rune. They began to scatter at his disturbance. Many appeared numb and shook their heads at the deadly sight before them. No doubt they wanted to return to their villages and tell the shamans of the mischief here, the *murder* here.

Instant relief at seeing the Scot alive brought Rune full back to the moment. He got up and stood by the slain dogs. The slain man would be seen to by his fellows, but the dogs, what of them? Where was the honor they deserved in death? The men who had hunkered around the scene had left; still in shock Rune was sure, and still afraid they might be next.

"Lad, I see your tears. I'm that sorry." Fox put a hand to Rune's shoulder, but focused on the dead at his feet, and who killed them. "I do *nee kin* who could do anythin' like this. So many *braw dugs doon* and no reason for it. I found *oot* some of the talk. They're saying the native Even had stolen the *dugs* from a local town, from a white man there. They're saying that's a lic. Word is the white man wanted this team and falsely reported this poor fellow, and sent the soldiers here for the *dugs. Nee* a moment of *blether* over it! They killed him with-*oot* any trial." Fox had to stop at this; the injustice curdled his emotions.

"Then, they killed his dogs," Rune gritted. "I think the soldiers were on orders to kill. We have to watch out for whoever gave them. The soldiers will come back. We need to get our dogs and get out of here before they do."

"*Aye*, lad, you're right," Fox said past an uneasy sigh.

A sturdy cart wheeled to a stop close by. Two locals, both expressionless white men, threw the dogs' lifeless bodies, one by one, onto their cart. They said nothing to Rune or Fox but kept on with their work, as if this was commonplace for them—as if they were used to picking up the sick and the dead. Cholera or small pox or any other plague would bring the same result.

Rune bristled when each brave husky was thrown onto the unfitting pyre. He wished them honor and peace in any storms ahead. To dishonor even one dog like this, to pile them up like so much rubble to be thrown away, cut him deep. No man or beast deserved this. He could see the native Even being lifted by his fellow tribesmen and carried ceremoniously away, no doubt to be given a fitting resting place.

Rune watched intently; the one gesture rang familiar, reminding him of Boris Ivanov's death. Then of Zellie's. His chest caught. The picture of Anya and her dogs in Nome flashed in front of him—then went dark. This couldn't be good. He tried not to think beyond that.

"Fox, have you traded for the rest of your teams?"

"*Aye*, lad," he answered soberly.

"Then let's gather them and get going. My crew will help. I don't want to stay here any longer than we have to. The midnight sun will guide us back to the *Nordic* in good time."

"I *d'nee* want to bide here *noo* myself, lad. I've got my three *dug* teams. *Didnee* need more than that but I've traded for seventy *dugs* in all. What say let's get them back to Nome safe and sound, lad," Fox said, then turned his back on the loaded cart of dead animals. He had to think about the ones still alive.

"Right," Rune agreed, reluctant to leave the scene but in a hurry to get to Anya. He followed the determined Scot across the open into the yet gathered crowd of dogs and men trading them. The thick tension in the air hadn't dispersed, but hung like a pasted wet curtain over the Markova Fair, enough to slow things down to a sluggish crawl. Each step taken sank deep into the slushy earth. People seemed in a hurry but without direction. Rune had the sense that everyone wanted to get out of there, the same thought on all their minds. No one wanted to be around when the soldiers returned. In a rush to get out of there himself, Rune forgot all about asking after Anya's stepfather, Grisha.

Flowers's breaths came quick, her stomach rigid. She lay down. She got up. She circled. She moaned; scratching her bed of straw, seemingly not satisfied with the spot to bear her pups. Anya knew the pregnant female husky wanted to find a dark, quiet place away from any disturbance. Still summer, the night was too light for her. Anya had untied her but meant to stay close, wherever Flowers might wander.

Xander fought his hide leash and strained against its binding hold, obviously upset over his mate. Anya didn't want to untie him, not yet. Flowers needed to be left alone. The rest of the dogs sat quietly at their posts, their eyes intent on Flowers. None tried to break loose; Midday and Magic least of all. The two female huskies, all-white Midday and copper-red and white Magic, almost at the same time instinctively folded into circles on their straw bedding and closed their eyes, as if neither wanted to watch. Anya understood.

Her spirits were damp, too, worried over whether or not they would ever conceive. She had the same worry for herself but kept it buried deep. This wasn't about her.

Anya needed to provide a dark place for Flowers to give birth, given how agitated the female husky remained. Never a good sign. Females usually settled by this time, ready to deliver. Flowers paced anxiously, a sign she wasn't ready. The pups inside her could die . . . or be dead now! Anya jumped into action and gathered up whatever she could find to make a yaranga big enough for Flowers to hide inside. Heavy wood crates from the great baidarkas were stacked conveniently nearby, no doubt placed there for storage. Rune's father had many ships, she'd learned, ships that transported large supplies of goods. For that, many of these funny crates were needed. They looked more like enormous cages to Anya than supply crates, but she didn't have time to think past that unnerving thought and rushed to the closest stack. Finally, she managed to pull one free.

No one was around to help her but Anya didn't want any help, not with Flowers. She didn't want anyone to know the husky was about to have her pups; especially Inga. The mean girl had a bad spirit. Anya knew *other* bad spirits, not of this world, watched. She didn't sense they would come at this moment, but she felt their presence nonetheless. Her knife was close, ready to strike down the enemy that ever held a monstrous whip over them. *Try to touch these babies and I'll cut you down, like before!* Her knife held the magic of Chukchi shamans, she believed; at least enough to give her the strength she needed to protect Flowers and her unborn.

Once the shipping crate was set in place, Anya grabbed up the cumbersome canvas blanket stored inside, then draped it over the wood slats, securing it where there were already ties. She managed to pull a portion of the canvas loose to create a closed doorway to keep out the light. Satisfied the makeshift yaranga would do, she turned to Flowers and not a moment too soon. The animal still paced, weaker, stumbling as she did. She was in pain . . . too much pain. Something was wrong beyond the normal anxiety of birth!

"Come, girl." Anya gently took up Flowers's collar and led her through the doorway of her birthing area.

Xander moaned loudest of all.

Miraculously, Flowers settled down inside the dark space and stopped her whimpers as if conserving her energy for what lay ahead. Anya put a hand to Flowers's stomach and could feel churning inside. Flowers almost nipped at Anya, at her touch. Anya understood. The dog did not want company.

"I will be right outside," Anya softly reassured as if the female husky understood her, then slipped the canvas flap closed to leave Flowers alone. In need of reassurance herself, Anya paced over to Xander and held him snug. His agitated moans broke her heart. "Hush now, my brave boy," she cooed. He licked her cheek and quieted somewhat. She stroked behind his ears. Their nerves matched, both forced to wait for what the future held, for the choice between life and death in Fate's hands—and not theirs.

CHAPTER TWELVE

Anya finally reopened the flap. It had been too quiet, too long.

Three of the four pups born were dead, all stillborn. Flowers licked her live pup, trying to keep the fragile puppy in this life. The damp odor of blood coated the air. The exhausted new mother didn't acknowledge Anya. Flowers had not consumed any of the placentas or amniotic covering of the dead pups. She instinctively knew the effort was futile. A brown liquid pooled beneath Flowers, beneath her female opening. Anya put a shaky hand to the gluey mass.

Puppies!

These were puppies that might have been.

The howls inside Anya screamed to the gods. How could they let this happen! Fighting her anger and upset, she needed to keep her head for Flowers's sake; for Flowers and her live pup. Anya knew the gods hadn't done this but she blamed them anyway. Nor had she done this, but she blamed herself all the same.

"No!" Anya whispered hard at Xander, trying to keep him away from the dead pups and the mass of tissue pooled.

He pushed his muzzle hard against her arm, each time more forceful.

"Wait, Xander. Wait," she begged, all the while somehow collecting the tiny bodies for transfer to dry straw. "They might come back to life, Xander," she whispered more for her benefit than his. "We must wait twilight to twilight, one full moon. It is the way of our ancestors. We must stay quiet. No drums in mourning. I will watch over them," she promised through her tears, and believed Xander understood her. He must have, since he no longer tried to push past her to his pups. One pup was black and white, like his father, and the others, spotted like their mother—three lives that might have been. No life breathed through them now but maybe tomorrow, Anya prayed. Yes, maybe tomorrow they would come back to life.

Xander rested his head on his paws, having slumped to the ground in a crouch. He barked at the lifeless puppies; at first soft, then louder.

"Easy, boy," Anya tried to soothe.

His barks dissolved into whimpers, much like her own upset. They both must stay quiet and watch reverently over the dead, wishing life back into the stillborn pups. Anya had witnessed ceremonies for the dead in her village, always over human life. To her, the huskies were every bit as human as she. She knew what to do. She'd witnessed many births of their breed but never one like this. It was common for at least one pup, even two on rare occasion, to be born dead. It had happened also, she'd witnessed, that a female's whole birthing delivered only a brown mass of tissue. But for Flowers to have both such unwelcome, heart-wrenching events in the same birthing; Anya had never seen this before.

The enemies in the spirit world didn't fight fair.

They hid in icy depths she'd never imagined could maintain life. Cowards! They bloodied the arctic waters using the unborn now, the innocent Chukchi pups, for bait. Dark spirits ascended from the Deep at every chance to surprise, to maim, to kill her People, her dogs, and then dove back down to hide in the hollows of frozen death. The ice storm brewed in those hollows. Every shaman instinct Anya possessed told her so. If only she could find the hollows beneath the ice where the ice storm breathed and cut off its air! If only she could find her way to the world of the Deep! The human part of her born to Native Earth told her she never would, but her Spirit didn't agree.

Flowers drew her head up from nursing and nurturing her only puppy, then gave out a weak bark to Anya and to Xander. She did not look in the direction of her stillborn pups.

Anya read the grief in her watch eyes, seeing the changed color, the broken lines of red crossing liquid blue. Afraid for Flowers and her newborn pup, Anya worried neither might make it, the lines between life and death ever redrawn. She determined to keep watch over Flowers and her pup, the same as the dead, wishing full life back into them all. Careful as she could, Anya reached to the newborn pup for a closer exam of its health. Flowers let her, staying calm. If not, Anya would have pulled back.

Xander sniffed at Anya's arm but didn't push her, seemingly content to watch her actions. He nestled close, all the same.

Little Wolf cried from his post, wanting to follow Xander, acting every bit the little brother. The runt in the pack, Little Wolf had found a safe place, nearby Xander.

The rest of the dogs stayed quiet; silent yet alert, Magic and Midday most of all. The females sat at full attention now while the males, Midnight, Mushroom, and all-gray Frost, folded down to a crouch, much like Xander, using their paws for chin rests.

Little Wolf didn't sit or rest, but danced in place, impatient for his big brother.

Anya waited for Little Wolf to quiet. She didn't want to leave Flowers and her pup at the moment or call out and create any more disturbances. She continued her exam of the newborn husky; the male had spots similar to his mother. His fur was predominantly black and white but Anya could see splotches of brown and copper. The mask would be dark, she thought. The pup appeared healthy, eyes closed, wanting to suckle, not shivering, able to flex its paws and legs. The animal, if he lives, will be well-muscled . . . like Rune, she suddenly thought.

She wondered now about any names of Rune's gods. The pup must have a name. She would wait for Rune to return and give the pup a name. It just felt right. They both shared in this, both guardians, both fighting together, both willing to die together for the same cause. Yes, Rune should name the first Chukchi puppy born here. He'd earned the right.

If all the gods were with Rune, Chukchi and Viking, he would return soon. The snows could come any time with the season beginning to change. The ice could start moving in earnest, and block Rune out and away from Nome's waters, and from her. Just as she needed Xander's nearness and support to sustain her, she'd come to need Rune's, too. Used to having him close by, she hungered to see him again. She needed him to help fight their enemies that hid in the shadows, mortal and demon. At least she told herself that was the only reason.

The Gatekeepers watched.

They watched over Rune and Anya.

They understood the human spirit must prevail over the darkness upon them.

Shadows recast over the *Nordic,* slowing its passage across the Bering Sea, stirring up the waters and moving the ice. What had been a calm late summer's day turned to blustery winter in a heartbeat; in the split second needed to give life or take it away.

"Ice ahead!" one of the crew shouted.

"Man your stations!" another yelled out.

"How could this be?" still another called in panic.

Rune knew exactly how this could be. He was ready for the enemy, for the ghosts coming, hiding in the ice field that approached. With one hand kept firmly on the ship's wheel, Rune shoved open the wheelhouse window for a better look at the ice and the fight ahead. Confident in his crew to hold just as firm, he knew they relied on him as captain to steer away from threatening floes; seen now on the horizon visibly formed into a solid wall of ice capable of crushing their ship, when reached.

The trouble relentlessly pursuing started to brew during the twilight hours of night, showing itself more in the full light of day. The midnight sun burned still. The serpent wasn't afraid of Rune, obvious in the way it snarled and snaked its way toward him in swift, icy patterns. Rune wasn't afraid either. He meant to slay the serpent at whatever cost to himself, but he didn't want anyone else harmed, man or beast. This was between him and the enemy of his ancestors; not the others on board.

"Men, see to the dogs!" he yelled through the open window.

"Make sure the huskies are secure below, and then stay below with them! I need full steam ahead! That's an order!"

Rune knew his men would obey his orders on the dogs, with the help of Fox Ramsey and Vitya, the dog trader Rune had agreed to bring along. His crew would make sure the two men and all seventy dogs were below and safe, and would make sure to fuel the engines, but he couldn't rely on them to all stay out of harm's way. The crew would want to help their captain fight the seas, ice and all.

No loyal crewman worth his salt would do less. Guiding the *Nordic* through rough, still-ice-free waters, Rune didn't have time to leave the wheelhouse to check on his men. If his ship went down, he would go with it. Uppsala was never closer. Unaccustomed to prayer, Rune tilted his head to the Viking heavens and silently asked for safe passage for the *Nordic* and all on it, save for him. Let me be your sacrifice, he pled to Odin, me and me alone.

An outsider, someone from outside the mystic arctic north, would say, "It's just a summer storm brewing; only ice." Even insiders, those from the region—not seasoned sailors—might say the same. Not Rune. He wasn't from either known place but was a seasoned sailor in the moment, fighting unknown enemies from a dark world far away, coming in after the dogs, Anya's dogs. *Nine serpents he must slay . . . or be slain,* he finished his thought. He kept one hand still, on the ship's wheel, and the other he used to withdraw his Viking sword, readying for the fight. The moment he clasped the blade's handle, he could feel the sunstone of the Vikings in the same grasp; fixed to the sword in a powerful union of wisdom and war. He swallowed hard, his muscles taut, his eyes peeled on the white line of death coming.

"No! No! No!"

Anya screeched at the armed soldiers who came after her dogs, relentless in their mission to untie each one from their posts and take them from her. Two of the blue-coat soldiers held onto her, and threatened to take her to their army jail if she didn't cooperate. She fought them, kicking and biting and willing their souls to a pitiless death!

"Hold on there, little lady," one of the soldiers tried to reason. "We're just following orders. These dogs belong to the Bonanza Mining Company. We're here to deliver them proper so don't be fighting us."

"How'd a little Eskimo gal like you get hold of these critters anyways? Did you go and steal 'em?" the other recruit holding her accused. "Hey, maybe you're part white. I'll be doggoned if you're not," his voice drifted off.

Were these men the shamans from her village, come back to plague her still with their accusations and threats! They acted the same. They even smelled the same, like fat left out in the sun to rot! She fought the soldiers even harder. The shamans hadn't let go of her until she'd lost her dogs.

"These are the dogs of the Chukchi! They do not belong to

you! They do not belong to me!" she cried. This was no time for the whispers of Chukchi women but the roar of Chukchi men.

"Well, now, there you done admitted it, gal. These dogs don't belong to you and we're taking 'em to the Bonanza Mining Company where they *do* belong," the same soldier who accused her of theft snarled; obviously annoyed with the upstart half-breed.

Xander growled at the man who held his leash line, at the whip in the man's other hand. He heard the cries of his pack, all fighting the same hold. He eyed his guardian, seeing she was caught the same. He eyed Flowers and felt her fear. The roar inside him bubbled over. The rage inside him fought back.

"Son of a bitch!" the soldier holding Xander yelped.

Xander had bared his teeth and used them on the man's arm, the one holding the whip.

"Archie, take your gun and shoot this son-of-a-bitch cur dog! He done attacked me straight out!" The injured soldier held out his arm as proof of the deed, torn bloody sleeve and all.

"Can't you even handle one damn dog?" Archie called over to his comrade, his own hands full, holding two retrieved huskies himself.

Xander sensed his opening and took it, jerking his body hard, away from his captor, enough to break the hold on him. But he didn't run; his eyes on the whip. He went for it and ripped it out of the man's hand this time. He didn't hurt the man again but tore at the whip until it fell in pieces around him.

The rest of the pack barked wildly. All tried to break free from the holds on them.

The soldiers shouted over each other to keep a grip on the dogs and their prisoner.

"Don't let the gal loose! Gotta take her prisoner for the dog bite! Somebody's gotta pay for this!"

Anya broke free from his hold. Fear for Xander gave her the

strength to act, to grab the gun from the soldier that aimed at Xander. She turned the pistol on the soldier instead. She'd never shot a pistol but clicked the barrel, ready to kill to protect Xander.

"Listen, little lady, there's no need for that," the man targeted tried to reason; his words guarded. "I won't hurt the dog, all right?" he lied.

Xander rushed to Anya's side, baring his teeth at the enemy, ready to kill to protect his guardian.

Then, hit from behind, the pistol fell from Anya's hands. She and Xander were overtaken at the same time by more soldiers. The moment this happened, all the dogs quieted, their fight momentarily gone.

"Well now, a fine ruckus you're all making." Margret Johansson had come outside with Inga in tow. "Is this how the army is supposed to help, making all this fuss?"

Despite her hold, Anya careened around, her eyes boring holes through Rune's mother. This was *her* doing, hers and Inga's! She remembered the paper where she put her mark, when she thought she was helping Rune. It wasn't to help Rune. It was to *hurt* her and her dogs.

"Sorry about the fuss, ma'am," the corporal in charge of the mission quickly came up and said. "We'll have the dogs out of here and the girl, too, in a jiffy. One of the dogs bit one of our men. We have to take the girl to Fort Davis to answer for it. I'll bring her back here personally if the situation is cleared up."

"When might that be?" Margret warily intoned. "My husband will return from Port Lay soon. I'd like this to be cleared up by then. No sense in having feathers ruffled, Corporal."

"Ma'am, beg your pardon, but you don't need to worry. We have your paper here giving the Bonanza Mining Company ownership of your dogs. Won't be any feathers ruffled over a fair and square trade," he assured.

"Of course not," Margret agreed. "It's just that the captain might not take to the girl being gone. He brought her from Siberia and will want to take her back. That's all."

The blow hit Anya hard, her insides never more churned up. She'd never felt so betrayed; not even by Grisha. Rune's *own* mother and sister had dealt her this blow. They meant to get rid of her and her dogs. Inga's anger at her ran deep, Anya realized too late. Ice water ran in the mean girl's veins, freezing any good feeling she might have once had. Anya would no longer think of Margret or Inga as Rune's family. They were dead to her, *both*. Turning back around and away from their menacing looks, Anya managed to put her hand to Xander and sink her fingers into his comforting fur.

In the next moment, her hand went cold.

He'd been taken from her, stolen with the rest of the pack in an unfair trade.

Spirit raced around the edges of the Great Crag, the expanse ever widening and changing with the movement of arctic ice. The world of spirits in which she dwelled churned in upset with the Good just outdone by the Bad. Every ghost of every ancestor mourned the day. The Raven god had deserted. The fires of *Hel* burned against them. There were no untouchables in this fight; not even the Gatekeepers. All in their breed, all in their thousands of years of ancestry, risked extinction; spirit and mortal. It was up to Spirit now, Spirit and her mortal counterpart, to do whatever in their power to save generations of Chukchi worlds from dying out. She and Anya had been born to their respective worlds for this purpose; both the first of their kind, half spirit and half mortal, able to travel between worlds—up to them not to be the last of their kind.

Shadows came and went. Ghosts swirled past. Some poked and prodded in mischief while others stroked and soothed in guardian touch. Spirit ignored them all. She ached to plunge into the depths beneath the Great Crag and rip apart the demons hiding there, but canine instinct held her back. She must wait for Anya to give the signal. Pacing and pawing the edges of the Great Crag, hungry and thirsty for the fight, the wait would be hard.

The no-name pup, Flowers's pup, stayed hunkered inside the upset crate, settling beneath what straw he could find for shelter. His watch-blue eyes had opened soon after his birth, fixed sure on the dark, empty space around him. No mother. No guardian. No one was there to help the no-name pup. Hungry, thirsty for any drink of life, the pup nestled beneath the straw and waited. His energy drained. The lonely pup whimpered, sensing no one heard; no one would come. Tired of this life just given him, the pup shut its eyes and waited for sleep. His newfound instincts cried for no more than that.

Beside herself with worry, Anya demanded her crude knife back from the jailer who just freed her. It hadn't been one week, but two, since she'd been put behind bars; left there in the dark with little food and water. For so many to be upset with her, throwing her into this prison because Xander bit one of them, no one appeared concerned about her at this time except the jailer letting her out. She'd received no punishment other than imprisonment and no word from any who had brought her here—no word on the dogs. When she'd tried to reach her Spirit to escape, she couldn't. All her pleas to all the gods had gone unanswered until now. The Gatekeepers opened the way for her, she believed. They controlled in this one thing on Native Earth, at last able to find a path for her. Her knife was returned. The season of snow would come anytime. She'd nothing to lose.

A thin channel separated Fort Davis from Nome. Grabbing up her seal-fur parka from its rumpled pile on the floor outside her cell, she rushed past the disinterested guard to the open air. She needed to cross the three miles to Nome. She breathed in the scent of musty tents, fishy quarters, burnt cookfires, and spent munitions, coughing past the unpleasant odors. Her keen senses led her to the pure, unmistakable scent of the danger ahead, on land and over arctic waters. The season of summer to frost had arrived. Two weeks of time lost and possibly lives lost drove her on, running fast, hard, and strong; pushing her past her limits.

The only lives she didn't fear for were Margret and Inga Johansson's.

She didn't think of them at all.

"Where is Anya and where are her dogs?"

Lars tried not to yell at his wife and daughter. Just returned from Port Lay up north, with the *Storm* securely anchored off Nome's shores, he was already agitated at not seeing Rune returned, too. By this time his son should have the *Nordic* anchored here. This wasn't good. His nightmares foretold of this. It wasn't good.

"I've told you, Lars," Margret kept up her lies. "Soon after you left, Anya did too; *with* her dogs. I'm as surprised as you, she's not here."

"Did you try to find her? Did you ask around?" he fired.

Margret hesitated.

"I did, Papa." Inga stepped in with the continued deception. "I asked *for* Mama. I asked white men and Eskimos . . . didn't I?" The daughter looked to the mother for support.

"Eh, yes. Yes you did," Margret said, her voice strained.

Lars eyed them both, suspicious but with no time to grill them anymore. Worry over Rune and Anya plagued him.

"Lars," Margret whined, seeing she had her husband's attention. Unwittingly she shook her head a bit, then straightened, as if she'd cleared away any nuisance cobwebs from her thoughts. "Inga and I are of the same mind. We want to return to Seattle. Summer is over and we need to travel before winter shuts us in this no-man's land. The frontier is just too much for either of us to take on. You should never have expected us to live in such a dreadful place."

"Not even for your son, Margret?" He turned his glare to his daughter then. "Not even for your brother, would you stay?"

Margret stepped protectively in front of Inga.

"Really, Lars, you don't have to be so dramatic. We just want to live in our home in Seattle. Is that asking too much?"

How was a husband, a father, to answer such a question with such a wife and daughter? They didn't speak the same language and right now didn't belong in the same family with Rune. His beloved son was out there facing God-only-knew-what, while his so-called family cared little about him. All they cared about were themselves. He finally saw that, clear as the alert bell on any of his ships. Soon as he could, he'd get them on one of his ships and leave them in Seattle for good.

"Where are you going?" Margret demanded of Lars's back, following him out the front door of their imposing home.

He didn't bother to answer.

He didn't want to bother with her at all.

Rune could hear the dogs bark above the gale-force winds despite their bluster, all seventy dogs at once, howling against the storm raging above deck. The *Nordic* rocked dangerously, hard to keep steady. Waves splashed onto the ship's decks and threatened to topple them. Anything not tied down flew overboard. The dark day grew darker, as if trying to shield the ice from view. Dark spirits ruled these waters, Rune knew.

Anything could happen. He was ready for Valhalla but *not to leave Anya.*

"May Odin and Thor and all the gods of my ancestors keep watch over this day," he found himself praying out loud. His rasped whispers quickly carried away on arctic winds. He prayed silently that someone would hear.

When the ice hit, the *Nordic* would either split under the crush and sink, or overturn and then sink. The only possible way to escape was to outrun the ice. Rune didn't think that was possible but he had to try.

"More fuel! More steam!" he yelled down to his engine room. The crew fueling the ship's power should hear him, waiting for such commands, their trained ears on the wheelhouse. He wouldn't have to keep shouting commands. The men knew well enough what they all faced. Rune focused on the edges of the approaching ice. Even in the now-dim light he could see the edges better than only minutes before. Concentration will do that.

Rune alerted every muscle in his body to remember everything he'd learned in a lifetime at sea. Focus and your vision will come, day or night. The sunstone of the Vikings pulsed in his hand and in his head. Keep your eyes on the horizon. When it shifts and sways and you lose your even keel, you must keep level the bearing in your mind's eye. Keep your focus on the enemy coming and keep your fears hidden. Only a clear mind will keep the blade and the broad ax razor sharp. Such was the lesson of his ancestors.

Rune watched the ice advance. He watched its edges *turn red.* It wasn't just one serpent laying siege to the *Nordic,* but many . . . too many to count, all dragging the ice to him. The Midgard serpent had risen from the depths of *Hel,* and had surfaced to feed. Animal horns of Rune's ancestors sounded in his head, signaling battle and sharpening his wits to the enemy coming.

He saw one serpent—he saw the many.

Fear threatened to choke.

He swallowed it back

His heart pounded the drumbeat of war.

The enemy had a clear face now. Yellow eyes were all on him, beady eyes pointing to death. Jowls opened below the eyes, thin mouths at first, then widened to reveal twisted blood-dripping teeth. The serpents kept coming, fusing together, the white line turned redder. The serpents conjoined their silvery blue and black-streaked bodies in killing force, and maneuvered swiftly through rough water, side by side, yet as one. None had scales, only what looked to Rune like gelatinous waste, doubtless glued there by the decay of time, by the death of its victims.

He couldn't see the end of the serpents; their long bony, red-dorsal-finned bodies blended with the misshapen juts of ice clumped together, to better strike. The giant serpents were part of the ice, Rune could see. Their heads had red fins jutting up in flaps and tips like cocky crowns. Each had two red-soaked pelvic fins that stood out, like oars, and gave the appearance of rowing toward him; likened to coming through the arctic waters on a proud Viking ship just to upset their victim all the more. Rune could smell their bloody intent. It didn't throw him off.

He knew now.

The Midgard serpent was one—and it was many.

It could divide and conquer at will.

The water appeared to spark electric ahead of the serpents, as it flashed across the seas like the borealis might in the skies. The sea monster seemed drawn to the light, to life, to feed on its victims and end their lives. This struck Rune hard, seeing the irony of the aurora borealis, the lights in the Northern skies giving life, used for such evil purpose. *Hel* couldn't burn brighter than these demonic streaks of lightning in the waters. Rune's fingers clenched the handle of his sword, itching for his own strike.

Setting the wheel of the *Nordic* on the safest course he could, he tied it in place. The men below would keep the steam up. The ship would have to weather the storm in this way, without him in the wheelhouse. The dogs, he hoped, kept a steady footing below. Fox Ramsey and the Chukchi dog trader, too. Whatever would come was on Rune's head, he knew; not theirs. If any below were to survive this onslaught, he had to get in the belly of the beast and kill it. Just how, he'd no idea. Racing down the slippery, wave-thrashed steps from the wheelhouse, he held onto his sword for dear life; his only lifeline, he believed.

The *Nordic* rocked too hard for Rune to keep any kind of decent footing. He managed to get to the ship's rail for a good hold and a better look at what was coming. Dazed by some of the waves, he shook his head to clear it and the hair plastered across his line of vision. He spat out the water in his face; not wanting to swallow any of it. The salt was polluted with blood, the iron taste, repugnant.

He *spat* at the serpent coming, at the one, at all of them!

CHAPTER THIRTEEN

The puppy had to be dead after so long a time.

Even if Anya found Xander and Flowers's pup, she didn't think Thor would be alive. *Thor!* How did the name come? She didn't have time to think on it with the young dog's life in the balance. The day had grown dark and her heavy step uneven. Tired from worry and the distance covered, fear for the dogs, especially the pup and Xander, added anguish to every direction she trod.

If only she could stop shaking. Her chills got in the way.

Just as worried for Rune, today somehow worse than others, she thought she heard him call to her across the Directions. Her emotional state clouded her thinking. She must stay focused. Stopping short, she forced a deep inhale. The frost-tinged air helped alert her senses. She exhaled, slow and sure. Her chills faded. Closing her eyes, she demanded calm. There was no time to wait for the trance of shamans. She must demand it of herself, *now.*

Shamans could heal.

That more than any other thought sent her straight to Rune's house, to the back dog yard he'd helped her create. In the time it takes for a heart to beat, giving life or ending it, she had the wood crate righted, the canvas flap thrown open and found little Thor. The pup was alive, barely; buried deep in a pocket of clumped straw.

To the untrained eye, the pup would be called dead on the

223

spot. Not to Anya. She sensed the life in little Thor even if she couldn't see signs of it at the moment. His little fur-spotted body was still warm to the touch, her first clue; a tiny wince at her touch, the second. But that was all. Anya knew he was close to death; too weak for anything but this final action. He'd no energy left for this life.

Anya thought she heard Zellie howl down from the heavens, calling in mournful acknowledgment. Anya heard the sorrow of what might have been in that call. So much life was left to live in Zellie when hers was cut short. She might have had the pup over which she grieved now. Anya gingerly scooped up the lifeless pup and put him to her cheek.

"There, there, little one," she whispered softly. "My Zellie watches over you like a mother. There, there."

Thor didn't suffer from anything naturally caused. Anya had lost other pups due to natural causes, having witnessed many births back in her village. It was never easy but she had to accept their loss. Not this time and not with this pup. There was nothing "natural" about what happened here. Something evil caused this. Something evil caused Thor's mother to be taken from him, then leave him abandoned for nearly two weeks. The pup was Chukchi. Evil didn't count on that.

Anya thought of Flowers, but even if she found Thor's mother, it might not be in time, and Flowers's milk might be dried. Anya wouldn't let herself think anything else might have happened to Flowers. Her pup was in trouble. Time ran out. Tucking the puppy into the deep pocket of her kerker, Anya followed her next impulse and hurried straight for Chinook's trade store. She made it there without being noticed or stopped by anybody.

★ ★ ★ ★ ★

The sight of a young, fur-clad, half-native girl running along the streets of Nome was not likely to strike any frontiersmen as odd.

The busy season of summer had ended and winter fast approached. No one had time for anything but going through their to-do list. The list was long. Residents had to lay in supplies and make sure of provisions; shut down summer mining and plan for winter drift work; weigh every speck of gold dust mined; shore up their homes where needed, fill in a chink here, a chink there; get out of Nome if home was in Seattle or otherwise, before the ice hemmed them in; settle into whatever winter work they might find; make sure of their business interests: make sure of their access to mail and freight lines; repair sleds for use over snow and ice; and collect their dogs to begin to train the huskies they intended to run in the next All Alaska Sweepstakes. The prize money and the status of winning the prestigious race were foremost on the minds of all veteran mushers and most first-timers in and around the Seward Peninsula.

The last storms of summer still blew fiercely, but the storms should have come and gone by this point. The August through September storms normally brought wind and rain like no other time of the year, yet no one expected this intensity to linger. This, more than any other issue before them, got notice from frontiersmen. Wind whipped down every street and through every crack and cranny in Nome. Buildings rattled and shook in the powerful conditions. Water poured in from the Bering Sea, creating new rivers to avoid and more mud in which to sink. The joke that much of Nome was water was no joke to locals; especially with these storms that wouldn't let go.

All of it would freeze soon enough, freezing them in time until spring thaw. Even residents in Nome, all stalwart and used to putting their shoulders to it, needed some break between seasons. The longer the summer storms hung on, the more locals realized they wouldn't get any break this time around. The water, the mud, the snow, the ice were all here to stay. There was always next year, many tried to tell themselves, after the big race coming in spring. That was something to hold on to, something welcome in the onslaught of relentless storms.

Locals already buzzed with names of dog drivers and their teams. They talked about all the dogs that might race, about all the malamute and mixed huskies who would compete. The Siberian huskies that came in so close on the heels of Scotty Allen, the "Siberian rats" who ran so impressively despite their smaller size and number, were all but forgotten. No one really thought of them and when they did, it was never to imagine they would run again in the All Alaska Sweepstakes. The big race was for big dogs, and for locals, not foreign breeds. The good showing made by the Siberian team was an exception to this rule. It wouldn't happen again.

When men met in saloons to talk over teams, they toasted their own; never the little Siberian team. Besides, there weren't enough of them around to be any competition.

"Canned milk? What is that?" Anya asked Chinook incredulously, at the same time she took little Thor from her pocket. He couldn't weigh much over a pound. He'd had milk from his mother but failed to thrive after that, when all nourishment had been ripped away. Anya had to get milk in the pup and give him enough to instill a will to live in him. She'd come to the trade store to see if any of Chinook's dogs had milk and would let Thor nurse.

Worried, she doubted the pup could even suckle.

Chinook took down a can of the guarded milk from his store shelf. No one else was inside to trade since the day for marketing had ended. No sooner did he set the can on his sawbuck counter, than he drew out his knife and stabbed an opening in the metal. The light on the counter was dying. Chinook pulled a lantern close and lit the oil. A whale bladder hung from a nearby peg. He yanked it down and filled it with some of the contents of the can, then handed it to Anya.

"Put a tiny hole in the bladder. The pup will suckle."

Mutely, Anya took the bladder bag in one hand and held Thor in the other.

Chinook took down a caribou sleeping blanket and arranged it on the counter.

Anya carefully lay Thor down and quickly made the necessary hole for him to drink. As she'd feared, when she tried to get him to nurse, he couldn't. He wasn't strong enough. This would take time, but she could do it. She would slowly drip milk into his mouth and force it down to his stomach. She needed a thin hollow of kelp root or animal sinew or bone or *something* to allow the passage of liquid to his stomach. Once, she'd seen this done by Grisha to save a sick dog, using a thin hollow to guide milk to the stomach to sustain life. Frantic for something to use herself now, Anya spotted a long, clear stretch of animal intestine, already dried; already thinned and supple for ties. With Chinook's help she rolled the paper-thin lining into a thin hollow, tiny and firm, enough to reach Thor's stomach.

She had to rely on the miracle of shamans to guide her, with no idea if this would work, or if she would kill Thor in her attempt to save him. The tube could tear his young insides.

Her hands trembled.

Chinook put a sure hand over hers, and offered a smile of encouragement.

Willing her hands to be sure, she let Chinook hold the puppy in position while she passed the makeshift tube down his throat.

Thor reacted reflexively but didn't come awake. Anya kept up her ministrations long enough to believe she'd reached his stomach. Once the tube was in, she slowly poured some of the canned milk into the tube, careful to have provided a funnel of sorts. After waiting the time she thought necessary, she repeated the same action, and did so until a portion of the can was gone.

"It is all we can do for now," she whispered to Chinook, steeped in doubt that she hadn't done enough to save Thor.

"Yes," the elder Chinook agreed, then settled the still-out pup on its bed of fur.

"Can I stay here with Thor?" Anya whispered her question.

"Yes. I will come back to open trade in the morning. You can stay and keep watch."

Anya smiled half-heartedly at Chinook and watched him close the door, then put her full attention back onto Thor. Relieved he hadn't died from her jarring his insides, she was ready with the hollow tube and more milk if needed. She was also ready with the bladder of milk if he could suckle. He had a chance at life; a small one, but a chance nonetheless. At least he wasn't alone.

He had her . . . and he had Zellie.

Cold fear shot through Anya. But did he still have his mother?

"*Just* dogs, you say," Lars Johansson called out the manager of the Bonanza Mining Company.

Lars had been searching for Anya and her dogs all day through in Nome, luckily finding out from some of the miners who worked at the Bonanza diggings that they'd recently gotten a team of "sad, small huskies" to help carry their loads. The men laughed around their whiskey table at the Discovery Saloon over the rat dogs that worked with them. They didn't seem to have any idea of the Siberian team, of the big race they'd run.

"They're no freight dogs; that's for sure. They stumble at the heavy loads," one said, chuckling after he did.

"Damned if the mine manager didn't up and shoot the one most injured. Won't have to carry nuthin' anymore," another man remarked without emotion. He didn't laugh.

None of the miners knew anything about a girl, Eskimo or otherwise, coming to their digs after the new dogs. Lars stopped asking around once he exited the Discovery Saloon, and headed straight for the Bonanza mining operation. Anya would never have let her dogs go willingly, he believed. Rune was away when they were taken. So was he.

He'd left Anya in *Margret's* keeping, thinking to make the trip up to Port Lay and back before now. The trade took longer than expected and he hadn't minded that. It made him feel better to work at full tilt. It helped him forget his troubles—his worries over Rune. Lars knew now that he should have been more worried over Anya.

Margret had done this, Margret and Inga. What he didn't know was why. He'd deal with them later.

Lars had hold of Jed Braxton's boiled shirt collar, in his face, angry at the mine manager. Lars stood nearly a foot taller and had more weight on him than the lesser man.

"You're coming with me and we're going to find each and every dog you stole from my daughter, Anya," he said without realizing his claim of her.

"I . . . we didn't steal—"

Lars cut Braxton off, the manager sputtered for air as it was.

"I know you shot one of them. You tell me which one. You show me the body and then you find the other seven Siberian huskies. If you don't I'll bring more than the United States Army down on you," Lars threatened. He let go of Braxton's collar, only to shove the man out the door of his mining office with no jacket.

Lars had brought his own pistol, not hiding it from anybody.

He wanted everyone at the mine to know he meant business and would use his gun on them if that's what this took. No one needed to worry about fetching the law. *He* was the law.

At first glance, it didn't look like anything was wrong. Men plowed into their work, sluicing and dredging and shooting water over hills of dirt, hydraulics still in full gear. Freight dogs pulled carts laden with rocks large and small, heavy supplies, and even men, to and fro through the thick slush. The busy season would have to come to a halt, thanks to the weather, but at present the men tried to keep up their work.

A few miners would hop in and out of dog-pulled carts as if for fun. That got Lars's attention. That was wrong. Then he noticed a whip in one of the men's hands. Then he saw it used on one of the dogs. This wasn't a freight dog. It was a husky, but too small. It had to be one of Anya's. On closer look, he recognized the copper-red and white husky. The dog slumped to the ground when the lash struck, and yelped in pain.

"Get up, you cur dog!" The man still held the whip over the husky but not for long. He fell to the ground next to Magic, out cold from Lars's fist.

"I swear I didn't know the dog supervisor had the damn whip. *I swear*," Jed Braxton tried to defend himself.

Lars knew better. Lars knew the man lied through his teeth.

"Braxton, I swear on all that's holy, if you don't help me find the rest of my daughter's dogs, I'll take care of you myself, here, *now*." Lars meant every word.

The threat wasn't empty and the mine manager knew it.

"Tell me first which one you killed."

"The . . . the other one . . . the other dog . . . that looked like this one," Braxton stumbled with his admission. "It couldn't work . . . it slowed us down—"

"Show me where the dog is buried, you bastard."

"I can't."

Lars clicked the barrel of his gun.

"What did you say?" he leveled.

"I can't show you the dead dog. I tossed it on one of our burn piles." Jed Braxton couldn't look Lars in the eye on this. Maybe his conscience had caught up with him.

Lars swallowed hard; the pain of what he'd have to tell Anya refused to go down easy. The cruelty of men overwhelmed him. Nature's cruelty, he understood. Not this.

Magic had gotten up. She stood on weak legs, enough to move away from the fallen man. Blood streaked across her back and hind legs. The whip had left its mark.

Lars kept his gun on Jed Braxton; at the same time he approached the injured dog.

Magic let him remove her harness, then slumped to the ground a second time.

"You," Lars yelled at a miner nearby who had been watching the scene. "Take care of this dog until I come back for her."

The miner nodded he would.

"I have your word?" Lars underscored.

"You do," the man said.

Lars switched his full attention back on Braxton.

"Find the rest. For your sake, they better be alive."

Jed Braxton continued to stumble, this time down the rocky paths of the Bonanza mining digs, praying on every misstep he'd find the rest of the no-count-rat-dogs . . . *alive.*

Too late for Mushroom; the valiant sled dog was dead and burned.

Thor began to suckle from the opening in the whale bladder bag, as if from his mother's teat.

Anya's fingers shook, she was so excited, but she had to hold steady to feed the young pup. *He will live,* she realized. At the same time she thanked all of her gods and Rune's for saving

Thor. What else but powers beyond this world could bring life back when it had all but disappeared, with the pup weakened so from want of nourishment.

To see him nurse at the bag and even put his little front paws to it, kneading as he would against his mother, was a miracle. Anya didn't know if he'd pull through until this moment. Pups could die from lesser problems. Oftentimes, any problem would cause the mother to neglect them, to let nature take its course, and take the life just given her. It was never easy to witness, Anya soberly recalled.

With one hand Anya kept the bag pressed close to Thor, and with the other she splayed her fingers over his body in an attempt to offer comfort, and cuddle him. Upset that something might have hurt Flowers, thinking of Thor's mother, Anya knew Flowers had not neglected her newborn pup. She'd been ripped away from Thor, torn away by something *unnatural*. Anya had to find Flowers and reunite mother and pup, anxious for them to bond again, for each to recognize the other's scent again, for each to know the other's warmth and unconditional love yet again—and for each to know the other hadn't left them.

Thor nestled inside the folds of the caribou sleeping blanket, still arranged on top of Chinook's store counter. Anya stood by him, as she had the night through. She continued to keep her hands circled around him; not his mother but the next best thing, she hoped.

"Don't you worry, Thor," she whispered over him. "I'll find your mother. I will."

At just that moment, Chinook opened the door of his trade store and walked in. He looked at the pup and then Anya.

"This is good," he said to Anya, his smile beaming. He could see the Siberian husky pup had survived the treatment, and also knew the treatment in this case might well be worse than the cure. The milk would strengthen the little husky, enough to get him past this tricky time. If no infection set in over the next days, the pup should be fine. He would love to have such a pup. The Siberian husky would add strength to his village dog breed. But it was not the time to put such a question to the Chukchi girl.

"Yes," Anya said to the Eskimo. "It is good that little Thor made it to this beautiful day."

Chinook smiled again. The day outside was far from beautiful. Sleet rained down, same as the day before, only today the winds howled louder and blew longer. He knew what Anya meant; that she was happy the pup lived still. *Thor,* she'd named him. He'd never heard such a name and wondered where it came from.

"Why do you call the pup Thor?" That question, he could ask her.

Anya stroked Thor's back with two fingers, gently, so not to stir him away from suckling, but enough to show him the love she felt. She stalled for time. She didn't have any answer for Chinook.

"I—I'd heard the name somewhere, that's all."

"Not from anywhere around here, I don't think," Chinook was quick to respond. He could see it on the girl's face. The name had come to her on the winds. She was special, this girl. All of a sudden he sensed something about her he hadn't before, as if she communicated with spirits and could talk to them. Chinook had the same feeling around the shamans in his village. They could talk to spirits. This little Siberian girl was no shaman and he shouldn't waste his time believing she might be.

"Where did you hear the name, Thor?" Chinook pressed, curious still.

Thor had finished suckling milk and had fallen asleep. Anya picked him up and held him over her heart, settling him close. His tiny heartbeats sped. This was normal for one so young.

"Wh—"

"I don't know where I heard the name," she said.

Chinook believed her. He also believed she *could* have some of the same spiritual powers of the shamans, seeing the trance-like look on her face. She'd also been able to *heal* the pup. Yes, Chinook had helped her, but hers was the touch of spirit needed to heal little Thor.

The pup roused and whimpered slightly.

Music to Anya's ears.

And to Chinook's.

"Thank you," Anya looked up at Chinook, in earnest.

He said nothing, and nodded back.

"I need to ask you something," she said softly in her Chukchi whisper. "I must find the rest of my dogs. Will you take care of Thor while I do? I have no one else to help me," she said, embarrassed she had to ask him. "When I can, I will come back for him. I will pay you back for the milk, too."

Chinook nodded his yes to her and held out his hands to take the pup.

"Go and find your Siberian huskies. I will keep Thor safe for you," he promised. While he wished she'd given him the pup for good, he would honor her wishes. To do otherwise would anger the gods, he suddenly thought. He felt spirits all around again, this time good ones. He'd sensed bad spirits around the boy, dangerous spirits that chased the boy and this girl. Chinook wanted to help if he could.

Chinook couldn't communicate with spirits, or see them, or hear them, but he could feel their presence, as many in his village often could. The Eskimo believed in the spirits and therefore were attuned to them. Chinook imagined the same held true for the Chukchi.

Anya reluctantly handed Thor over to Chinook. Having just found the pup, she hated to let him go but she'd no choice. She trusted the Eskimo. She *had* to. Right now she'd no choice in this, either.

"The mines," Chinook said, holding Thor a moment before he replaced him onto the caribou blanket. The fur acted as a safeguard against any chill for the young pup. Chinook arranged it close.

"What do you mean?" Anya didn't understand.

"Most dogs that are lost show up at one mine or the next. The white man will do anything to get dogs and keep them for work to get the yellow metal. Your dogs could have been taken to work the mines," Chinook advised.

The mines. Anya remembered how strange and terrible some had looked, built high with rivers of water gushing over steep drop-offs into deep, dark mud pits. *Graves,* she thought, graves opened up for her dogs! A worse chill shot through her. Was she imagining it or did she really hear the dogs yelp in pain? The winds outside the trade store blew strong, she finally noticed. It wasn't a beautiful, calm day as she'd first thought. It was an awful day.

"I must go," was all she could manage to say before she opened the door and squeezed it shut behind her. She didn't think of Thor now, but of his mother. She couldn't think of one of the dogs in danger without realizing they were *all* in danger. She couldn't think of Xander over the others. Where? Which mine? Where to start? Winds whirled and whooshed by so swiftly she couldn't get a read on any Direction! She must. This wild territory was too big and there were too many mines to search to find the dogs before . . . before something might happen to them. Already, she'd lost two weeks.

If Anya had been able, she would have prayed in a proper way to the Morning Dawn and to all the gods of the Chukchi to help her. Too anxious to stop and pray, too upset when she realized Rune couldn't help her, she ran to find the first trail that led out of Nome. She couldn't read any of the signs, but she could follow a path well enough. The poor weather wouldn't stop her. Before, she'd found the dogs from their howls across the open. She'd been able to read the signs given in their howls, given through the sounds. It took all of her concentration to sort out what sounds she could hear while she rushed along the trail.

She'd no way of knowing it, but the first path she'd decided to take took her to the Bonanza Mining Company. Inside of an hour she'd been reunited with six of her dogs, thanks to Lars Johansson.

"*Dead,* you say?"

Anya tried to understand what the captain told her, but she refused to believe it. His words didn't want to register. He'd said "the other copper-red and white dog was dead." Anya went numb. The truth suddenly hit: Magic stood in front of her. Mushroom *did not.* Neither did Xander.

"Where is Xander?" she heard herself ask, numb inside and afraid to hear more bad news.

Lars had to go easy. He could see how upset Anya was becoming.

"You mean the black and white husky?" He hoped he'd given a correct description.

"Yes, Xander," she answered, barely above a whisper. She looked over the rest of the dogs the captain had with him, but had trouble pulling them into clear focus, and keeping her mind steady. Fear will do that. Flowers was there. So was Midday, and then Midnight. Little Wolf and Frost, too. Six. That makes six—six *without* Mushroom and Xander.

Anya tried to process what this meant. She fought her upset and her guilt. Grief over Mushroom's death blanketed her in mourning but she tried to throw it off. She had to. She had to find Xander before she let herself cry over the beloved copper-red and white twin to Magic.

"I don't know where Xander is, child," Lars explained. "No one at the mine could tell me. They hadn't seen the black and white Siberian husky for a couple of days."

"A couple of days . . ." Anya's voice trailed, caught over what to do. She didn't want to leave the six surviving dogs but she wanted to try and find Xander. He could still be alive. That thought alone was all that kept her on her feet, when she wanted to drop to the ground and cry out her heartache to all the gods of the Chukchi. The Gatekeepers had to be upset with her for her poor watch over the dogs, but she didn't worry about that. She wanted their comfort and their guide to help find Xander.

"Anya," Lars began. "Come with me back to my house. You can keep the dogs there."

"No!" She lunged for the ties to the dogs and tried to grab them from the captain's hands. When he didn't let her have them, she got madder. "I do not trust Margret and Inga! They are bad. They traded my dogs away. They are not good. I do not trust them!"

Any feeling Lars still had for his wife and daughter died in that moment. He'd suspected as much but didn't realize how far Margret had gone in this bad business. Anya didn't lie about this. Margret and Inga had.

"What happened to you when the dogs were taken?" he asked soberly.

"You mean stolen! The dogs were stolen!"

Lars tried to keep steady and not reveal to Anya how upset he was for her, and at his wife and daughter.

"What happened to you when the dogs were *stolen?*" he asked again.

"The soldiers from the fort took me to their jail. Two weeks I was there. Two weeks away from my dogs. I let Mushroom down. I should have been there. I should have saved him. It's my fault," she began to cry.

"Child, it's not your fault. If you could, you would never have let your dogs be sent to the hard mines. Some of the men who work the dogs mistreat them. They caused this. Margret and Inga caused this. *Not* you, Anya." Lars wanted to say how sorry he was but he couldn't find the right words, any way to apologize for such evil and trickery. Anything he thought to say sounded empty to him.

Anya didn't feel any better. She felt guilty. She was shaman. She was supposed to heal! *Some guardian* was all she could think; some guardian she made. Downhearted and tired, with no sleep for days, she did her best to focus on the six dogs in front of her.

They all looked worn, she could see now. They'd been whipped! The telling marks covered each one. Spirit or mortal, it made little difference to her at the moment. She cursed whatever and whoever did this to the valiant, hardworking Chukchi dogs. This was a cruel place, this land of Alaska, she said to herself.

Magic whimpered; her watch eyes looked as sad as Anya's.

Midday and Midnight opened their jowls and yawned out their whimpers, almost talking.

Frost sat, and kept his watch-blue eyes fixed on Anya.

Little Wolf looked lost without Xander near. Anya knew just how he felt.

Then there was Flowers. Anya crouched down to her.

"Your little one is all right," she whispered, as if the husky could understand. Anya rubbed behind Flowers's ears and gave her a kiss on her mask. "Thor is waiting for his mother."

Flowers licked Anya's face, as if in answer.

Anya realized the miracle in front of her, that at least six dogs had survived the cruel whip. At the hands of a mortal, yes, but driven by the bad spirits after them.

"Captain, the dogs must not go back to your house. It is not safe." She stood up and faced him.

"All right," he said, understanding why she didn't want to return to his house. He didn't either. "We can find another shelter for them, a safer one this time." Rune would do the same thing, he realized.

"I know a village, an Eskimo village, the village of Chinook, who runs the trade store in Nome. He will help us," she told Lars and hoped she spoke true. It was the best place she could think of, and she trusted Chinook by this time.

"Captain, when we get to the village, will you stay with the dogs and watch over them until I return?"

"Yes."

"Promise me?"

"Yes, Anya, I promise you I will stay with your dogs." He didn't have to ask where she was going. He knew. Believing she was too young to battle such problems, Lars wished he could keep Anya with him at the Eskimo village and try to protect her, along with her dogs. But he knew better. With the awful news that one of her dogs had been killed, she didn't want to risk the same thing happening to another. She had to find Xander.

Lars hoped the animal would still be alive when she did.

CHAPTER FOURTEEN

"For three days they ran, and the ice field relentlessly followed, always gaining . . ."

Yuri Rytkheu, *The Chukchi Bible*

The red serpent hadn't overtaken Rune and the *Nordic,* yet.

The ice had tried to push and shove and grind the ship down
into the sea, battering at its hull, being able to move in ways
meant to strike the most fear. The icy beast acted with cunning
and arrogance, almost human in its show of might over those it
targeted. Close to the ship for days, the ice hadn't moved in for
the kill, seemingly wanting to torture and terrify first, as a crazed
murderer might with its victim.

The sea had already claimed two of Rune's crew.

The struggle with the ice had been exhausting for all of the
men. Most ignored their captain's orders to stay below deck
and, instead, tried to help him save the ship. Those in the engine
room didn't leave their post and fought to power the *Nordic* out
of harm's way. Fuel ran low. Some of the men couldn't help,
too injured after accidents caused by the ship's crushing blows
from the enemy ice. It was amid such an attack that two of the
crew died. One was bludgeoned by a loose mast and fell
unconscious to the deck, and when his mate tried to save him,
they both slid into the frozen depths, gone in a heartbeat. Helpless to do anything, others watched in horror.

Most in the crew had heard tales of such ice fields giving

chase but few had experienced a time that rivaled these relentless days of peril. There was no escaping the ice, they realized. The ship couldn't make enough headway to outrun it. It had them encircled; at least that's what the men felt in their gut. The ice might not have completely caught them up yet, but it was only a matter of time. Some wanted to give up. Some already had; the greenhorn rookies especially. Death was no stranger in the Arctic. The veteran crew signed on for this, and didn't blame their captain. The boy was able, like his father.

That first day, with the first hit of the ice field, Rune Johansson proved he was no coward when they saw him leave the wheelhouse and come down to fight in the belly of the beast. What he did on that day still had them scratching their heads. Those who watched couldn't believe what they saw! Like a pirate might, Rune put a blade of some sort in his mouth and lowered himself to the water over ropes on the starboard side of the *Nordic*. He managed this, despite the rough seas.

To a man, no one thought Rune was a captain deserting his ship, suddenly gone mad and deciding to jump into the eye of the storm to a certain death. They instinctively knew he was in the fight, not just for his life, but for all of them. There's no explanation for why they knew this. Call it wishful thinking. Call it years of traveling the legendary, mystic arctic waters. Call it myth and folktales handed down over the years. Caught up in such disbelief at the sight before them, anything was possible. As crazy as Rune looked to them, they didn't think him crazy. Still, they all said their own goodbyes to Captain Rune Johansson the moment he disappeared over the side. The seas stayed rough. They all had a job to do if any expected to live through this.

Forced to, they had to forget about their captain.

But Rune didn't forget about them, or Anya and her dogs on that fateful day.

Since these sacrificial moments would be his last . . . he saw Anya's image before him, the girl he loved. He would take this image to the golden halls of Valhalla, into eternity. Not for a second did Rune think he could slay this greatest of serpents, but he had to try. He believed in the Viking sword he'd been given. He believed he carried the might of war in one hand and the power of wisdom in the other. Most of all, he believed he had to somehow save the men and the dogs on board ship. They were his responsibility and he would save them, or die trying.

When he'd hurtled over the side of the *Nordic,* he followed his instincts to slay the beast but didn't have any plan beyond that. His mortal being had already left this world, gone to the fight ahead. Electricity shot through the heavens and sparked and spat at the unbroken, unending thickness of ice. This emboldened Rune; the gods are with me, he'd thought.

Rune had reached the bottom of his ropes, where the great red serpent waited for him, its thick, icy jowls open and dripping blood. Rune took his sword in hand. In every direction, he could see the freeze thicken and cement together in a killing field of solid ice. A sea of yellow eyes fixed on him. The enemy wasn't afraid. The blood of war polluted the air. Rune tightened his fingers around the blade's handle. He wasn't afraid, either. In one quick strike he aimed, then sent his Viking sword into the serpent's mouth, his hit sure. The ice field suddenly whined and creaked, then cracked, causing the great field to break up into a sea of ice floes; still dangerous but less so.

Sea smoke covered the scene. To the naked eye, the arctic storm had changed and veered direction, enough to cause cracks and schisms to break up the pack ice, and enough to allow an avenue of possible escape. Rune knew better. His work was still cut out for him—to navigate away from the treacherous ice floes and avoid them—but he knew the truth of what just happened. It defied reality. He scrambled up the swaying and knocking

443 N. 6th St
Grand Junction Co 81501

CAYLARA

ropes, then climbed back over the rail and planted both feet firmly on the *Nordic's* deck.

Besides the men on board, he feared for the dogs.

The weather still chased them. The winds blew fierce and the temperatures dropped, unseasonably colder. Ice floes nipped and jarred where they could. No, this wasn't over, but at least the beast had been injured enough for its forces to break up and cause it to be weakened, Rune believed.

He held out his hands in front of him.

His Viking sword was gone; a sacrifice at Uppsala to the gods when he thought his life was to be the sacrifice. Rune swallowed hard at the realization. It unsettled him. With or without the sword, he doubted himself. But without it, without the weapon of his gods, would he be of any use to Anya? It worried him that he would not.

Xander stood his ground. He hurt. He bled. He waited to die. The hostile environment in which he found himself was too cruel, too ferocious, for him to keep up the battle. Disoriented and alone, the call of the wild rang in his ears as a death knell. The fight had been taken out of him by his enemies. They were too many and they kept coming, one after another, stalking him, hunting him, thirsty to kill. He wanted to strike back. His canine instincts were still alerted to the enemy, but his body couldn't fight them much longer.

Broken from his pack, he didn't have a chance and he knew it. His body was giving out and giving up on this life. On a level unknown to humans, when Xander scanned around him for any way to escape, he thought of his guardian and how she had always cut his ties and set him free. Her hands meant life, not death. But her hands were not here to free him. The only hands he saw held whips. The whips hurt him and meant to kill him. The men with the whips sent others to hurt him—other dogs like him but not like him. They carried the scent of death, same as the black birds of fire that killed the wolves.

The wolves were gone.

Zellie was gone.

His pack was nowhere near.

The cruel hands with the whips were.

Xander instinctively recognized one of them, the same human shape that had attacked before. Xander had taken the man's whip and torn it apart, just like he wanted to do to the man now. The man sent the enemy dogs to fight him. The man meant to kill him. The dogs would keep coming at him. It would end soon.

But as long as he could hold his ground, he would.

By some miracle he was able to pivot around and put his blurry watch eyes to each figure that entrapped him. His senses had dulled. The last attack left his vision clouded. Men shouted at him. Dogs barked at him. He couldn't see them all clearly, but he could still make out shapes. The light had dimmed. His body had numbed to the point of pain. His paws slipped on his own blood and he had to struggle to keep standing.

Then silence.

Xander tried to circle again. He tried to face the enemies he knew were coming for him, but he didn't have the strength. So he waited in the center of the ring of death for what would come. What senses he had left went to Zellie. He let out his last cry to her—

The shocking bite of death cut off his cry. Fangs sank into his neck, his back, then into a leg, all at once from more than one attacker. He tried to fight them off, baring his teeth and biting where he could at the enemy. Then he collapsed. The pain of death held him down. He couldn't move. Fresh wounds bled. His attackers weren't done. They wouldn't leave any life in him. Xander made sure to keep his watch eyes open for the final attack, even though he couldn't see.

Moody's dogs went in for the kill.

Spirit suddenly jumped into the fray and ripped open the throats of both dogs going for Xander. Her bite to each was deep and deadly. Neither dog got back up. With surprise on her side, she'd been able to jump through the ring of men and ropes to get to the dogs after Xander. In two quick strikes she killed the big dogs, just as if she'd taken a blade to their throats.

"G-damn cur dog!" Moody yelled and took out his gun instead of his whip. "I'll shoot you dead for killing two of my best!"

"*No* you won't," one of the men next to him said and grabbed Moody's gun away. "This is bad business, all of it, Moody. It's over."

Moody started for his whip.

Spirit growled at him.

Xander whimpered—he wasn't alone anymore.

Chester Atkins turned his anger onto Moody.

"Drop the whip," he demanded.

"Yeah, well maybe I will and maybe I won't," Moody leveled back, spitting mad that he didn't hold his gun. He'd like to put a bullet in Chester!

Chester watched Moody. He could have another gun hidden on him, or a knife. Chester wouldn't put it past Moody to kill him for breaking up his fight game.

Both men itched for a fight. They didn't waste time and rolled up their sleeves, then went fist to fist, throwing bruising punches at each other. The crowd that had gathered for the dog fight all watched the men brawl now, no one paying attention to the dogs, dead or alive, on the floor of the ring.

The fight didn't last long. Chester knocked Moody out. The crowd cheered, as if they'd wagered on it and won. Moody would be sore as hell when he came to. Then one by one, the men drew their attention back to the dog fight ring. The freight dogs were dead, lying in pools of blood. The "Siberian rat" looked almost dead, lying in a bloody mangle himself. But the dog that came out of nowhere and charged in for the kill, taking down both of Moody's fight dogs, was gone? Instead of seeing *that* husky they saw an adolescent girl!

"Chester, where did that plum-loco dog go?" one man said.

"Who let that half-breed gal in here?" another sounded off. "This ain't no place for her."

"I don't know about the dog," Chester panted. "But I'll tell you what, I'm glad it's outta here so you fools can't kill it with these damned fights. This is it for me. I'm done. You all should be too. Look at that poor animal; he's barely alive thanks to all of us. We should never have let Moody take things this far. I'm as guilty as the rest of you."

Chester looked at the girl. She couldn't be more than fourteen or fifteen. He thought he'd seen her before. Then he realized where. She was the same girl he'd seen out back of the Nugget Inn when Moody tried to mess with the dogs, the same girl who likely owned the dog brought here to fight. Too bad the hurt animal wasn't going to make it.

"This your dog, girl?" he asked.

Anya's heart pumped inside her chest. She'd raced here from a place of dreams, where only shamans traveled. Out of breath and on edge, she remembered how upset she'd been when she hadn't found Xander. She remembered going over every bit of ground where she thought he might have been taken, but came away empty-handed, without even one sign to guide her to him. Then, just when she thought all was lost, desperate and alone, she felt pulled out of her body and into another.

She wasn't alone.

Spirit had found *her.*

That's what had just happened—she'd become *Spirit.* It was

the only way to help Xander. Spirit had found him when she hadn't been able to. Now Anya was returned to her mortal body, to her human spirit, and she could see all too clearly the frightening sight in front of her.

The dark void of death loomed. Zellie had died in such a place.

Xander was unconscious. Passed out from blood loss, Anya believed, seeing how many wounds on him bled. The effect on her was immediate. She felt her own life's blood drain, willing to die with him, not wanting to leave him alone. It was asking too much of Xander to try and live with such horrific wounds. She'd no right to ask him to, to put him through anything more. Tears wet her face and ran down her neck. Grief rippled through her. She shut her eyes and ears against the pain closing in. But then . . . distant howls pierced through her senses and brought her back to the moment and back from the dead. Perhaps the ancestors, perhaps the Gatekeepers, called to her, to not give up on Xander.

Snapped into action, in a desperate race with death, Anya had to get Xander back to Chinook's village and sew up the wounds and stop the bleeding . . . before he awakened. The pain of it would be awful if he woke up! But what if he didn't wake up? She refused to let herself think that. She refused to think his wounds were too many and too gaping. She *refused* to believe Xander wouldn't pull through this.

"Girl—"

Anya didn't want to be bothered by anyone or anything. She didn't have time.

"Girl, is this your—"

"Yes, yes," she yelled out impatiently, but still didn't look up. "He's my dog. He needs help. You have to help me," she demanded of the male voice, more aware of her surroundings than a moment ago. She finally looked at the man who talked to her but didn't move from Xander's side.

"Get a sled or a wagon or something to help me get my dog onto it. *Now*," she begged.

"You bet," Chester said and hurried out of the ramshackle building. He pitied the girl since her dog would die, and he cursed himself for letting it happen.

Anya watched the man leave before she looked down at Xander again. She didn't bother with any of the press of men still gathered, silently watching her. They were no threat. The bad spirits had left this place, she could sense. Cowards, all of them! Full of anger and upset, she fought her emotions. If she let herself cry even one tear for Xander, she would be no good to him. He needed her to heal him and she needed to stay strong to do it. His wounds were horrific, torn and bleeding, his insides ruptured in places. She wanted to scream to the Morning Dawn and blame all the Directions for this. They hadn't helped her and Spirit get to him in time.

Anya straightened her spine and shut her eyes against what she'd just thought. This carnage wasn't the fault of the Chukchi gods. It wasn't her fault or Spirit's, either. The men who did this were bad men—bad men driven by bad spirits.

The Raven god plotted against them.

The fires of *Hel* burned against them.

The unknown Evil after them did this to Xander.

How Anya wanted to kill at this moment—to strike at the heart of such an Evil and cut it apart into strips of useless mold and decay!

Xander started to stir.

Anxious for him, Anya prayed he would not wake up in pain. She had much to do to try and save him before he regained consciousness.

It was just a reflex. Xander didn't awaken.

Relieved, Anya put her hands to his wounds and repeated

chants of ceremonial healing she remembered from long ago. This was a time for shaman healing, a time to call on help from all generations of Chukchi, then and now. There were no drums. There were no trances. This ceremony she did alone. The ancestors came close. She could feel them. The Gatekeepers whimpered their upset. Anya prayed for them to stay close and try to hold back time. Xander had precious little left. Unable to waste even a moment, Anya repeated the mystic chants meant to heal and didn't think of anything else.

"He won't pull a sled again, but he will live," Chinook said soberly. He'd finished helping Anya bandage Xander's stitched-up wounds and had lost count of how many the young husky had endured. An average dog would have died. That this one had not was a true miracle of the gods.

Xander stirred a little but did not come fully awake. His body twitched as if beginning a fit, but soon settled.

Anya put a hand to his husky mask, then splayed her fingers over the bandage there, gentle-like so not to cause pain but enough to let him know she was there. She didn't know how long she'd labored over his wounds. Chinook stood by her to help. The Eskimo had a good and true spirit. The words, "he will live," were all she heard Chinook say.

Weary over Xander's struggles, grief-stricken over Mushroom's death, upset Rune was still gone, and worried Spirit might not have returned safely to the world beyond, Anya tried to think about Thor and Flowers and the rest of the surviving pack. They were all in the village. The captain stood watch.

"Ouch!" Her necklace suddenly burned hot. Too distracted to give this any thought, she grabbed hold of the necklace and tore it from her, then absentmindedly shoved the husky carving in a pocket; the same one that held her knife.

Her mind went back to the dogs that survived. For the moment, they were safe in the village with the captain. Unable to do anything more for Xander, and unable to stay awake, she curled next to him and fell fast asleep. Her hand stayed gently pressed to his face, unable to let go.

Fox Ramsey made a careful count of all of his newly-traded-for Siberian huskies before he'd agree to off-load them onto the large lighter boat that would ferry them from the *Nordic* to Nome's shores. The boat was flat with rails and big enough to carry hundreds of men and dogs. In this case the load would be seventy dogs and what crew Rune Johansson would give permission to go ashore. Fox was anxious to get his huskies offloaded and to safety in the dog yard outside the Ramsey mines he'd planned out before he left for the Markova Fair in Anadyr, Siberia.

The Scot was determined to make this passage and this group of huskies count. He didn't plan on another trip across the Bering Sea in all its storms again. There had been too many times on board the *Nordic* when Fox didn't think any of them would survive the battering from the ice and the fierce winds and waves that constantly assaulted them. Sure of one thing, however, he'd picked the right captain, in the lad Rune Johansson. With such a wicked crossing, Fox admired Rune for seeing them all through to a safe arrival in Nome waters. He admired the dogs, too. They'd made it without complaint, as if used to such squalls and poor conditions.

Of course, Fox had the Chukchi lad, Vitya, to help him. The lad knew how to handle Siberian huskies and they responded to him. Maybe he'd ask Vitya to help him train up the dogs for racing. Fox hadn't decided on that, yet. Anyway, Fox didn't know any Chukchi and Vitya didn't seem to know much English. The lassie Anya had obviously learned English, and so Fox hoped Vitya would learn in the same way she had. If not, it would make any communication difficult, at best.

A more serious concern troubled Fox. What happened back in Anadyr wasn't right. The Even native being killed and all of his dogs with him—it wasn't right. It was *murder* and Fox didn't think anybody would pay. He still couldn't understand the cruelty and sheer evil of such a foul deed. To go after a man and kill him for no reason was incomprehensible to Fox, but then to go after dogs and kill them for no reason was just as hard to fathom. It didn't add up, none of it. In all his life, Fox would never forget the sight of the dog driver and his dogs, slaughtered, and strewn across the slushy ground like so much rubbish left to be cleaned up, and then forgotten. This memory would stay with him and make him treasure the dogs he'd just traded for, all the more.

They were special, these Chukchi dogs—these Siberian huskies. He meant to prove it to all the race watchers in Nome. Sure, he wanted to win the next All Alaska Sweepstakes for himself, but now he wanted it for these Siberian dog teams. They deserved to be recognized for their unique ability to run. These animals had heart and soul beyond any dogs he'd seen.

It felt extra good to Fox, all of a sudden, to have brought his teams of Siberian huskies to Nome, to run in the biggest race of all in the District of Alaska.

"When Rune gets back here, Margret, when I know he's safe, you and Inga can return to Seattle," Lars told his wife.

He used the same tone he would in closing any business negotiation. He felt nothing more for his wife and daughter than he would a casual acquaintance. Lars had gone over this many times in his mind since he'd found out what Margret had done to Anya and to her dogs. It was hard for him to stand in the same room with his wife of so many years, much less in the home he'd bought from Jafet Lindeberg for his family—for

Margret, Inga, and Rune—to live together in Nome.

Recalling Margret's deception, he didn't want to live with her in Seattle or Nome. He didn't want to live with her, period. He wanted a divorce.

"Well good, Lars," Margret said and smiled at him as if nothing were wrong between them. "Inga and I can prepare for the winter season in Seattle. How wonderful that your daughter won't have to miss any of the parties. You're a good father, Lars Johansson."

Lars couldn't believe her! She didn't ask one thing about her son, and only cared about their daughter's social life. Worse, Margret didn't even realize the wrong she'd done to Anya and to her dogs. Sad for his wife and her poverty of heart and mind, he was also sad for his daughter.

Inga was a shallow girl, a spoiled girl, and a girl capable of causing hurt to others. Ashamed his daughter had such a mean spirit, he didn't know what to do about it at this point. She was grown. His fault as much as Margret's, he supposed, being away so much when maybe if he'd been home more, Inga would have turned out differently. Too late now; she wouldn't change. He didn't have the will or the inclination to help her try; too late for him to change, too.

"Lars? Lars?" Margret whined. She didn't know why her husband looked so distant, so removed. "Which ship will take us back to Seattle, the *Storm* or the *Nordic*? It's a shame you let Rune sail the *Nordic* to Siberia. Why, I'd much prefer taking that ship back home. When did you say our son will be back?"

Our son, Lars winced inside at her reference to Rune. She didn't have a right to say that.

"Lar—"

"My son will return soon," he interrupted Margret, then doubted whether he had the right to call him *son*, either.

"I'll start packing our trunks this minute," Margret happily announced, about to leave the parlor.

"Not so fast, Margret, we have more business to discuss," Lars said calmly.

"Business?" she repeated and laughed, though hesitant.

"Sit back down, Margret." He was all politeness. "Please."

Margret sat on the velvet settee and ran shaky fingers over the smooth fabric on each side of her. Her nerves kicked in. Much as she didn't want to, she finally looked up at her husband.

"I want a divorce," he said as a matter of fact.

She'd suspected he wasn't happy but few rich husbands were. They always worked and were never home. It was the same with most all of her society friends. Never in her wildest dreams did she think Lars would actually say the word, divorce! But he just had.

"I won't give you one," she heard herself say.

"Oh, yes you will, Margret. If you want yourself and Inga to be taken care of in the manner in which you've become accustomed . . . *you will.* If you fight me on this, you'll lose," he told her with authority.

She knew he meant it, and she knew he was right. Slowly, she rose from the settee and started for the entryway to the upstairs of the stately house, then turned to Lars.

"Inga and I will be ready the moment Rune arrives," she said quietly. "Whichever one of you in whichever ship can take us back to Seattle, will suit." In the next few moments, she'd disappeared upstairs.

A chill ran through Lars at the coldness of Margret's words. They were spoken without feeling, without any hint of emotion for Rune or for him. Lars tried to be sad about this bad business, but for the life of him, he wasn't.

★ ★ ★ ★ ★

For all his efforts, the golem didn't have much to show for it. The dogs were stolen right out from under him—from *his* Russia. The punishment must be severe.

Only two Chukchi dogs were dead when all nine that escaped Siberia should be.

Only one man was dead from the escape, the man who had stolen them. But another had taken his place and taken more dogs.

Only one Chukchi pup lived, but it was one too many.

The golem paced in his iron cell, upset and thirsty for more blood. Despite his powers in the world of dark spirits, his powers weren't strong enough yet on mortal earth to break through the stone walls of his prison. Once free, and the time fast approached, his mortal sword would strike down the Chukchi dogs and rip the heart from its people. The dogs kept the Chukchi strong. The golem could not allow it. The iron taste of their blood fueled his plans and calmed him.

He still had time to get at his victims.

He still had time to send the ice storm.

He still had arctic forces that obeyed him.

The guardians of the Chukchi dogs must be emboldened since they had escaped his grasp. Not for long. All of the *kulaks* could be stopped. *Any* who dared challenge him could be stopped.

Two waves of dogs had escaped; the second was larger and harder to control because of their numbers. The first wave of nine dogs had been hit and weakened; two dogs were dead and soon three. The golem would keep after the rest, the pup especially. The pup must not get into the wrong hands. Only the hands of death will welcome the pup, the golem vowed.

The second wave of Chukchi dogs that escaped Russia presented more of a problem since there were more of them.

The golem didn't doubt he'd win in the end, but he hated losing any battle in this combat. The red serpent had failed him. The dogs still lived and so did the man who took them! The ice serpent had been struck by powerful forces from worlds beyond the golem's dominion. This war of ghosts was not over.

The golem began to pace again, unable to quell his growing worries over the enemies that gathered to fight him. He'd been able to spirit some of their gods away, to fight on his side, but not all. He hadn't been able to convince them yet.

Those he couldn't convince, he must destroy.

Those he couldn't destroy in the spirit world, he would *execute* in the world of mortal men.

Soon he would show them all—in all the worlds—who held dominion over them. He would be Master and no one else, from any reach, would stop him. This certainty calmed him enough to stop his pace, but not enough to quench his fanatic thirst for absolute power.

CHAPTER FIFTEEN

"Where is she, *Far*?"

The moment Rune set foot inside the house in Nome, he came face to face with his father. Thoughts of Anya had kept Rune going on the voyage to Siberia and back. Scared to see her again—scared she might not have missed him—he couldn't wait to find out. Deep down, he believed Anya had missed him, and maybe loved him, too. He'd tried to hide his feelings from her before, but now he thought he could risk telling her. He'd made it back safe. The dogs had made it safely to shore. He'd slain the serpent, at least enough to stop its attack. The danger had quieted, maybe gone for good.

For the first time in a very long time, Rune felt hopeful about the future.

"Anya is in the Eskimo village of Chinook," Lars answered his son, astonished that Rune had actually walked through the door. His chest tightened with emotion. Tears threatened, but he wiped them away before Rune could see. Lars realized in that moment he must be doing something right in this life, to have his son returned safe. But how could Rune have escaped the Midgard serpent? Lars had feared his nightmares would come true. They hadn't.

"What's that for?" Rune accepted his father's hug, too surprised to react otherwise.

Lars pulled away and looked at his son.

"I'm glad to see you. I thought you might be *dod*. I thought the *hav* or the *isen,* the *glass,* might have taken you," Lars admitted.

Rune shifted uncomfortably. He wasn't used to thinking his father thought of him at all, much less that he worried the sea or the ice would have killed him. Turns out, his father was close to the truth. That's not what upset Rune. His father's attention had him bewildered. Suspicious, Rune changed the subject to the only one that mattered.

"Anya is all right? Are you sure, *Far?*"

"She is."

"And the dogs?"

Lars couldn't look his son in the eye. Lars wasn't supposed to leave Anya or her dogs, and had promised Rune he would watch over them. Well, he hadn't. He'd sailed up to Port Lay and left Anya in Margret's care. He felt responsible.

"Things happened, son."

"Look at me, *Far.* Tell me. All of it." Rune's cool voice belied his upset, his anger. He needed to be forewarned when he saw Anya.

"*Ja, Run'a,* I will." Lars owed his son the truth—all of it.

"I'm sorry, girl," Chinook said quietly. He regretted what he'd said earlier, that her dog would be all right. The animal could not walk. Anya would have to put the dog down. It was the arctic way. There was no other. He wanted to put his hand on Anya's small, trembling shoulder to offer comfort but left her alone, bent to her gashed and wounded dog. On this day the spirits could not help her. Her dog would not heal.

Xander had awakened from his stupor and come fully alert but when he tried to get up, he couldn't. His senses were keen but his body wasn't. Still weak and too injured to try another attempt to lift himself off the ground, he put his head on his paws and whined softly. His blurred watch eyes closed to the situation in which he found himself. Pain shot electric jolts through him. Memory of the fight flooded his awareness. Stirred by this recall, he opened his eyes and raised his head enough to peer all around and make sure the enemy wasn't waiting to attack. He sensed no whips or bared teeth. He felt no claw of death. Yet death was close—his own. Generations of husky breeding and life in the arctic wilds told him as much.

Aware his guardian stayed close, Xander did what he could to move his head, to find her hand and push his muzzle into it. He wanted her comfort and he wanted to comfort her, too. Their time together would soon end. His canine instincts sharpened at this realization. The hurt built inside him. With the strength he had left he suddenly let out a howl to the heavens, a soulful cry to the Gatekeepers to keep watch over his guardian for he could not. Like his body, his clouded vision failed him.

"Xander, shhhhh," Anya tried to soothe. "You must stay still and rest. You must save your strength," she whispered over him and gently stroked his back.

"I am sorry—"

"Why, Chinook?" Anya angrily spat at the Eskimo. "Why are you sorry?" She glared at him accusingly, but kept by Xander. Chinook had given up. She dared not.

Chinook did not answer. The girl needed time to grasp what she must do. He would not upset her any more than she already was. She must bargain with the spirits and them with her. His eyes on Anya, he gave her a nod, then backed out of the tented shelter and closed the flap behind him.

Alone with Xander, Anya lay down next to him and put her arm over his torn back. The lump in her throat stung. Since a pup, he'd hated being alone. She couldn't imagine them parting, in this life or in any other.

"Sleep now, my brave boy. Dream of your days ahead when

we will run together across the ice and tundra. I am with you always. Zellie is with you always. Do not fear that you are alone," she quietly tried to reassure.

Xander whimpered, then rested his head on his paws but kept his failing watch eyes open.

Anya couldn't close her eyes, either. Their time together was too precious.

Frustrated with Vitya and their poor communication, Fox Ramsey thought of Anya. She was part Chukchi and could speak the language, he was certain. He didn't know anyone else in the area who did. Vitya didn't understand the Eskimo tongue, Fox had discovered. Fox had let the young dog driver come with him from Anadyr to help with the Siberian huskies and could still use his help. For that to happen, Fox needed Anya. Especially now, since Vitya acted like he wanted to leave the Ramsey mining operations and what . . . leave?

"*Haud* on *noo*. You *cannae* go yet," Fox said, and stepped in front of Vitya to block his path. "You need to bide here with the *dugs*. It *will nae* do for you to take off. I want you to stay with us," Fox implored, and spread out his arm over the fenced dog yard. "All of these *dugs* need to be trained up. I could sure use your help, Vitya."

Vitya followed the direction of the dog trader's arm and surveyed the landscape of native Siberian huskies. He understood, or thought he understood, what the dog trader wanted: for him to stay and help with the dogs. Vitya should, he knew, since the man had helped him cross the great sea to this new land. But the dog trader didn't understand what *he* wanted and needed: to find Anya.

She was the only reason Vitya had traveled so far away from his homeland. He was determined to find her and take her back to their village. She would become his wife. They would raise

Chukchi dogs together and children of their own. Anya would never have to fear Grisha again. Vitya would take her as his and protect her from harm. No matter that she spoke with the spirits, she still needed protection. She was his responsibility, and his alone.

"Come on, lad," Fox said, and tried again to get his point across to the Chukchi. "Back with me *noo,* come on." Fox started walking toward his house at the mine, then stopped when he realized the lad didn't follow. He gestured for Vitya to come with him.

Vitya shook his head in a firm no.

"Anya," he mumbled, talking to himself.

"What?" Fox shouted.

"Anya!" Vitya shouted back.

The dog yard came alive with yelps and barks. Something stirred them. Maybe predators. Maybe nothing. Fox and Vitya hopped over the enclosure wall and tried to settle them down. Neither man carried a weapon. Both regretted it at the moment. Whatever was out there causing this upset among the dogs wasn't friendly. Uneasy, Fox and Vitya sent each other a nod, then took off through the field of huskies in opposite directions to better scout the situation.

The skies eerily darkened. Snowflakes drifted across the light winds, hinting of a new storm. Summer rain and sleet storms had pounded Alaska's coast for weeks but had begun to let up. Winter storms brewed early. Time to prepare was short, the hour late.

Miners poured outside of their barracks, awakened by all the noise.

"Grab your guns!" Fox yelled to them. "Could be wolves or bear!"

Half-asleep, the miners followed their boss's orders and soon had their rifles pointed into the darkness that surrounded the dog yard. No one had to order them to shoot if necessary. To a man, they'd been on the frontier long enough to know the dangers that threatened. Hell, if the weather didn't kill you, there was always something else that might.

When the dogs settled down, Fox believed the danger must have passed for the moment. Just like the storms, the danger wouldn't let up. He needed more men to help keep watch over the husky teams, but he especially needed Vitya to help him. Call it coincidence or plain luck, Fox wouldn't question his good fortune that Vitya must know Anya since he'd just called out her name. Fox was certain Anya could get the lad to stay and help with the husky teams he'd traded for, at the Markova Fair. Fox couldn't do this alone. If he wanted to win the 1910 All Alaska Sweepstakes and stake his claim on the biggest race in the District of Alaska with these special huskies, it would take all of them working together, man and beast.

First chance he got, Fox would take Vitya with him and locate the Siberian lassie.

"Yes, let them come inside, Chinook," Anya said when she realized the dogs waited outside.

This might be the last time the dogs would see Xander. Anya swallowed hard. She felt sick to her stomach. It would be the first look and maybe the last for his pup, Thor. Anya had prayed and thought the night through about the choice she must make—about Xander's chances for survival. The Chukchi way seemed so cruel, to let him die on his own out in the open. It was also the Chukchi way for a child to end its parent's life if the mother or father were too ill or too old. If a suffering child is not meant to live, should a parent then end its life? The choices left her were impossible ones. She had no right and yet she had every right. The heart of a husky, the heart of a Chukchi, rested within her breast. Xander was her family, her responsibility. Xander entrusted her with his life, as she did him.

Thor scampered over to Xander and flopped down in front of him, then opened his mouth and playfully gnawed on Xander's paws. When there was no response from his father, Thor barked in protest and tried again for attention. This time Thor attempted a howl. The little pup knocked himself over, trying to let out a howl. Xander slowly raised his head and whined back, which got an immediate response from Thor. The pup froze a few short seconds and then lunged at Xander's paws again, gnawing in play. Xander licked the pup's face where he could and even barked slightly at Thor's antics.

Anya ran out of the Eskimo tent.

None of the other dogs followed.

Once she cleared the village, she kept on running. She didn't want to stop and have to face the truth of the moment: that Xander wouldn't live to see his son romp and play another day. This day was Xander's last, and Anya knew it, for she was the very one who must end his life. It would be inhumane to force him to live with such pain, unable to stand, to walk, to run across the ice and open tundra. He was going blind, his life already shutting down. She couldn't allow him to suffer. His moments now with his pup would be his last. Anya stopped running and fell to her knees.

Could she use her knife on him?

Could she deliver him to the open and leave him at the mercy of the wild?

If he must depart this world then so must she. This had been her plan but . . . she had the others to think about. Heaviness hit Anya unlike anything she'd experienced before. She felt numb from the weight on her. What she must do on this day killed all feeling inside her. She would never recover from such a deed and she knew it.

Nana-tasha was gone.

Zellie was gone.

Soon Xander would be gone, along with her own *Spirit*. She couldn't imagine having any life left in her Spirit.

Only she would be left on Native Earth, and she would only stay long enough to help keep the rest safe. After that . . . she didn't really care what happened to her. Her days as shaman were numbered. What use would she be, empty and alone with her loved ones gone? None, she realized.

Rune's image forced its way into her troubled thoughts. He wasn't a loved one. He wasn't family. She tried to push his handsome features away but couldn't. Then Vitya's face appeared before her. He wasn't a loved one or family but he was her forever friend and companion. Funny, but Anya couldn't conjure emotion for either Rune or Vitya. She was too drained. Their images faded.

Anya mechanically walked back to the Eskimo tent where Xander would be sacrificed. That's just how this sad business felt to her, a sacrificial killing. The Great Crag loomed overhead, its shadow unforgiving.

Chinook came outside the shelter and shut the door flap.

"It is time," he said.

Anya didn't ask for an explanation. She knew exactly what he meant. The words were familiar. Her grandmother had said as much to her, a lifetime ago. Snowflakes drifted across Anya's line of vision. The winds picked up. She ignored the Directions. She didn't want to hear from them. They held no answer, no hope. The drumbeat of the ancestors coursed through her thinking, and she couldn't ignore their call to the Gatekeepers and the worlds beyond. They were trying to help prepare her for what she must do. Generations of Chukchi alerted to her. They did not judge. They understood where she, still, did not.

"It is time," Chinook said again.

Anya opened her eyes.

"Please take Thor and the dogs out. I do not want them to see," she whispered. Her stomach pained. Spirits closed in. Some were there to help, some to lay blame.

Chinook nodded to Anya and went back inside to the dogs. There were no words for such a time.

Anya fixed her gaze on the closed door flap. Something should adorn it to mark this place for Xander. She owned nothing worthy of him, and had nothing on her except . . . Vitya's necklace was in her pocket, she just remembered. It was made of walrus tusk from home, *Xander's home.* Reverently putting her hand inside the pocket of her kerker, she pulled out the husky carving, still on its hide chain. Her fingers had brushed her knife, which rested beneath the necklace, but she recoiled from its touch. The blade sent cold shivers through her and made her doubt her purpose all over again. She must have more time with him. She must!

"Chinook!" she called through the hide-tented wall, panic-stricken.

One by one, she watched the dogs, all tethered to the same line, come outside in single file. Their tails sagged, all curl disappeared. Flowers came out first, followed by Magic, then Midnight, Midday, Frost, and Little Wolf, the runt whimpering softly. Their watch eyes hooded their upset. Chinook held Thor against his chest with one hand and held the dogs' line in the other. The subdued, orderly dogs led the eerie procession as if a practiced ritual, as if they knew what would follow.

Anya couldn't look at any of them and quickly pulled back the door flap and disappeared inside the tent. Xander lay as she'd left him, still and quiet. The thin air made her cough. Dust scattered when she did. There was enough light shining through slits and spaces in the hide walls to see it.

Xander lay so still?

Had he died?

She shot over to him and knelt down. When she put her hand to his back, it rose and it fell in shallow waves. She blew out a hushed breath. Her chest ached from loving him. He was aware of her, she knew, though he showed no outward signs of acknowledgment. Frightened by his composure, she realized he waited for her to take out her knife and end his life. He'd said goodbye. He was ready. He waited for her, trusting her hand in life and in death.

"My brave boy," she tried to soothe. "I love you—"

Unstoppable tears washed down her face. What could she possibly say to Xander to make this moment right? It felt wrong to her . . . to let Xander go like this . . . by her hand. Her clammy fingers shook as she methodically took up her knife. Would the cut hurt? Was her knife sharp enough to kill in one stroke?

"Anya! Anya!" A call came from outside.

She dropped her knife at the sound of the unmistakable voice and ran outside, instantly relieved to have any reason to run from this awful moment.

Xander opened his eyes then, aware his guardian had left.

Vitya, Anya mouthed, but couldn't say anything to him. She wasn't happy or sad or even surprised to see him, so caught up still with leaving Xander alone. What should she do? What was the right thing to do? To leave Xander at such a time? No, she decided, and turned to go back inside the hide tent.

"Anya," Vitya rasped in a hoarse voice and rushed over to her. He immediately grabbed her arm to hold her to the spot. This wasn't the response he expected after so long a time apart. She acted like she didn't even know him. Something was going on here that he didn't understand. That had to be the reason for Anya's snub, he told himself.

Anya held herself still.

"Let go, Vitya," she said coolly, in Chukchi.

He let go, but he didn't back away from her. She looked changed. Still his pretty girl, his *gitengev*, she wasn't the girl he remembered. When she turned to him and looked up at him, he realized the change: she was a woman now, more beautiful than any arctic flower or magical northern lights dancing across the sky. The sensation charged through him, stirring his urge to be the man to match such a woman, his *gitengev*.

Anya let the reality of Vitya standing in front of her in the flesh set in. Full awareness returned, of Xander especially. She would go back inside to him soon. For the moment, let him sleep peacefully, she prayed silently to the Morning Dawn. Let him sleep.

"Vitya," Anya finally said out loud. "What miracle has brought you here?" she whispered weakly and put her hands to his strong shoulders.

He put his arms around her and pulled her close.

"You are the miracle that brought me here, *gitengev*," he breathed against her hair.

This is the scene Rune came upon when he arrived at Chinook's village looking for Anya and her dogs. Too late to turn around, Anya had already spotted him.

"Rune!" she called out, and pulled herself out of Vitya's embrace.

Vitya. Rune cursed the name. He'd sensed a rivalry with the Chukchi dog driver when he first met him and now he knew why: Anya. The two knew each other. That was obvious enough.

Anya ran over to Rune.

Vitya watched her. Jealousy took hold. His hands balled into fists and his jaw tensed, ready for the fight. It killed him to stand there and wait for Anya to come to her senses and come back to him. A Chukchi, she couldn't care for a white boy! Vitya would never believe she did.

"Rune," Anya said quietly, then instinctively put her arms around his waist. She felt at home with him near again and pressed her flushed cheek against the familiar wool of his sea jacket. He would help her with Xander. He would know the right thing to do. His gods and her gods had battled together and could trust each other, she believed. The feel of him, the look of his golden Viking countenance, the smell of the sea on him, the tension of his well-muscled body against hers, all gave her the strength she needed to lean on his, and show him her affection—how much she loved him.

Rune didn't put his arms around her. It took everything in him not to touch her. The hurt from seeing her with Vitya cut deep. He'd been a stupid fool to think Anya might love him! Old hurts die hard. His own family didn't love him. Why should she? That he loved her was his problem, not hers.

Anya could feel Rune pull away. She didn't understand. Frightened by his lack of response to her, she hugged him tighter, afraid to let go. She loved him and thought he loved her and had missed her as much as she'd missed him. She couldn't have been wrong about him, she couldn't! So much had happened since they'd been apart. She had much to tell him and was desperate for his advice.

"The dogs," Rune said in a curt tone. "How are they?"

Crushed by his cold indifference to her, Anya eased her arms from around Rune's waist and took a step back before she looked up at him. She couldn't read any emotion on his handsome face. What had happened to him? What had changed? Her heart sank at this unexpected reunion with Rune. She'd hoped for more, so much more.

Rune tried to concentrate on the question he'd just asked her and not on her lovely countenance, her shapely mouth, her soulful brown eyes, her soft cheeks, the sculpted curve of her chin, the way her hair shimmered in the evening light, and the way her slender body felt so perfect against his. The sweet smell of her charged the air.

"Where are they?" he forced himself to ask.

"The dogs, you mean?" Anya tried to sound as indifferent as he did.

"Yes." Rune unintentionally blew out a heavy sigh of regret over all of this.

"Do you even care what happened to them, Rune?" Anya spat out, interpreting his action as unconcerned.

"Look, Anya," Rune said, trying not to get upset with her. None of this was her fault, but his. "I just want to know if the dogs are all right." He wanted to say more but stopped himself. He wanted to find out why the hell she would even ask such a question of him. His father had already broken the news to him. It was upsetting enough that Mushroom had been killed at the Bonanza mine and Xander torn apart in a dog fight ring . . . and now Anya doubted he cared?

Rune shrugged his shoulders. He tried to shut her away. It hurt too much, how little she really thought of him. He shot a look at Vitya. The Chukchi dog driver was the reason. Vitya had Anya's heart and her trust, not Rune. She'd never let him hold her the way Vitya just had. He'd lost her to the Chukchi. The image of Anya in Vitya's arms ate away at Rune. He'd never shake it. Led by his heart and not his head, feeling betrayed and defeated, he needed to get out of there—he needed to forget Anya.

Vitya would help her with the dogs.

Vitya was Chukchi. She was Chukchi. So then they belonged together.

Fine.

What did he care?

"Xander?" Rune made himself look at Anya, suddenly worried like hell over his trusted wheel dog. "Will he be all right?"

Anya shook her head in a no.

Rune felt gut-punched. Tears caught in his throat and stung at his eyes. The black and white Siberian husky had always recovered before. Not this time. Rune had stopped the serpent in the sea, but it wasn't enough to slay the evil after them. His gods and Anya's, none of them had kept Xander safe. Rune blamed himself. He shouldn't have left Anya and the dogs alone. His family hadn't protected them, either.

Angrier at himself than his family, Rune cursed the day he bumped into Anya at the Markova Fair. If he hadn't met her, maybe none of this would have happened. Maybe the ghosts of her gods and his gods would have left them well enough alone and all the dogs would still be alive! Doubt set hard in his bones.

No matter what, Rune felt responsible for Anya and her Chukchi dogs. He guessed they would be Vitya's responsibility from here on. They would have to be, for he meant to leave Nome and not come back. Anya would be better off without him, he firmly believed. Xander's dying was proof enough for Rune that he should go. The sooner he did, the safer Anya and the surviving dogs would be. The number nine rang in his head then went deathly silent.

"Thor, Rune? Do you want to see him?" Anya whispered, scared she couldn't read Rune's thoughts. She saw his tears and wanted to comfort him. They must be for Xander. Seeing the pup might help to take away some of Rune's pain. She didn't worry over Rune's indifference to her. Xander mattered. Thor mattered. All the Chukchi dogs mattered. Not her.

"Thor?"

"I named Flowers and Xander's pup Thor," she said, and tried to lighten his obvious upset with a smile.

Had his father said anything about a pup? Rune couldn't remember.

"Thor is a good name," Rune pronounced. The corners of his mouth crinkled into the hint of a smile.

"He's a feisty pup," Anya hurried to say. "He's handsome like his mother and strong like his father." Then her smile faded the moment she thought of Xander and what he faced.

Rune caught the change.

"Thor is Odin's son, an important god of the Vikings." He tried to keep their conversation going . . . anything to bring back Anya's smile.

"Truly?" she said in disbelief. She didn't know how the name came to her. She'd wanted to name the pup after one of Rune's gods and couldn't believe she actually had.

Rune took in every detail of Anya's captivating, naturally mischievous smile. It would have to last him a lifetime. When he left this place, he would not see her again. Their time together had come to an end. His days as a Viking warrior were over, ghosts be damned. His war with them was done. He brought bad spirits to Anya now, he was certain. To stay and fight for her would be a mistake. She and the dogs couldn't afford the risk.

Vitya charged over to them, and possessively put his hand to Anya's arm, linking his fingers there.

Anya barely noticed with her full attention on Rune. She didn't bother to shrug off Vitya's hold.

Rune's heart sank even lower, seeing the Chukchi touch her. Upset all over again, he had to get out of there.

"Keep her safe," Rune gruffly told Vitya. "If you don't, I'll find you."

Then Rune turned his back on them both and walked away in the picked-up snowfall.

Vitya didn't understand English but there was no mistaking Rune's threat.

"Rune," Anya called out. "Rune!" She started after him but

Vitya held her to the spot. "Let me go," she begged Vitya. "Let me go," she whispered into the sharp breeze. "Rune," she whimpered. "Rune." He was leaving. He wouldn't come back. The light in her life went with him. Overcome and drained, she felt faint.

Vitya caught her before she fell to the ground. He was pleased the sea captain had left, for good, he hoped. Anya would be all right now that they were together again. He meant to get her back to Siberia, to their home village, at first chance. They would be happy. They would have a good life.

Rune Johansson had no claim on her. *He* did.

Summer storms poured into winter, begun early in the frontier city of Nome. There had been a break between seasons, enough to switch gears in the mines and change the method of extracting gold to suit the incoming weather. The days of fifty-degree temperatures were over. The days of access via the Bering Sea to Nome were ending. All travel would shut down, all except by dogsled. Everything depended on the sled dog. Mail, vital supplies, hunting, and any travel. Things didn't change in the Arctic, no matter on which side of the great Bering Sea.

Once the last ships left Nome waters, none could return until the next summer. Nome would be isolated. It was the routine this time of the year, and yet it was never routine to locals to be shut away from the rest of the world. Veteran frontiersmen and miners dug in for the long winter. Families in Nome and the surrounding Eskimo villages prepared their homes and made sure of their provisions, what they had and what they needed to hunt. Mercantile and trade store shelves were stocked with goods, ready for purchase. Most tourists had left. Vacancy signs gave proof. The saloons in Nome started to come alive with men who had more time on their hands in winter. They had gambling, drinking, and dog racing on their minds.

The next All Alaska Sweepstakes, to be held the following April, already occupied the main topic of conversation. Which dog teams and which dog drivers would best the other sparked spirited debate. Gold rush days had produced gold rush dogs and made sled dog racing the premier sport and recreation in Nome. The outside world had begun to take notice. But to residents dog racing was a part of them, of what they did and who they were. Sled dogs were their life. Sled dog racing had become an all-important part of that life. It gave residents reason for joy during the long months of isolation and desolation in the frozen winter.

Some still talked of the little Siberian rats that ran third in the last All Alaska Sweepstakes, but few thought the small huskies would dare attempt another race against their mighty Eskimo huskies and freight dogs, powerful mixed malamutes, all. They'd heard that one of the owners of the Ramsey Mines off-loaded a bunch more of the Siberian rats and refused to let this sway their thinking that the little dogs had *no* reason to be here. Most thought the dogs would be used to work the mines and laughed at this. What good were they? How much freight and supplies did Ramsey expect the little huskies to be able to pull? There was no saloon talk in any corner of Nome where men put any of Ramsey's dogs in front of a racing sled period, much less hitched to run in the biggest race of the winter season.

Ships were leaving Nome waters. The ice thickened. Time ran short. This subject also ran the saloon circuit, dampening spirits enough to make some down another shot of whiskey. It would take two months by dogsled to get to Nome from the Outside once the ships left. A sobering thought, to many.

"He's gone!"

Anya dropped to her knees and then prostrated to the ground in the spot where she'd left Xander inside the hide tent, only moments ago she thought. But then . . . she couldn't think, she couldn't remember anything except the awful choice she'd had to make for Xander: to end his suffering on Native Earth. Had she done it? Had she killed him? Panic-stricken, she sat up and peered into the dead space around her. When she saw no body, nothing giving any sign of Xander, she closed her eyes and prayed for calm, for clear thinking, for her memory to return.

In the next moment, it did, all of it.

Alone and unashamedly afraid, Anya mechanically got up and tightened her kerker around her and checked for the blade she always kept in its pocket. She must keep her weapon close. It was all she had left to help her protect the dogs. There was nothing else, no one else. She doubted her own *Spirit* and even the Chukchi gods.

Her loved ones were gone . . . Nana-tasha, Zellie, Xander, and Rune.

"May the Gatekeepers watch over you," she whispered into the void around her, sapped of everything but her simple prayer.

This was an awful day.

It had no end.

GLOSSARY

Alianaiq— good to meet you
Awrite— hello
Aye— yes
Baidarka— Chukchi walrus-hide boat
Blether— long talk, chat
Braw— good
Cheerio— goodbye
Dod— dead
Doon— down
Dotter— daughter
Dug— dog
Fru— wife
Glass— ice
Golem— an artificial creature created by magic; an animated personified being created entirely from inanimate matter; attribution of human form to anything other than a human being
Hallo— hello
Haud— hold
Hav— sea
Isen— ice
Issorartuyok— leader dog
Ja— yes
Kanosak— gold
Ken— know

Kerker— Chukchi outer fur coverall

Kin— understand

Kringmerk nakkertok— dogs are fast

Kringmiluardjuk— pup

Kulak— wealthy peasant (Russia)

Makoktok amarok— young wolf

Noo— now

Pialaksaurtut nakkertok— race fast

Piktaungitok tonrar— evil spirits

Qamutik— basket sled

Shaman— communicates with native spirits; a healer; a holy man or woman

Skepp— ship

Sibirskiy haski— Siberian husky

Sivudlit— ancestors of the wolf

Siwash socks— socks cut out of Hudson's Bay blankets for wearing inside moccasins

Tikikrautauwok— finish race first

Wean— babe

Wee— small

Yaranga— Chukchi home; walrus-hide covered tent with large center pole

ABOUT THE AUTHOR

A wife, mother, and grandmother living between Colorado and California, **Joanne Sundell** is retired from nursing. She has six published works, all historical romances with Five Star Publishing: *Matchmaker, Matchmaker,* 2006; *A . . . My Name's Amelia,* 2007; *The Parlor House Daughter,* 2008; *Meggie's Remains,* 2009; *Hearts Divided,* 2010 (The Quaker and the Confederate, Book 1); and *Hearts Persuaded,* 2010 (The Quaker and the Confederate, Book 2).

In 2014, the first book in the Watch Eyes Trilogy, *Arctic Storm,* was released from Five Star Publishing in their Frontier Fiction line. *Arctic Shadow* is the second book in this young adult, arctic adventure series. Joanne has raised and loved Siberian huskies for over forty years and believes it's time to tell their story.

Joanne holds membership in Women Writing the West and Western Writers of America.